LEGEND OF THE BLUEGRASS

LEIGH BORDEN

Legend of the Bluegrass

1977

Doubleday & Company, Inc., Garden City, New York

Library of Congress Cataloging in Publication Data

Borden, Leigh.
  Legend of the Bluegrass.

  I. Title.
PZ4.B727Le   [PS3552.07]   813'.5'4
ISBN: 0-385-12308-6
Library of Congress Catalog Card Number 76-56266

For Those Who Have Loved Me

LEGEND OF THE BLUEGRASS

CHAPTER ONE

The day she arrived in Lexington to take up her duties at Manford Manor, Leslie Tallant little realized the beauty and the terror she would encounter here. Nor did she have the slightest inkling how profoundly not only her life, but her very self, would be changed.

After all, Leslie was a modern, common-sense sort of girl. There had been loneliness in her life, and defeat, yes, and even fear. She had wept tears, she had loved both wisely and too well. But a deep, bone-shaking terror is not expected to enter into our lives in these times when all the corners are well lighted, and ghosts no longer walk.

Certainly, being driven in a chauffeured limousine along the Paris Pike toward her new home, there was nothing in the passing scene to evoke a sense of foreboding in even the darkest soul. This Kentucky world, its rich bluegrass paddocks and pastures enclosed within white fences, was beautiful. She was enchanted by the sight of long-legged Thoroughbred foals so actively playful beside their sedate dams. In one paddock she saw a great chestnut stallion, his magnificent head in profile as he gazed at the horizon. Perhaps, Leslie thought, he was remembering those pounding runs into the stretch, bracing into the roar of the crowd as he strained every muscle, every ounce of will, to cross the finish line ahead of his rivals.

A lush and beautiful place in which to begin a new life; not since she had been a girl, fortunate to spend Maryland summers on a horse farm, had she known a land so lovely. The Paris Pike was an undulation of gentle dips and curves, passing stone-gated entrances that evoked a presence of great houses in spacious grounds, their privacy shielded by stone fences and serried trees.

Only hours ago, in New York City, she had locked her tiny apartment for the last time, carried her bags down to the street to hail a taxi, checking her wristwatch as she got in to make sure of ample time before her flight. Through all the movements of departure there had dwelled in her the feeling of adventure in which she had made the decisions necessary to bring her to this place at this time of her life.

Leslie Tallant was twenty-eight years old. She had gray eyes, directly honest in their appraisal of the world, a firm-lipped mouth that yet revealed a hint of will and passion in the sculptured line of the upper lip, the sensual, though controlled, fullness of the lower. Her ivory skin was extraordinarily clear and luminous.

Her body had been made strong and lithe by tennis and walking. She was wearing a denim-blue skirt and a white, plain—even severe—blouse; and brown Gucci loafers . . . expensive, elegant shoes were her one extravagance.

The loveliest thing about her beauty was her unconsciousness of its impact. Indeed, Leslie had never been able to think of herself as more than moderately attractive; which was as far from the truth as the innocence of adventure in which she was coming to her new job.

There had been—no denying it—one moment of intuitive foreboding. As the shadow of it flickered across a corner of her mind, she turned her gaze from the passing landscape to look at the back of the chauffeur's head.

At the airport, he had approached her tentatively. "Miss Leslie Tallant?"

She had turned to see a small, wry-bodied man. He was wearing a red checked shirt and khaki pants, the cuffs down over the uppers of flat-heeled Kentucky boots. She could not read his precise age in the wrinkled face. Indefinably, he exuded the air of a long-time horseman; it was in his compact body, his light weight, the size and strength of his hands. He held his body with a youthful-seeming gracefulness.

His eyes sent through her a tremor of uneasiness; they showed the flat, shiny blackness of a crow's eyes, so blank in seeing they seemed malevolent rather than merely watchful. The impression was enhanced by a mannerism of holding his head stiffly on a twisted neck, one shoulder raised slightly, so that he peered up at her from an awry viewpoint. Surely, she thought involuntarily, he must view the world most strangely from such an angle. *And me?*

"Yes," she said, her voice, from the apprehension his presence had aroused, rising more sharply than she had meant. "I'm Leslie Tallant. Were you sent to meet me?"

"I reckon so," he said. "Which is your bags?"

She pointed them out. The man extracted the suitcases and started, without further word, toward a tan Lincoln Continental arrogantly waiting in a nearby No Parking zone. After stowing the luggage, he turned, with seeming deliberation, to survey her again.

"So you're gonna live at Manford Manor."

The adumbrations of tone quivered in her. "Yes," she said, again speaking too sharply.

She braced herself against the impact of his flat, black gaze. Then: slowly, very definitely, he shook his head. It was a considered movement, as though he had pondered the question of whether he should, or should not, give her a needed warning.

Overhead, the Kentucky sun shone brightly on a bright world. About her was the bustle of a busy airport, a jet taking off on a long run, people in cheerful movement, animated by the excitement of travel.

Within Leslie Tallant's soul, however, a dark and chilling cloud had, without warning, covered the sun. She shivered, and thought: *Someone must have walked over my grave.*

"What do you mean?" Again, her voice was too sharp; she was irritated to hear herself speak so apprehensively.

He regarded her steadily for another long moment. Then, with deliberation: "It ain't for me to say, miss," and turned finally away.

She knew it was useless to pursue the subject. Silently she got into the car as, politely, he held the door, then closed it behind her.

Leslie Tallant was committed to Manford Manor.

The automobile left the highway in favor of a curving drive, broaching between twin stone pillars which bore the brass-plaqued legend MANFORD MANOR. Leslie's breath caught in her throat. The driveway wound grandly between ancient oaks in a parklike setting, the open spaces an enormous expanse of greensward. A great mansion, tall though wide, waited ahead; broad steps, guarded by couchant stone lions, rose to a porch graced by white columns sweeping upward with massive grace. Over the heavy oak doorway was a fanlight fashioned in delicate tints of stained glass. The architectural details, in keeping with the fanlight, were elegant and restrained, the columns Doric, the austere lines taking nothing from the uplifting masses of shaped stone.

Leslie, as she stepped from the limousine, was extraordinarily moved. Yet there was . . . something . . . Yes. Beneath the grandeur lurked a shabbiness that could only have come from neglect. The paint was thin, sun-dry, scaling in tiny slivers. This air of long abandonment puzzled Leslie; it did not fit with the imperious telegraphic summons, with the limousine sent to meet her at Bluegrass Field.

The contrast instilled a sense of uneasiness. She shook off the feeling with an impatient movement of her shoulders. Resolutely, behind the chauffeur carrying her bags, she mounted the stone steps. The door opened to reveal a black man in a white jacket. Nodding a friendly greeting, he stooped to take up the bags, stood aside for her entrance.

Leslie stepped across the threshold. Then she turned, her gaze drawn against her will. The wry-bodied little man, standing again beside the limousine, gazed at her fixedly. As though involuntarily, his head moved in that same gesture of negation, of warning. When he realized that she had seen, he got behind the wheel of the car and drove away.

Leslie took a deep breath. She walked into the house that was Manford Manor. She had begun the new life.

The hall was broad, well illuminated. On each wall hung oils of race horses, the paintings so old they showed the exaggerated elongation of head and barrel characteristic of the earliest period of Thoroughbred portraiture.

"Miss Mary Ben is waiting in the living room." The houseman spoke in a soft voice, one hand signaling her direction through an archway that broke the left-hand wall. "I'll put your luggage in your room."

"Thank you." Leslie smiled. "What is your name?"

"My name is Martin, ma'am."

"Thank you, Martin."

She passed through the archway. There was not time in which to absorb an impression of the room, only a fleeting recognition of ancient sofas and chairs in patterns of faded brocade, a library wall of books in leather bindings. No time; for Mary Ben Ashe, the invalid wife, was rolling eagerly forward in her wheelchair, stretching forth one hand.

"My dear, you can't know how glad I am that you have come."

Leslie gazed down upon the tiny woman whose welfare was being placed in her hands. Mary Ben's features, as delicate as Dresden china, revealed that same fragile luminosity; as with so many invalids, a light seemed to glow through her flesh. Though her heart-shaped face was young, streaks of gray showed in her tidily groomed hair, tied back with a girlish ribbon. Behind her stood a robust, thick-bodied woman, with a broad, pleasant face, wearing a nurse's uniform.

Mrs. Ashe's voice had trembled in speaking the words of greeting. Her hand, trembling also, clutched Leslie's with a fierce gripping.

"Now, Miss Mary Ben," the nurse said in a chiding voice. "You mustn't excite yourself."

Mary Ben, visibly calming herself, looked toward the nurse, saying with a tremulous smile, "Will you ring for tea, Mrs. Nunn?"

The nurse crossed to the fireplace to tug at a brocaded bellpull. With remarkable agility, Mary Ben's thin, veined hands maneuvered the wheelchair, turning it to move to one end of a long coffee table, where she locked it once more into immobility.

"You may sit there, Leslie," she said, indicating the sofa. "Next to me." She smiled appealingly. "I know you would prefer to go to your room to freshen up. But I want so much for us to get to know each other. You won't mind, will you?"

"Tea is so refreshing," Leslie said. "Especially after a journey."

Martin entered, pushing a tea trolley. Instead of placing the tray on the coffee table, he left the trolley beside the wheelchair, within reach of Mary Ben's ministrations. The nurse had departed, leaving them alone.

Mary Ben seemed to enjoy the meticulous preparations for the ceremony of taking tea. "How do you like it, Leslie?" she inquired. "Sugar? Milk? Lemon?"

"Just milk," Leslie said, and accepted the cup.

She waited until Mary Ben had served herself, then took a sip. An excellent and warming beverage, soothing the uneasiness that yet remained.

Mary Ben drank deeply, sighed in contentment. "I'll leave it to Whitney to outline your duties," she said. "I know he'll be pleased; you look exactly as I pictured you in my mind." She smiled wistfully. "I hope we shall be friends."

"Of course we will be friends," Leslie said strongly.

Mary Ben's lips quivered. "I've never had a woman friend."

Leslie leaned forward to place a warm palm on Mary Ben's hand. "Let's not worry about it," she said, smiling. "I don't think we shall have any problems in that direction."

Mary Ben's return grip was unexpectedly strong. But that, Leslie thought, would come from years of maneuvering the wheelchair.

"It was Whitney's idea to place the advertisement in the *Blood-Horse.*" She smiled frankly. "I didn't think much of it at first, to tell the truth. I have not needed . . . companionship. Except for that of my husband." A shadow came into her eyes. "He's so terribly busy now, of course, and . . ." Her eyes came clear. "Now I'm delighted I gave in."

"We'll have good days," Leslie assured her. "We'll do exactly what you like best . . . reading, embroidery . . . have you tried macramé? I did macramé for a while last year. Perhaps we should take it up."

"Oh, yes," Mary Ben breathed. "That would be marvelous." She added modestly, "Of course, I've never been clever with my hands. But I'm sure you can teach me."

Leslie, as her hostess poured fresh cups, lifted her head to look about the room. Her attention was trapped by the portrait over the fireplace: a beautiful young woman, bearing a striking resemblance to Mary Ben, in a riding habit. Against her shoulder was the magnificent head of a black stallion, the wide-spaced eyes limpid with intelligence, brave with the courage and the will of the breed.

"Such a beautiful house," she said to Mary Ben. "Is it your family home?"

"Yes," Mary Ben said. "Manford Manor is one of the oldest horse farms in Kentucky." She gestured toward the portrait. "It was established, really, by my great-grandmother, Brooke Manford. A marvelous horsewoman; she had an international reputation as a rider."

"I spent my summers, as a child, on a breeding farm in Maryland," Leslie remarked. "A beautiful place, but not nearly so great as Manford Manor."

"It's terribly run-down, I'm afraid," Mary Ben said. "We've . . . been away a long time. One can't leave a house empty for so many years without expecting it to deteriorate."

"Yes, a house must be lived in," Leslie agreed.

So that explained the air of neglect; the Ashes had only just returned after long absence.

Mary Ben picked up her cup. It chattered in the saucer as she held it with both hands. She's trembling again, Leslie thought, wondering at the agitation.

"It's . . . we didn't expect to return," Mary Ben said, almost whispering. "It was for sale. I . . . prayed every night that it *would* be sold."

Strange words, spoken in a strange manner. They infused a chill into the warm coziness of teatime. Leslie sensed suddenly what her job would entail. Mary Ben's spirit, her mind, was as vulnerable as her crippled body. She's a nervous woman, Leslie told herself. Perhaps, a bit neurotic. Who wouldn't be? Confined to a wheelchair as she is, cut off from the active life a woman of her age should be enjoying, a loving husband, children, household activity. She studied her charge again, aware that she did not know what ill fortune had befallen to make her an invalid for life. Of course, one could not ask.

Mary Ben, she realized, steering the conversation away from the dangerous boundaries, was talking about a card game.

"Yes," Leslie responded with an effort. "Russian bank is a nice two-handed game."

"Wonderful!" Mary Ben said enthusiastically. "It's just my favorite."

"We'll have a continuing tournament," Leslie said gaily. "Keep a running score."

Mary Ben's eyes gleamed. "I warn you, I'm a gambler, I . . ." She hesitated. "Of course, you may set the stakes."

"I'll have to think about that." Leslie laughed. "I'm not much of a high-roller, I'm afraid. But I'll try to make it interesting."

The atmosphere was warm again. "More tea?" Mary Ben inquired.

Leslie laughed protestingly. "Enough for me. I . . ."

A movement at the end of the long living room caught her eye. She was startled; a man was there, on the last step of a tight spiral of staircase that, tucked neatly into a half-hidden corner, she had not noticed before.

The tall man, lean and dark, stood regarding her with a fixed intentness. He was dressed in a riding outfit, the black coat broad in the shoulders, tapering to a slender waist, the boots showing a soft luster. In one hand he carried a riding crop and helmet. At his side stood an enormous white German shepherd, his head lifted like his master's, his eyes betraying that same intent concentration upon her stranger presence.

Leslie, transfixed, was unable to move. Mary Ben, becoming aware of the direction of Leslie's gaze, turned her head.

"Oh, there you are," she cried. "Come, Whitney, you must meet Leslie. She's exactly what the doctor ordered."

The man did not move. Only the dog. Silently he padded forward, his head thrust out at a questing angle. He was not growling, but a low sound rumbled in his throat which could easily become a menacing growl. Leslie waited for the man to call off the animal. He, however, remained silent, only watching as the white dog prowled toward her. Leslie, on the edge of panic, rose, took a step toward the archway.

The movement elicited a deeper note of warning. At the same time, the German shepherd quickened his prowling pace.

The maneuver, executed so neatly, trapped Leslie, so that she dared not move. The animal was too close, obviously too dangerous. Standing in rigid fear, she waited for the master to call off the household guardian. But he did not speak. Mary Ben, Leslie noted out of the corner of an eye—she dared not turn her head—had shifted the wheelchair to observe the drama.

The dog must not be dangerous after all, Leslie thought with clear-headed logic. Surely they wouldn't allow this, even in jest, if there were a possibility I could be bitten.

So I must react quite naturally, she told herself sternly. I must lean over, pat the dog on the head. His tail will wag. All I have to do is bend at the waist, extend one arm, let my fingers feel the coarse hairs on the top of his head, rub his ears. The tail will wag, he will be happy, I will be happy, and . . .

She couldn't do it. She could not command her muscles, her will. For the low sound continued to live in the white throat and she was terrified that any movement she might make would deepen it into that menacing growl she had already heard once. And now he was so much nearer.

All right, then, she told herself. First you have to look at him. Bow your head slightly, direct your gaze; know your enemy. It's said that animals can read the human eye. If I show no fear . . .

But in her heart there *was* fear. Stark panic. And the white beast would know it. One look into the depths of her craven soul would launch him at her throat. She experienced a vision of his massive body hurling against her, bearing her to the floor beneath sheer weight, his great jaws fastening themselves into her throat, the blood spurting as the red tide of violent death took possession of her life.

She had to look. Deep inside, she began painfully weaving the tatters of her courage into a whole cloth. Rescue from the peril must come from within her; the man with the dark brow and the burning, intent eyes would do nothing. Even Mary Ben, her new-found friend, had not made a move.

Slowly, in spite of the great fear, Leslie turned her gaze down upon the white animal.

A jolt of terror shocked through her. The dog had lifted his head, his massive throat gleaming whitely, to look directly into her eyes.

In the first moment, she could see only the snare of white teeth; his lip, quivering under controlled tension, curled slightly. Then— his eyes overwhelmed her.

They were yellow, a color cold and true. Absolutely impersonal;

in them no hot glow of animal rage, simply a clear, cold seeing she found intolerable.

Their gazes remained locked. In the background sounded the low rumble that was not quite a growl and, for that very reason, far more menacing than an open threat.

Now I must touch his head, Leslie thought. It will be necessary to stretch out my arm, bend slightly—such an enormous dog, he stands nearly as high as my waist—and, holding my hand palm down, let it rest on that broad white expanse of skull.

Her arm was heavy. Vainly she strove to force the command through the numbed nerves. It seemed beyond her; she had squandered her tiny courage on directing her eyes.

Somehow, her arm moved. Like the arm of a mechanical doll, lifting jerkily even as she bent stiffly from the waist. She watched, bemused, as her hand crept through the air toward the dog's head.

His eyes did not shift. They remained fixed on her eyes, locking her gaze so that she could see her own movement only peripherally.

The rumble in his throat deepened. She had not been able to begin. Now she was unable to stop. Agonizingly her hand crept nearer, the palm slightly cupped, the fingers tingling in anticipation. She could already sense precisely how it would feel, the coarse harshness, the bony skull underneath. And then—the tail would have to wag.

Her palm was now within an inch of touching. It required a separate act of will to think about lowering it into actual contact. Just as the act of will took place within her soul, the man's voice crackled harshly from all the way down the length of the room.

"Don't do it!"

It was impossible to stop the movement. She stopped it; she had read the deadly meaning of the words. The moment she touched the dog, she would feel his fangs.

Her hand hovered. Then, slowly, as agonizingly as it had gone forth, it withdrew, her body straightened, she stood rigid as before. Even her head was lifted, so that she could no longer see the white beast.

She stood like a statue; she did not know for what she waited.

What did occur was entirely unexpected. The dog flowed upward in one lithe, irresistible movement to place his paws on her shoulders. She braced herself against the impact, determined not to take even one step backward to keep her balance.

She was helpless. Something within her wanted to cringe, cry out, crumple under the onslaught. But something else, a stronger part, would not allow such a surrender. She could only stand braced, rigid, awaiting the violence the white beast would wreak upon her flesh.

Unbelievably, the great dog ceased the not-growling. Incredibly, his tail wagged.

Not with enthusiasm, in sudden friendliness; simply one majestic sweep of the white plume before he lowered himself to all fours and turned to pace majestically to the side of his master. Once there, he brought himself precisely to heel and lay down, stretching forth his head on outthrust forelegs. Idly, he yawned a magnificent yawn, lifting his head to do so, then let it drop again to rest.

Leslie was safe; in some inexplicable manner, she had conquered the great white German shepherd. She directed a burning gaze toward the man who had stood by while she had dwelled in such danger.

"You could have stopped him."

The words were cold, irrefutable. They seemed to have no impact on his steely composure.

"I didn't need to," he said. "It seems Dragon decided to like you."

"But you couldn't have known that."

They were looking into each other's eyes, as she and Dragon had looked, with much of the same quality in the sword-crossing of gazes. His eyes, like the eyes of his dog, held the same cruel appraisal; an equal depth and availability of violence.

"Once so near, even you couldn't have stopped him in time," she said. "Isn't that true?"

"But I didn't need to."

He was unassailable.

She assailed him. "It isn't exactly the friendliest introduction to your household, Mr. Ashe."

Something moved in his face. No. In his eyes. Something that, she knew intuitively, she did not want to understand.

"Perhaps it was a test of your qualifications for the position you have come to take with us."

Her reply came hotly. "What kind of test is it to be threatened by an enormous white beast like that?"

The movement *was* in his face this time. A tight smile.

"You handled it rather well, I think."

Through with the conversation, he began walking down the length of the room. She turned, as watchful as if the dog, rising to move at his side, were still a menace to her safety. Whitney Ashe stopped beside his wife's chair. Courteously, he took her hand, pressed it to his lips.

"I'm going riding, love," he said. "You'll be all right, won't you, now that Leslie's here?"

"Yes, of course," Mary Ben assured him; though the tone of her voice betrayed nervousness. "But won't you have tea with us, so you can get acquainted . . ."

"Sorry," he said crisply. "I'm late now."

Without another glance toward Leslie, he exited through the archway, the German shepherd padding at his heels. Leslie, making an effort not to follow him with her eyes, read anxiety in Mary Ben's expression as she watched her husband depart.

The two women turned simultaneously toward each other.

"I . . . I hope Whitney didn't frighten you too much with Dragon," Mary Ben said. "Surely he wouldn't have let him hurt you."

Leslie, drawing a shaky breath, tried to turn it into a laugh. "It wasn't exactly the *friendliest* greeting I've ever had."

"But he did want you to come to us," Mary Ben assured her hastily. "Indeed, he insisted. It's just that . . ." She paused, as though doubtful she should utter anything that sounded like criticism of her husband. "It's just that . . . often, it's hard to understand what Whitney means by something he says or does."

A silence fell. Leslie broke it by saying wryly, "Yes. I can see that."

The silence returned. Along with it, the anxiety showed again in Mary Ben's beautiful, ravaged face.

She almost whispered in the speaking. "Whitney was the one who insisted on coming home to Manford Manor." Her mouth was trembling. She put up one hand to cover the betrayal. "I had to come with him. I had to. He wouldn't have it any other way."

CHAPTER TWO

Leslie awoke, the next morning, with a phrase so strong and certain in her mind it was as though someone had stood at the foot of her bed speaking the words with a peculiar urgency.

I am a stranger in a strange land.

Alarmed by the force of the message, she sat up abruptly, for the moment so disoriented it was as though, somehow transported during slumber, she had come awake in a different place.

Last night, after coming to terms with the reception accorded her—she had simply decided to ignore the inexplicable incident—she had taken spiritual possession of her quarters. Meticulously she had hung her clothes in the large cedar-lined closet, stowed her bags, laid out her things in the old-fashioned bathroom with blue porcelain tile banded waist-high around the walls. She had brushed her teeth at the marble lavatory stand, meanwhile running water into the claw-footed tub. She had remained in the tub for a long time, comforted by its womblike depth.

Never would she have cause to complain about the accommodations. Her bedroom was large, high-ceilinged, the two outside walls graced with tall, narrow windows that looked out upon the southern expanse of grounds surrounding the mansion. Beyond, still within view, she discovered, was a great stone barn and a stallion paddock.

She also had a dressing room, smaller than the bedroom but equally high-ceilinged, furnished with a marble make-up table backed by a mirror. There was also an extraordinarily flossy chair, chintzed and furbelowed, that was entirely out of context with the character of Leslie Tallant.

The bedroom was dominated by a canopied bed, the rich cherry of its wood shining softly with the patina of years. The canopy top, with a short valance on all three exposed sides, was an elegant burgundy fabric. An oriental rug, a cedar chest against one wall, two comfortable armchairs arranged around a floor lamp and an elbow-height table, completed the furnishings. The lighting was subdued, yet excellent for reading purposes. The incongruous note was a small Sony color television set.

Leslie had felt quite at home, the night before, as she reached one arm to plunge the room into darkness, herself into a deep and dreamless sleep. Why, then, had she startled awake in the early morning with a warning ringing so loudly in her mind it might have been spoken aloud?

She rose, went to the window. The sun was just up, casting the first rays of light against the stone façade of the great barn. The paddock between was empty, the rich greenness sparkling with dew. Why do they call it "Bluegrass"? Leslie thought. It's the *greenest* grass I've ever seen. Then she remembered someone had told her, once, that at a certain time of the year one could detect a bluish sheen. July it was, when the Bluegrass was at its ripest. Well, it was June now; maybe she would observe the phenomenon.

As she watched, a squirrel scampered across the expanse of lawn and darted with quick energy up the broad trunk of an ancient oak. A blue jay swooped to a nearby limb, its inquisitiveness attracted by the movement, and scolded the squirrel. The squirrel halted halfway up, twisting the upper part of his body around, even as his feet clung tenaciously to the rough bark, and gave the blue jay as good as he got.

Leslie laughed delightedly, feeling herself restored to a wholesomeness of mind by this view of nature's wildlife pursuing its morning ways. Going into the bathroom, she scrubbed her face vigorously before putting on the minimum of make-up that she had long since discovered showed Leslie Tallant off to the best advantage.

As she selected her outfit for the day, Leslie allowed her mind to revert to the echoing message: *I am a stranger in a strange land.* Only to reject it. After all, she told herself sturdily, I've *always* been a stranger in a strange land. Aren't we all?

The strangerness had always, indeed, been a part of Leslie Tallant. At home, an only child, she had lived a solitary life; her father had died before Leslie was old enough to retain a memory of him, and her mother, who had never remarried, had devoted herself to an intense social life based upon good works, leaving little time for her child.

Even the Maryland summers on the horse farm, Leslie reflected, though she remembered them warmly, made no essential difference. Despite the kindness of her rich uncle in inviting her to spend the months of July and August with her cousin Halene, she had remained forever a guest in a household of strangers.

There had never been a great love in which she could find herself at home for a bittersweet time. The boys who had courted her as a girl, the men she had known as a woman, had not counted. When, as inevitably as their appearance on the periphery of her life, they had departed, she had dutifully sought to muster up a broken heart in order to give the event a significance it had never possessed of itself. To no avail; within a week, even the memory had faded.

And New York?

Before the morning when she had, on impulse, purchased a copy of the *Blood-Horse* from her neighborhood newsstand because the cover showed a marvelous photograph of the great and ill-fated Ruffian, Leslie had not been aware that a certain restlessness, a secret yearning for change and adventure, had been growing in her.

She had, indeed, felt herself completely—well, *almost* completely—contented with her life. In her own terms, she was doing well with what fate and circumstance had yielded. Arriving in New York at the age of twenty-two from her hometown, Baltimore, within two days she had landed a job in the typing pool at the old-line Rennick Brothers, Publishers. From that menial beginning, she had climbed steadily until, three years ago, she had become the invaluable executive assistant to the young president of the publishing division, Michael Rennick IV.

Michael Rennick—lean, aristocratic, intensely involved in his work—was the kind of boss an ambitious young person could be proud to work for. Because, in addition to assuming the administrative burden of the executive post, he insisted on continuing to function as the editor for selected authors, he desperately needed Leslie's organizing talents.

Leslie had never quite let herself realize it, but, if not already in love, she was *ready* to fall in love with her boss at the first sign such a passion might be welcomed. Much of the eagerness with which she rose to face each working day could be credited to the happy knowledge that the next eight, ten, sometimes even twelve, hours, would be spent in the company of the most fascinating man she had ever met.

Michael Rennick IV, scion of an old New York family, could easily have chosen to become one of the idle rich. Instead, after graduation from Yale, he had started in the family firm as a lowly copy editor, commuting from the elegant family estate on Long Island as daily as a wage slave. During the intervening years, he had worked in every department, from the printing division to traveling throughout the Midwest presenting the current list to bookshops and department store buyers. He had found his true niche, however, as an editor, and only reluctantly had he accepted the post he now occupied . . . as he would, eventually, succeed to the management of the firm when his father chose to retire.

Leslie had been his first, and only, executive assistant. Quickly they had established a basis of intimate, though impersonal, friendship, often remaining in the office after the rest of the staff had long since departed. Invariably, on these occasions, they dined together in a small restaurant just around the corner; cherished times in which Michael was so gallant, so charming, as though they were out for a true evening of companionship, that Leslie would return to her lonely apartment with an ache in her heart she could not allow herself to recognize.

For one simple reason: the most prominent decoration on Michael Rennick's desk was a silver frame which held the photographs of a lovely wife and two delightful children.

Not that Leslie would have, could have, accepted an invitation toward a more involved relationship. Never, under any circumstances, could she have yielded herself to a dingy, clandestine relationship of hole-and-corner romance. Especially with *this* man, who embodied so completely her ideal of manhood. Far too demeaning for her, for him; so much out of the question that she never even searched him for a glimmer of passionate interest. It was enough to be valued so highly that daily he spoke openly her praises.

Except for the unalterable fact that he was unavailable as a man, it was a perfect job. Yet, though she felt herself fulfilled as she had never been even in her reasonably happy childhood, there remained a curious emptiness. For too long, now, the eligible men with whom she happened to come in contact were so predictably unexciting that she had ceased to date at all.

Yes. Leslie's life had, unnoted by her, narrowed in until it consisted solely of work and of solitude. After the interminable weekend of cleaning the tiny apartment—a task that could, at best, be stretched over a couple of hours—perhaps a Saturday night movie or, extravagantly, a concert or theater ticket, a Sunday afternoon visit to the Whitney or the Metropolitan, returning to work on Monday morning was something to be looked forward to. It was not an existence for a woman as vital, as forthright, as Leslie Tallant.

Perhaps the residual memory of good summer days spent on a Maryland horse farm had caused her to notice the magazine cover photograph of the renowned filly. Like almost everyone, she had been moved by the tragedy of Ruffian. Watching the match race on television, she had gasped when the magnificent animal took the bad step, anguished over her pain as she gallantly continued trying to outrun the champion colt which had been her rival.

A secret part of Leslie Tallant believed in fate. She felt touched by that fate when, leafing through the magazine to look at the grand stallions advertised in conformation photographs, she came across, in the back pages, the discreet, line-bordered advertisement:

> *Wanted: Private secretary-companion for invalid wife (no nursing duties required). Salary open; full-time residence on horse-farm estate. Some knowledge of Thoroughbred horses desirable but not essential. Reply to: MANFORD MANOR, PARIS PIKE, LEXINGTON, KY., 40505*

It was, somehow, a message for her, a way out of the blind alley her life had got itself into. *Some knowledge of Thoroughbred horses desirable but not essential.* Even that fitted; as a girl, she and her beautiful cousin Halene had romped through the barns and paddocks of her uncle's farm, petting the foals, helping to shake the stalls and groom the yearlings.

In Leslie's memory, those halcyon days of her girlhood had assumed the lineaments of an idyllic time. No matter that her cousin was rich and beautiful and willful; Leslie was only too happy to follow her imperious lead, grateful to be permitted a share in such magical Maryland summers.

Halene, as a girl, had been small but buxom, with lovely blue eyes and long blond hair. Even at a tender age she had borne within herself the serenity of the woman she would become, demurely feminine, smug in the certainty that, now and forever, only good things could happen. Leslie, in contrast, had been gangly-limbed, tomboyish in behavior, subject to sudden impulses and enthusiasms and bursts of violent activity that, somehow, she did not know how to control.

Halene had *possessed*, Leslie had *yearned*; this was the essential difference between them, the reason why, after childhood, they had drifted apart. Halene had attended a private boarding school, then an exclusive junior college. Six months after graduation, she was married to Robert Stilwell, Jr., the impeccable choice. Leslie had graduated from the state university, then had gone to New York. She never knew that, from those idyllic summers, there remained in her soul a dark residue that never allowed her to believe that she was a beautiful woman.

For all these reasons, secret yet real, one rainy Sunday afternoon Leslie had written a letter to Manford Manor, applying for the job as private secretary-companion to an invalid wife. At the time, it had been only a ritual gesture toward a new life's adventure, after which she would undoubtedly subside comfortably into the accepted routine of dedicated work and noble solitude.

Three days later, she received a telegram requesting the earliest possible arrival: first-class airline fare to be reimbursed. The name of the sender was Whitney Ashe.

Only then did it become necessary to make the decision. That day she arrived at work in a strange frame of mind; it was as though she had awakened this morning into a new world. The friendly faces confronting her with morning greetings were suddenly the faces of strangers. The six years of my life passed in this building might as well not have existed, she thought.

As she entered Michael Rennick's private office, he glanced up, the smile warm but as brief and abstracted as his gaze.

"It's a heavy schedule today," Leslie began. "There's the Publishing Committee at ten, with a long agenda, and Kurt Van Wezel is coming in at eleven. You know how he hates to be kept waiting." She smiled, the movement of her face as brief as his greeting had been. "Remember, the last time, he walked out in a huff because you were delayed five minutes."

They shared a silence, contemplating the advent of the best-selling author.

Michael sighed. "Yes, and he's being very difficult about the paperback split on his next contract. Have you noticed, Leslie, the more *literary* a writer is, the more difficult he can be about money?"

Leslie laughed in satisfactory response. "Your luncheon is with Roger Ward from the Tyrrell Literary Agency."

Michael frowned. "Let's play a small game with our eminent author," he said. "I shall become so engrossed in our conversation I will insist that we must continue our talk over lunch. I will summon you, tell you to cancel my previous appointment. Give Roger a ring now, tell him it'll have to be tomorrow." He frowned. "Where should I take Kurt for lunch?"

"La Grenouille," Leslie said promptly. "He couldn't stop talking, last time, about how much he liked the food."

Michael grinned. "Yes. He shall feel valued. It may make all the difference to his next book."

Throughout the quietly efficient conversation, Leslie had been studying her boss. Such a nice man. Such a handsome man. A sharp ache had come into her this morning at the first moment of greeting. Suddenly she realized that every day, for a long time now, she had experienced that pang of deprivation.

The ache was acute and real and permanent. And, she realized, he was totally unaware. As he was unaware of Leslie Tallant as a person. To Michael Rennick, she thought with a quiet fatefulness, I am a typewriter . . . no, more complex; a computer, say, an intricate but reliable bundle of talents and skills, with sensitive nerve endings attuned solely to his professional needs.

He is a man, Leslie thought. Then, with utter clarity: But he is not my man. He never will be. And I would not have it any other way.

Michael had been speaking, but she had not heard. "Yes?" she said.

"Have we covered everything I need to know for now?" he repeated. "While I'm in committee, check on how the copy editing is coming along on *The Torrey Testament*. Make sure I have it by Friday at the latest. I must go over it again before it's returned to the author."

Leslie sat looking at him for a moment. "There is one thing more," she said tentatively.

He had already turned his attention toward the papers on his desk; a tinge of impatience showed in the way he lifted his head. "Yes?"

"Michael," she said. "I am leaving New York. So . . . you'll have to think about finding someone to take my place."

In their long relationship, she had never addressed him by his given name. She did not know why, at this moment of farewell— farewell to so very much, she realized, far more than she had known it would be—the affectionate "Michael" had come so accustomed to her tongue.

He was seeing her now. In his eyes was revealed a disconcerted panic. Her heart thumped painfully; but immediately she recognized that he was disturbed only by the thought of how his daily routine would be disrupted by the necessity of breaking in a new executive assistant. Within the week he would undoubtedly be served in devotion and unrequited love by someone quite as efficient and unselfish and dedicated as Leslie Tallant had been. And Leslie Tallant would be only a dim, though friendly, memory.

"Is it . . . because of anything that isn't working between us?" he asked.

There had been, as he spoke, a flicker of awareness in his eyes.

"No," she said steadily. "Not at all. It's simply a private decision, for private reasons."

Immediately he placed her unexpected action into a category he could understand. "So many people are leaving the city. Where will you go, what will you do?"

As she explained, Leslie watched him come to terms with the idea of her departure. It was with a sense of relief that she finished. "I'm afraid, Mr. Rennick, they want me as quickly as I can come to them."

He was silent for a moment. "I have no wish to lose you, Leslie," he said quietly. "I think you know that. Neither do I wish to stand in your way." He smiled slightly. "I don't quite understand. But I sense, somehow, that this decision is important to you."

She felt a rush of gratitude. "It is," she said. She made a small laugh. "Though I don't quite understand it myself."

Now, sitting on the side of the bed experiencing her new state of being, Leslie wondered if she would ever understand anything about life. Especially herself, as a woman and a person.

CHAPTER THREE

This feeling of strangeness, then, is nothing new, Leslie Tallant told herself soberly. It's simply that the atmosphere of this old house is strange and brooding and fateful, engendering these emotions of out-of-placeness. Only to be expected. Very old houses have a *presence*; too many people over too many decades have laughed and loved and lived and cried and died within these walls.

A house, through the passage of many lives, acquires a soul.

Leslie felt herself strangely cheered. She was not, had never been, an introspective sort of person. Perhaps such introspection was a neglected development of her character. Perhaps this new life she had chosen so impulsively—or that had chosen her, she wasn't sure which—would develop in her that unlearned art of living in which one reflects deeply on the hidden meanings and purposes of one's actions and feelings.

Certainly, this morning's quiet reflection had restored Leslie's sense of herself. She felt cheerful, alert, ready for whatever the day might bring. Not to mention hunger—she realized that she was extraordinarily ravenous.

Leslie lifted her head, searching for sounds that would indicate people were astir. Only a deep silence. Well, these were thick walls; perhaps they were all belowstairs, wondering why the new employee, her first day on the job, was so slugabed.

With brisk decision, she rose, opened the bedroom door. The hallway was empty. She went to the landing above the entrance hall. Silence. She walked with careful quietness down the broad stairs into what seemed to be an empty house. Perhaps the dining room, the kitchen . . .

The dining room was to the left, a large, square, windowless space. Seeing Whitney Ashe alone at the table, she hesitated. He looked up, a flicker of . . . something . . . in his eyes. Leslie wondered, uneasily, if it were annoyance at having his solitary breakfast intruded upon. But then he smiled, saying, "Good morning. I see you're an early riser, too."

"Good morning," Leslie said. "Yes, I've always been." She hesitated. "Is Mary Ben . . . ?"

He made a careless gesture with one hand. "She's never about before ten-thirty, eleven." He added, indicating the sideboard, "Breakfast here is English style. Help yourself."

Leslie lifted the heavy silver covers—they were, she noticed, crested by two large *M*s, intricately interlinked by a massive flow of scrollwork—to discover kippers, country sausage, scrambled eggs, ham, toast, fluffy biscuits.

"If you care for a poached egg, or sunny-side up, I can ring for Martin," Whitney offered.

"This is fine," Leslie said. "Marvelous, in fact. I scarcely know where to begin."

She loaded her plate with a generous assortment and turned to walk to the far end of the table.

"Come, sit closer," Whitney said, smiling. "I need to talk to you, anyway."

Leslie had experienced an obscure necessity to put space between them—and not simply out of a desire to avoid disturbing his morning privacy. There had not been, really, any communication between them since the incident of the white German shepherd, though the three of them had shared the dinner table, and small talk afterward, before Whitney withdrew into the library, leaving Mary Ben and Leslie to play Russian bank. He had devoted his attention to his wife, treating Leslie simply as an accustomed figure in the ménage.

Remembering how deeply disturbed she had been by his attitude toward the dog's assault upon her, she turned to look at him. His head was bent as he folded his newspaper, put it aside. Whitney Ashe was such a similar type to her erstwhile boss, it startled

Leslie each time she saw him anew. Yet there was a difference. Whitney Ashe betrayed a darkness of spirit and experience that had not been in Michael Rennick IV. A *power*. That was the only word to describe it.

"Come, come," Whitney said. He smiled thinly. "Don't be afraid. Dragon won't bite you. He proved that at first meeting."

Somewhere in the back of her mind, Leslie had been wondering where the white dog could be. Now, as she came around the end of the table, Dragon, lying beside his master's chair, raised his head. He made a solitary sweep of the plumed tail—that one majestic gesture which seemed to satisfy his enthusiasm for communication—and laid his head again on his paws.

"You see," Whitney said gravely. "You two are quite friends."

"Good morning, Dragon," Leslie said, bravely determining not to bring up anew the issue of being tested by the fierce beast. Dragon did not deign to reply, except by the rolling of one eye.

"He *is* a magnificent animal," Leslie said, putting down her plate and taking a chair. "What is his breeding?"

"Impeccable—except that a German shepherd of his type is not acceptable, according to the official standard of the breed. Champions are prominent in his pedigree, but Dragon would have been put down but for me."

"How did that happen?"

"By a stroke of luck, I was spending the weekend with my friend Eric, who owned the kennels where Dragon was born. He took me, that Sunday morning, to view the new litter."

Whitney dropped his hand to Dragon's head. "Six beautiful pups—even I, who knew nothing of the breed, could tell that. I congratulated Eric.

"'Yes,' he said. 'They're all good but that white one with the yellow eye. He's a throwback, and no judge would give him a second glance. He'll have to be put down.'"

Whitney looked down at his dog. Dragon, in response, alertly lifted his head.

"While Eric explained about German shepherds with white coats, this little fellow found my hand, blindly nuzzled at it." He smiled deprecatingly. "I managed to talk Eric into letting me take him. He finally agreed; but, of course, Dragon came to me without papers."

A new and unexpected aspect of Whitney Ashe had been revealed. Leslie said gently, "So, in every sense of the word, he is
your dog."

"Yes," Whitney said. "He answers only to *Dragon*; and only to
me."

"Is he trained?" Leslie asked.

"Guard!" Whitney said, not altering the quiet tone.

Dragon sprang immediately to his feet, white ruff bristling,
upper lip curling to reveal the fangs. A growl rumbled in his
throat.

"Down," Whitney said, and Dragon immediately resumed his
lazy posture. "You see?" he added proudly.

"Yes," Leslie said, in spite of herself a small tremor in her voice.
"I see."

To cover her agitation, she began eating. Whitney pressed a
button with his foot and Martin came to take away his plate.

"This morning I'll show you the barns," he said. "Not that
there's much yet to see; but soon there will be mares and foals,
and a stallion is being shipped from England."

"You are planning to make Manford Manor an operating Thoroughbred nursery again?" Leslie asked. "Mary Ben told me it used
to be a great breeding establishment."

His eyes lighted. "Yes. When I came here originally, as farm
manager, I saw all that it could be. Now I shall have the opportunity to make it the showplace of Kentucky." He paused. "You,
Leslie, will be an important factor in my plans."

Leslie raised her head. The man was suddenly more animated
than he had shown himself so far. An enthusiasm was revealed in
his eyes, in the eager gesture of his hands. It awoke in her an immediate response; one could not fail to respond to a dream so
manifest.

"You will not only be a companion for Mary Ben, you will
also be our office manager," Whitney said. "You can't imagine
the paperwork that goes into a breeding operation. All those interminable Jockey Club forms, records to be kept on each mare and
her produce, the stallion's book for the breeding season."

He smiled. "Of course, at the beginning, there won't be much
to it. But, when horses arrive, paperwork arrives with them . . .
foal registrations, Coggins Test certificates, veterinary records.

There'll be the payroll every two weeks, health insurance, social security, withholding. We'll be boarding mares brought here to be serviced, so there will be monthly bills to the owners. Since Mary Ben sleeps late, then has Nurse Nunn with her for the physical therapy regimen she must maintain, your mornings will be spent working with me in the office. When it becomes too much for you to handle on that basis, we'll hire an assistant, because you will want to spend the afternoons and evenings with Mary Ben. But you will be in complete charge of everything."

Leslie smiled. "It sounds exciting."

"Terribly dull, I'm afraid. But essential to a successful operation. When I saw that you had been executive assistant to a company president, I knew you were just the right person." He looked at her. "And when I saw your photograph, I knew you'd be just the right sort for Mary Ben."

"Thank you," Leslie said. "Yes, I think we shall be friends."

His voice hesitated. "Mary Ben needs constant reassurance. She is so often . . . afraid."

"Yes," Leslie said steadily. "I saw. Have you talked to a psychiatrist? Sometimes . . ."

He waved an indignant hand. "All the time in Europe, she was under the constant care. It didn't help at all, not that I could see."

"But her fear seems to be centered on living at Manford Manor."

"Coming home has sharpened it, focused it," he said. "We must make her understand, you and I, that there is nothing *to* fear."

"I only hope that I can help. After all, that's why I'm here, isn't it?"

"I know it will mean a great deal to Mary Ben to have your companionship." His smile was charming. "You're just the ticket." He pushed back his chair, stood up. "If you've finished with breakfast, come along."

Leslie could have done with a second cup of coffee. But she rose obediently to accompany Whitney Ashe. Dragon rose also, to pace at his master's heel.

Their first stop was the stone barn. As they entered the broad doorway beneath the stone arch, Leslie's nostrils widened. So early in the morning, the scents were delightfully fresh; dewy grass in the nearby paddock, here the stronger odors of horse sweat and horse manure. The barn was redolent with the past presences of Thoroughbred horses; it gave Leslie a marvelous sense of *déjà vu*, translating her instantly into the Maryland summers of her childhood.

"Oh, it's wonderful!" she breathed.

Whitney smiled at her in understanding. "Just wait until our stallion is in residence, and we have a full band of broodmares, with foals at their sides. Right now, all I can show you are two Irish hunters, and a couple of barren mares I picked up on the cheap because they're problem breeders. Next year we shall see them in foal."

She liked the sound of quiet confidence in his voice. Here was a man who knew his worth as a horseman.

He opened a stall door and led out an Irish hunter, extraordinarily tall and long-legged, with well-muscled hindquarters. He was lean in the belly, his chestnut coat glistening with well-being. He tossed his head, making a sound of greeting. Leslie put out one hand, let him snuff at her palm.

Whitney was watching her manner with the steed. "Do you ride?"

"I have, a bit. A long time ago."

"I'll teach you. That is, if you care to learn."

"That would be marvelous," Leslie said, thinking, It'll solve the problem of exercise. Her game had always been tennis; she had already noted there were no courts at Manford Manor.

"Excellent. So busy with getting the farm into operation, I don't have time to exercise these two as much as I'd like. I want to school them for shows." He looked at her. "There's a Lexington hunt, you know, they have point-to-points and drag chases."

"I've only ridden in exercise rings," Leslie said dubiously.

"Not to worry. We'll work you up to it. I'll have you performing in horse shows in no time. And just wait until the first time you take a real fence . . . there's nothing like it. Mary Ben used to . . ."

He stopped abruptly. When he spoke again, it was to change the subject. "This next is a colt, he's just learning."

He returned the chestnut to his stall and brought out a bay nearly as tall, but lighter in the hindquarters.

"I'll put you up on Irish Sailor first. He's a gelding, a very kind horse. Tara Boy is something else."

Leslie could tell; he arched his neck, tossing his head, a white rim showing in his eye as he pranced backward against the constraint of the chain shank.

"Easy there, boy, easy," Whitney murmured soothingly. When Tara Boy had quieted, he patted him fondly on the neck.

"Got a mind of his own, this one," he told Leslie. "When he decides not to take a jump, he can be difficult. But he'll be a great one, give him time to get his head right." He patted the bay colt again. "We'll get it sorted out, won't we, son?"

The colt snorted, pawed at the hard-packed clay floor. He surged forward suddenly and Leslie shrank against the wall. She was grateful when Whitney released the wayward colt into the stall.

"Needs work," Whitney said. "Lots of it. He'll *get* work as soon as I finish showing you around. Perhaps you'd care to watch."

They turned at the sound of a step. The wry-bodied little man who had driven Leslie from the airport appeared, carrying a pitchfork in one hand.

"Good morning, Tom," Whitney said. "You know Miss Leslie, don't you?"

"Reckon I do," Tom grunted, not looking at her.

"Tom Musgrove," Whitney said to Leslie, ignoring his attitude. "Been working at Manford Manor since before God began. Isn't that right, Tom?"

"That's right," Tom Musgrove said. "Want me to turn them horses out? I need to shake their stalls."

"I'll be riding Tara Boy, so tack him up." He turned to Leslie. "Shall you get up on Irish Sailor today?"

Leslie protested, "I don't even have the proper clothes yet. No, I'll just watch, if you don't mind."

"Come on, then, I'll show you the rest of the place," Whitney said. "Tom, you can turn out Irish Sailor."

As Whitney drove them in a pickup truck to the next barn, Leslie found herself dwelling on Tom Musgrove's surliness. He had kept his gaze averted, his voice had been not even grudgingly polite. So often, old hands feel themselves privileged to rudeness. But this was more than rudeness. He doesn't like me being here, Leslie thought uneasily.

A pity he must be so hostile, she reflected. He could help me to understand Mary Ben. What happened, for instance, to put her into the wheelchair. So many things. She sighed. No chance. Distrust, dislike . . . even, perhaps, a degree of hatred . . .

Leslie glanced at Whitney from the corner of her eye. Does Tom Musgrove think . . . ?

She wouldn't allow herself to entertain the thought.

Certainly, she told herself, Whitney Ashe is livelier, more cheerful, than yesterday. Talking with animation, using one hand for expansive gestures, he outlined his plans for the restoration of Manford Manor. As he conducted the tour, ranging from an old coach barn surmounted by a green copper weathercock showing a horse and rider, to a colorless modern construction of board-and-batten, his eyes glowed, his face was more youthful, he laughed and talked with great charm.

Even Dragon seemed to enjoy the tour of inspection. Each time they returned to the truck, he leaped with one smooth bound into the back, to stand on Whitney's side, his head thrust out to catch the breeze of passage. At each stop, he descended to walk at his master's heel, seeming to listen to Whitney's explanations as attentively and intelligently as Leslie.

The barns were yet empty, though redolent still with the smells of horses. As Whitney talked, however, the easy jargon of "outcross" and "hybrid vigor" and "dosage diagrams" delighting Leslie's unaccustomed ear, his words seemed to populate the paddocks with grand broodmares and their playful foals. Leslie could envision a painstakingly selected staff of yearling grooms and stable help going about their myriad duties of tending the expensive horseflesh assembled here for the sole purpose of producing stakes winners which would, in turn, become valued sires and dams.

Leslie understood, even from her scant knowledge, the enormous gamble involved in a Thoroughbred breeding operation. Of all the foals dropped this year, no more than half would win any kind of a race; less than 3 per cent would ever win a stakes. This, after the attrition of barrenness, spontaneous abortions, the birth of twins, all the accidents and diseases to which every crop of foals is subject.

Whitney stopped the pickup truck on the crest of a small knoll. "Let's get out. You can see the estate best of all from here."

Leslie stood at Whitney's side. Below were the extensive grounds surrounding the mansion, the building nestled amid the great oaks as though it had grown out of the earth instead of having been erected upon it. On each hand, the pastures and paddocks, outlined by white fences, made a pleasing pattern upon the earth, shaping it into a purpose and meaning equivalent to the purpose and meaning of Whitney's ambition.

As they watched, Tom Musgrove led out Tara Boy from the stone barn toward the exercise ring. The hunter reared, taking Tom's feet off the ground with the mighty surge, and whirled in a rapid circle. Tom, with skill and firmness, brought him under control.

Whitney took his eyes away from the action to gaze at Leslie. "Well," he said. "What do you think?"

"I think it's wonderful," Leslie said, speaking only the truth. "It must be terribly exciting to have such a dream. Such a beautiful old place, it deserves to be . . ."

"Never should have been allowed to run down," Whitney said. His eyes smoldered. "When I first came—I'm English, you know, came to Kentucky originally to manage Manford Manor—the rot had already set in. The Manfords clung too long to the old bloodlines, which had been successful in the past, even after they were demonstrably thinning out with too much inbreeding. There's ample inbreeding, at best, with the Thoroughbred. Every runner alive today is descended from one of three sires—Matchem, Herod, and Eclipse—the overwhelming majority from Eclipse alone." He paused, not thoughtful but intense. "It became a matter of principle, you see, to continue the bloodlines which had made Manford Manor great. Even when it got to be dog's years since Manford Manor had produced a major stakes winner."

He drew a deep breath. "I couldn't believe this estate on first sight. I've been around horses all my life, started as a stable lad in order to learn from the ground up, became a successful steeplechase jockey, a gentleman rider at first, but then, when money was needed, riding professionally. Then I was a broodmare foreman, a stallion manager. Manford Manor was the first job with all authority in my own hands."

He stood, thoughtful, for a long moment. Leslie watched in fascination. She felt very close to Whitney Ashe as he betrayed so vulnerably the genesis of his dream. She yearned to let him know somehow, perhaps with the silent touch of a hand, how much it meant to hear him talk so openly.

Instead, she stooped to pat Dragon's head. He lifted his muzzle, pushing his forehead strongly against her palm.

"I could have done it then," Whitney said. "It ought to have been done. When Mary Ben and I were married, I had it all. The task, and the means to accomplish it."

His face became shadowed.

"Fate, plain accidental fate, cut it off. But now . . ."

He drew another deep breath.

"*Now* the great plan shall be carried out. Manford Manor will again be a recognized breeding establishment of the Kentucky Bluegrass. Whitney Ashe will have brought it about."

Leslie took her hand from the dog's head, straightened to look him in the face.

"Mr. Ashe, I want to help," she said. "All that I can."

He smiled. "I know, Leslie. And I am grateful."

She frowned. "But to help, I've got to know. Why is Mary Ben terrified to live in her old home?"

His voice cut sharply, so that for an instant she felt the whiplash of his anger. But it was directed toward a larger target.

"Superstition," he said, the words abrupt, harsh. "A tissue of old wives' tales. That's all it is. She believes that rubbish, it's stained into her soul."

"Perhaps it wasn't wise to bring her home, Mr. Ashe," Leslie said steadily.

He put a hand on her arm. "Some people aren't cut out to live a rootless life. She was dying in Europe. All that time, Manford Manor was dying too, as real and true as the death of any human being. I couldn't have it. Not for her. Not for the estate."

His eyes were burning. "Here, she will live or she will die. But she is *at home*, as she can never be anywhere else."

"But . . ."

He turned away toward the pickup. As quickly as he had taken her into his confidence, he was closing the gates. "I've got to give Tara Boy his work," he said coldly. "Are you coming?"

"I think I'll walk the rest of the way," Leslie said. She did not wait for his reaction, but started down the small hill.

It was at this moment that a strange event occurred. Feeling a presence at her side, she looked down to see the great white German shepherd, heeled on her, accompanying her down the slope.

She stopped, turned, looked at Whitney Ashe. He was staring at the dog, a startled expression on his face.

His voice snapped. "Dragon! Heel!"

The dog, having turned also, lowered his head, crouching slightly.

"Heel, damn it!"

As though he were waiting for a countermanding order, Dragon lifted his eyes to look into Leslie's face. When it did not come, he started obediently toward his master, moving in a slinking gait, his tail tucked tightly.

When he reached Whitney, the man slapped one hand against the truck body. "Up!"

In one leap, Dragon landed in his accustomed spot. Leslie turned, walked on. When Whitney passed, she did not lift her head to acknowledge him.

As the pickup rattled on at a pace too fast for the road, Dragon faced around, gave one sharp query of a bark. Then man and dog and truck were gone, leaving her to make her way to the mansion alone.

CHAPTER FOUR

When Leslie climbed the stairs to her room, it was still too early in the day for anyone to be about. She was grateful for this small time in which to be alone. Leslie Tallant needed to think.

She closed the door behind her, stood looking at the big, comfortable room. Her clothes were hung neatly in the closets; bedroom slippers showed their heels under the edge of the still unmade bed; her robe was thrown across the foot.

What I ought to do is pack my things and get out, she told herself. The words in her mind carried the thin, silvery sound of a warning bell, and she knew that the more sensible, everyday part of herself was telling the other Leslie Tallant the wisest move. Yet who, exactly, *was* that other Leslie Tallant?

Compulsively, she busied herself making the bed, though she knew the maid would be along sometime this morning. Only after the room was tidy did she sit down in a comfortable armchair to survey the situation.

Since I may leave, I might as well enjoy the amenities of the establishment, she told herself rather belligerently. Rising, she went across the room to yank on the bellpull. Sooner than she would have thought possible, Martin knocked discreetly.

"Yes, Miss Leslie?"

"Martin, may I have a pot of coffee here in my room?"

Martin smiled. "Why, of course, Miss Leslie. How about some toast to go with it?"

Leslie laughed protestingly. "I've already had a *huge* breakfast."

He went away, to return quickly with a heavy silver pot on a tray . . . and the toast. He placed the tray on a small coffee table and asked, "Is there anything else, Miss Leslie?"

"No, thank you."

Martin quickly closed the door.

Leslie poured coffee, drank gratefully. All right, girl, let's deal with it, she told herself. Let's just look at it coldly in the cold light of day.

She put down the coffee cup, lit one of her rare cigarettes. After the early morning rising, the exercise of walking, it tasted good indeed. What I'd like to do is play a fast and furious set of tennis with someone who's better than I am, she thought. Singles, where one must cover the whole court without the aid of a partner—and without excuses when one fails.

She drank again, knowing that her mind was evading the larger questions.

All right, she said sternly. Let's face it. There's something dangerous and fated in the atmosphere of Manford Manor, something too aweful to contemplate.

Whatever it might be, because it had already defeated him once in his plan for restoration of the estate to its former greatness, Whitney Ashe was as afraid of it as Mary Ben Manford Ashe. Yet his very strength compelled him to the struggle, even at the risk of the sanity—perhaps the life—of his wife. *And*, Leslie thought, *Mary Ben knows it*.

She drank again, finishing the cup, and stood up, going to the window to gaze into the distances of white-fenced paddocks. Empty paddocks, now, for the most part, but soon to be graced by noble horses. Whitney, in the exercise ring, had just mounted Tara Boy. Tall, lean, elegant in the riding outfit, he looked to the manor born.

We shall now contemplate Mr. Whitney Ashe, his character, Leslie instructed herself.

In the enthusiasm of introducing her to the projected breeding establishment, he had revealed much of himself. Leslie knew, for instance, that he had come to Manford Manor as a hired hand. A valuable employee, true; the manager of a Thoroughbred breeding farm is a key element. Nevertheless . . .

Whitney had been an impoverished English gentleman, following the immemorial pattern of emigrating to the New World to seek his fortune, his only baggage the previously acquired talents and skills, along with the character formed through the vicissitudes and triumphs of the old-world existence. And the courage—perhaps the recklessness—to accept the challenge of making a new life in a new place.

Whitney Ashe made his fortune, all right, Leslie thought. A wry, almost bitter, twist of her mind . . . had he truly loved the woman who had become his wife? Or had he first loved the land, only later the girl who could, who would, yield it into his masterful hands?

I don't know, Leslie told herself. So I shouldn't speculate. Certainly I have seen nothing to indicate that he feels anything less than the most cherished regard for Mary Ben. And there is this, Leslie told herself. Do I *wish* to discover that only his ambition, not his heart, is involved in the marriage? If it *were* true, what could I hope to gain?

Stopping herself from exploring that avenue of thought, she focused her attention on the activity below.

She had not seen Whitney ride until now. He was spectacular in the saddle. An excellent seat, a strong pair of hands, an empathy with his mount. Even with her limited experience, Leslie recognized immediately the quality, the style, of his performance.

Beautiful to see, and from her concealed vantage point Leslie absorbed herself in watching. Only after some minutes did the spectacle presented by the man and the horse begin to arouse in her an uneasiness.

At first she could not pinpoint it. Then, as he finished a series of jumps and turned Tara Boy to begin again, she recognized it; though with reluctance.

Yes. He rode beautifully. He handled his mount with perfection. But there was, also, a controlled ferocity that communicated itself to the young stallion. Tara Boy was lathered with sweat, foam streaking wetly along the sides of his neck. Whitney did not abuse the animal with whip and spur. But he put his steed at the jumps in daredevil abandon, imbuing Tara Boy with his own lust for treading the narrowest borderline between perfect accomplishment and terrible disaster. The man and the horse were one; not in the serenity of performance but in the reckless disregard for everything except the demands of a spectacular exhibition of skill and daring.

This strange duality was demonstrated most graphically when Tara Boy, swerving aside at the last moment, refused the highest jump. The sudden maneuver almost unseated Whitney. He succeeded in bringing himself and Tara Boy under control; then, turning the horse with a harsh pressure of knees, he trotted back into place and, with savage will, launched again the steed.

Instead of taking the command, Tara Boy reared. This time he did unseat his rider, Whitney landing in the dust with a sudden thump. Leslie, in dismay, put her hand to her throat. But Whitney was immediately on his feet, turning as Tara Boy, free now, frantically circled the arena, loose reins flapping. Tom Musgrove, who had been sitting on the fence watching the performance, jumped down and, as the horse lunged past, caught one rein with a quick snatch of hand.

Whitney came to Tara Boy, patted the lathered shoulder. He seemed unshaken as he shifted the saddle back into place and tightened the girth. Tara Boy stood with heaving barrel, his nostrils distended. Whitney stepped into the saddle, as Tom Musgrove straddled the fence again, and trotted the young stallion in a circle until he was calm.

Then, without warning, Whitney straightened the jumper with rein and body, launching him once more. This time, compelled by the man's will, Tara Boy took the jump in a soaring rise. Whitney leaned to speak into the horse's ear; then, ruthlessly, he took Tara Boy back to the beginning, putting him over the jumps one by one in the intricate crisscross of pattern until they had arrived once more at the most difficult.

Tara Boy tried to quit again. Whitney wouldn't allow it; with hands and body and will, he kept him true, lifted him up and over, the great animal flying as light as a bird. As he allowed Tara Boy to trot twice around the exercise ring, a grim smile of accomplishment showed on Whitney Ashe's face.

Standing far above, Leslie could not take her eyes away. She had been shown the darker side of Whitney Ashe, not in demeanor, this time, but in action; to her horror, she was enthralled. He'd be like that with a woman, she thought involuntarily. Fierce and violent, demanding of the woman's will and passion as of his own.

Whitney dismounted, Tom coming forward to take the reins and lead the sweat-blackened animal to a thick patch of grass where, after unsaddling, he began washing him down with meticulous care, the sponge and scraper moving with expert strokes. Whitney stood watching for the moment, chatting with Tom before he turned away.

As he strolled toward the house, one hand idly tapping the riding crop against a breeched leg, suddenly he raised his head to look directly at her window.

Leslie drew back. Had he been aware all along that she was watching? Had he, out of some desire she did not care to define, deliberately demonstrated something—which she did not care to define, either—to Leslie Tallant?

Returning to her chair, she put one hand against the silver coffee pot. It would be lukewarm by now.

That was all right. She didn't want more coffee, anyway. She wanted only to suppress, deny, the warmth that had suffused through her body.

Girl, if you know what's good for you, you'll shake the dust of Manford Manor from your shoes, the common-sense Leslie told that other part of herself. There's no way you can love this man as you loved Michael Rennick, she thought with fateful clarity. Safely, comfortably, secretly; neither wisely nor too well.

She sat up straight in the sudden shock of awareness. Until this moment she had not admitted the depth of her feeling for her former employer. Beyond the shock of recognition lay another understanding, dark and strong. There could be no safety, no comfort—most awful of all, no secrecy—in what she felt for Whitney Ashe.

To take her over the jumps, as he had taken the Irish hunter, he would only have to put out his hand. She would be rebellious perhaps, but, like Tara Boy, ultimately responsive to his will, his need. For something within her dark and violent, whose existence she had not realized, responded to the challenge.

Leslie Tallant had never known a man capable of dominating her will; directing it, coercing it, yet ultimately only compelling her to fulfill her own primordial nature. As Whitney Ashe had compelled the Irish hunter to fulfill both his instinct and his training by taking gallantly the most difficult jump of all. Not once, but twice . . . And again and again and again, when the necessity, the desire, should arise.

Leslie was trembling. Not outwardly, visibly; but deep within her soul there was a quivering. She knew now; there could be no departure from Manford Manor. Only by remaining could she hope to know the trueness of Leslie Tallant. For, though she did not understand exactly *how* she knew, Leslie had come to the Kentucky Bluegrass for one vital purpose: To find out who she was. Who she could be.

Like Whitney Ashe, she had emigrated into a New World, her only baggage the character formed by the vicissitudes and triumphs of her old life. To seek a fortune that would consist only of knowing herself, with all her human potentiality for good and for evil.

Know thyself. And the truth shall make you free.

For this, she had also dared the New York adventure. We are all seeking for wholeness, searching for our total selves, trying to attune ourselves with the universe; for without such completion we are only fragments of the whole person we were destined to become.

It was no accident, Leslie knew now, that had brought her to Manford Manor. And so, until the very end—whatever that end might be—there could be no retreat.

Leslie tapped lightly on the door to Mary Ben's suite of rooms. Nurse Nunn opened immediately, for Leslie was expected; only moments before, the nurse had rung to say that Mary Ben wished to see her if she were free.

"Good morning," Mary Ben said with a bright smile. She sat in the wheelchair, blond hair freshly combed, her heart-shaped face beaming a morning welcome. She looked cool and fresh in a happy, gingham-checked blouse.

"You must have had a good night," Leslie said, smiling in return. "You look absolutely top of the world."

"I slept better than any night since we've been back." Mary Ben put forth a hand, and Leslie took it. "I think it was because I knew you were in the house, Leslie."

"Surely not," Leslie said lightly.

Mary Ben's voice was serious. "Yes. I really believe it." She had not relinquished Leslie's hand, but held it tightly. Gazing upon her charge with an extraordinary fondness, Leslie thought, I suppose she's never really had a chance to grow up. The fears she knows are so very much the fears of a child.

Mary Ben was continuing. "I went to sleep thinking about what we shall do today. Do you know what I've decided?"

"Of course not," Leslie said, laughing. "But you're going to tell me, aren't you?"

"I thought of the macramé first of all," Mary Ben said gaily. "I really want to get into that. But of course you'll have to go into Lexington, first, to stock up on supplies, won't you?"

"Yes. I'll do that, first chance," Leslie promised. "Maybe this afternoon the chauffeur can run me in."

Mary Ben smiled mischievously. "So what I really lighted on, and it'll probably be a total surprise, but I'd love to read Kipling all over again. Do you like Kipling?"

"Haven't read him in years," Leslie confessed.

"There's a beautiful leather-bound set in the library," Mary Ben said. "Shall we begin, then, and see how far we get?"

"Marvelous," said Leslie. "It'll be great fun to discover Kipling all over again." She chuckled. "Have you kippled lately? Remember that old joke?"

The phone rang. Nurse Nunn picked it up, listened, said, "Mr. Whitney wishes to speak with you, Miss Mary Ben."

Mary Ben took the phone. "Hello, darling," she said. "You were up and out early today. Even earlier than usual."

She paused to listen. "Oh, wonderful!" she exclaimed. "We'll be right down."

She hung up. "Whitney says the English stallion was released from quarantine yesterday and is being vanned from the airport right now. He wants us to come down." She turned toward the nurse. "Shall we go, then? Come along, Leslie. You'll want to see, too."

Leslie felt a reluctance to face Whitney again, so soon after this morning's small contretemps, so soon after secretly watching him ride Tara Boy with such ferocity and finesse.

"Oh, I'll have a chance to view the stallion later," she said.

"While you're doing that, Mary Ben, I'll get ready to launch us upon the Complete Works of Rudyard Kipling."

"Whitney specifically instructed me to bring you along," Mary Ben cried. "He'll be dreadfully disappointed."

"Well, in that case . . ." Leslie said, still reluctant but aware that, to get out of it, she would have to make an issue of her absence.

"Let's go, then!" Mary Ben said excitedly. "It's been *years* since a great stallion has stood at Manford Manor."

Nurse Nunn, grasping the handles of the wheelchair, pushed Mary Ben toward the door, while Leslie held it open. They proceeded down the hallway to the small elevator installed especially for Mary Ben's use. After seeing her and the nurse safely inside, Leslie walked down the stairs, to meet them again at the front door.

When they reached the stone barn, the horse van was being positioned against the loading ramp. Whitney, Leslie was relieved to see, was so preoccupied with directing the operation that he scarcely had time for more than a glance in her direction.

When the driver opened the doors, Whitney himself went up into the van. As they waited for him to lead the stallion forth into his new domain, Leslie felt herself gripped by an inward excitement. Mary Ben, she observed, looked ready to leap out of the wheelchair from sheer impatience at Whitney's long delay.

At last they came. The stallion was precise, almost dainty, about the placement of his feet, keeping balanced as he picked his way down the ramp to solid earth.

Gazing upon him, Leslie felt her heart catch into her throat. The sheer beauty of a great male animal.

He was enormous in size, fully mature, with a great bowed crest to his neck, and massive hindquarters. An arrogant head, but a calm and lambent eye. Yet, beneath the calmness, lurked the look of eagles that all great runners are said to have.

His coloring was the great surprise; Leslie knew that the Thoroughbred never has a truly white coat, so he must have been born a gray. But now he showed almost pure white, though, of course, he would never be called "white." The coat carried a glossy sheen; he did not look in the least as though he had spent many days in the cramped quarters of a quarantine station before being allowed to enter the country.

Leslie caught her breath. "What a *grand* stallion!" she exclaimed. "What is his name?"

Whitney shot her a glance of warm approval. "King's Man," he said. "Yes, he *is* a grand individual, isn't he? Just look at that conformation . . . he passes it on to his offspring, too, let me tell you."

He turned the stallion, posing him. Leslie gazed dutifully, but, because she had not studied the conformation of the horse, she could not see how perfectly balanced, even in full maturity, King's Man showed himself to be.

"He's a Herod-line stallion. Traces back in tail-male through Tetratema and The Tetrarch—who was nicknamed "The Rocking Horse" because of his peculiar coloring—and Roi Herode. This is the great gray line; nearly every gray you see owes the color to Herod. Incidentally, there used to be considerable prejudice against gray Thoroughbreds."

Whitney paused to stroke possessively the massive neck. "He'll be a complete outcross to nearly all the most prominent Kentucky bloodlines, such as Princequillo and Bold Ruler broodmares. That means he'll bring hybrid vigor to his Kentucky get." He nodded his head in satisfaction. "I've been advertising his arrival in the *Blood-Horse* and the *Thoroughbred Record*. His book is already half full for next spring."

He turned to his wife. "Come, Mary Ben. Introduce yourself to King's Man."

She shrank into the wheelchair. "Isn't he . . . dangerous? When I was a child, we were always told to leave the stallions strictly alone."

"They can be, of course, but I'm holding the shank," he assured her tenderly. "Come along, let him get the smell of you. He's a very kind horse, for a stallion, I've been told."

Mary Ben's voice firmed into decision. "I'd rather not, if you don't mind."

Whitney glanced toward Leslie and she, as though reading his mind, knew he had thought of inviting her to approach the great stallion. He did not speak, however, only turned to Tom Musgrove, indicating that he was to take the shank.

While Tom held it, Whitney stooped to lift each hoof in turn, feeling the ankles, the knees, with sensitive, probing fingers. As he did so, with a quick flick of a tool taken from his hip pocket, he cleaned out the frogs of the feet.

"King's Man is twelve years old, a proven sire. Good runner in his time, won some important stakes, though not absolutely the best of his crop. Like most English runners, he could get a distance of ground . . . that's something else that's needed in American bloodlines. Most breeders go for sprinting ability . . . so many rich two-year-old stakes at less than seven furlongs. The English breeder has always believed in developing classic potential, which takes staying blood."

He stood back, studying all over again his proud acquisition. "It took some doing to persuade his owners to sell." He smiled slightly, his lips compressed into thinness. "But money talks, and a lot of money talks loudly." He looked at his wife, his glance straying over Leslie as he did so. "King's Man represents an enormous investment; he carries in his seed the success or the failure of Manford Manor as a Thoroughbred breeding farm."

Leslie was moved by the quiet declaration. And, as she gazed upon the gray—almost-white—horse, she felt a confidence that Whitney, out of his wisdom, had made the right choice.

She could not refrain from speaking her subliminal conviction. Looking directly at Whitney, she said, "But he will do it. I know he will."

Whitney's eyes were warm again. "I cut the odds as much as possible. After all, he *is* a proven sire, which makes him so much more expensive than a colt just coming into stud from a racing career, no matter how successful. But still . . ."

He stopped, his face brooding into suddenly graven lines as he contemplated the enormous gamble.

Shaking himself, he said to Tom, "Let's turn him out while he's still tired. Been a long time since he's run free."

Leslie watched with fascination the meticulous preparations for loosing the stallion. Tom led King's Man into the paddock, from which he had already removed the Irish hunters, taking him toward the middle of the enclosure. In the meantime, Whitney stationed himself in a near corner of the fence.

"He's not as likely as a young horse to go wild with freedom," he said. "But it could happen. If he injured himself, immediately upon arrival, I . . ." His mouth quirked harshly as he stopped the unlucky words.

Quietly Tom unsnapped the shank. Quietly he stepped away, moving backward, keeping his eyes on the stallion. Only when he had reached a safe distance did he turn to hurry into the other corner of the board fence.

King's Man stood still for a long minute. Then he walked, with sedate steps, to a pile of manure left by one of the Irish hunters. Putting his head down on a long neck, he stood with legs braced wide to snuff at the odors. Suddenly he tossed his head high, nostrils widening, the crest of his neck seeming to thicken as he realized that this paddock, so immediately his territory, had recently been occupied by another horse.

Quickly he surveyed the expanse of green grass, seeking for the rival that, within these confines, would be his deadly enemy. To his satisfaction, the paddock was empty. Still, he snorted, pawing at the ground with one quick-flashing hoof.

Suddenly he seemed to realize his freedom. With startling abruptness he launched into a full run, going straight away in a long gallop before curving back toward them; hoofs pounding, mane flowing, nostrils flaring.

For a fraught moment, it looked as though he would crash through the board fence. At the last moment he turned, putting his head down to dig in for the stretch run along the rail, his heels throwing clods of grass. Finally, swinging away from the fence, he headed for the center of the paddock, where he stopped as abruptly as he had started.

His sides were heaving; sweat showed wetly on the almost-white coat. He stood with head high, gazing at the horizon; then, gathering himself once more, he came racing toward them.

Directly for her, Leslie realized in panic. She stood frozen. In her ears was the fateful pound of his hoofs, the harsh sounds of his breathing. Nearer now, then nearer still, until she was overwhelmed by the mass and speed and smell of him. She knew, as well as she had ever known anything, that he would crash through the fence to destroy her.

He came to a scattering halt, his nose almost touching the barrier. He blew his breath at her, gusty and warm, then trotted away. In the center of the paddock he stopped, dropped his head, and cropped a mouthful of grass.

"He's all right," Whitney said with satisfaction. "He's home now."

Leslie gazed at the man, as he was gazing at the stallion. They were much the same: proud males, bearing within them the past and the future.

"This is the beginning, isn't it?" she said quietly.

He turned. Their eyes met over Mary Ben's head as she sat in the wheelchair between them.

"The beginning," he said. "Of everything."

CHAPTER FIVE

It began a week later.

The time in between had been a period of serenity, during which Leslie had settled into the pattern of her new life. She devoted the morning hours to organizing the farm office, which occupied a small stone building adjacent to the stallion barn. This task necessitated a daily relationship with Whitney Ashe.

There was, however, an extra dimension of propinquity. A diligent student of Thoroughbred bloodlines, Whitney had the nightly habit—as Leslie and Mary Ben read, or played Russian bank, in the living room—of withdrawing into the library for a solitary session with broodmare records and stallion registers over a bottle of port.

Every night, when ready to retire, Mary Ben insisted on being wheeled to the door of the library. Leslie would knock, Whitney would say, "Come," and Leslie would open the door.

In this quiet time of his long day, Whitney Ashe smoked a pipe, so that the spacious room would be fogged with blue whorls of smoke. He wore an old smoking jacket of faded burgundy, and his hair was disheveled from the concentration of study. He would look up from his desk, eyes still abstracted.

"Good night, Whitney," Mary Ben would say in a soft voice. "Don't stay up all night."

"Be along shortly" was his invariable reply.

More often than not, the promise was not kept. These were the evenings when, as they looked in upon him, instead of working at the desk he would be sitting in a leather armchair, booted feet thrust out upon a footstool, the bottle of port at his elbow nearly empty. At such times his countenance, turning to accept grudgingly their intrusive good-nights, would show the dark and brooding look.

As long as he was downstairs, Leslie could not find the safety of sleep. Something within her was always aware when Whitney Ashe remained wakeful in the night. Lying with achingly tense muscles, she kept vigil until she had heard his belated step up the stairs and down the corridor past her bedroom door to the suite of rooms he shared with his invalid wife.

Whitney was never less than correct. Working with her through the morning hours, he was, indeed, quite friendly and communicative. He seemed anxious for Leslie to share in the daily progress of the breeding establishment. Far more than Mary Ben; the invalid woman, though she listened dutifully as her husband spoke of plans or accomplishments, seemed to avoid the subject, as though such matters were part and parcel with her fears.

However, the time of true closeness came when they rode together. Whitney started her on jogs and trots and slow gallops in order to toughen her muscles for future show ring schooling. Weather permitting, almost every day, with Whitney on Tara Boy and Leslie on the sedate Irish Sailor, they explored the far reaches of the estate. There were long-abandoned bridle paths, a few strategically placed fences and hurdles.

They scarcely spoke, except when Whitney corrected her seat or instructed her in the finer points of posting. He would not allow her to take a fence until her long-dormant skills had returned. When she jumped for the first time, though it was only a low hurdle, Leslie experienced a great lift of exhilaration as she felt under her the gathering of the horse's muscles, the explosion of effort.

Though in the first days unaccustomed muscles ached stiffly, Leslie gloried in the rides at Whitney's side. It was a time of communion, not through speech but through the silences of action. Such pleasure enabled her to ignore the disapproving scowls of Tom Musgrove as he saddled her mount. If Mary Ben was aware of their daily rides, she did not speak of it.

Immediately after the great gray stallion, King's Man, had taken up residence, other Thoroughbreds began to arrive. Whitney, having determined the bloodlines he wished to cross with the Herod-line stallion, had commissioned a bloodstock agency to seek out the individual broodmares which would fit into his scheme.

Though the best opportunity to purchase breeding stock would come during the fall auction sales, from time to time a few mares, often from points as far away as California or Florida, arrived at Manford Manor. Leslie, more often than not, was present at the unloading. She adored the look of these matronly broodmares, broad of hindquarters, often sway-backed, so large-bellied it was hard to believe they had once been athletes of the track.

This year's breeding and foaling season was over, of course, now in July, and most of the purchased mares were barren. Few horsemen, Whitney explained, could bring themselves to sell a mare with a foal *in utero*. Or with a foal at her side. Breeders were great optimists; they believed in their hearts, despite the irrefutable statistics which proved otherwise, that every foal would be a champion. They were fearful that precisely the foal they had been persuaded to sell would prove to be the greatest runner of their lifetime production. More than once, it had happened so . . . often enough, at least, to prove the point.

A few mares, however, arrived with foals at their sides. So there were new workers about the barns now, young people in the main, both boys and girls—the girls, Whitney informed Leslie, were often much better with horses—and Tom Musgrove had been elevated to the position of broodmare foreman.

It delighted Leslie to see the foals led out, these Kentucky mornings, to be turned into the pastures. They were frisky, playful, inquisitive; extraordinarily affectionate, because they were accustomed from birth to daily handling. They placed as much trust in the kindly people about them as in their own mothers.

Already they revealed the competitive spirit that would, hopefully, make them runners of heart and stamina. Daily they grew in size and strength. Sparring with nipping teeth and flashing hoofs, or racing side by side to the far fence and back again, their long legs seemed so fragile that Leslie often held her breath at the danger of injury.

Leslie observed how carefully Whitney supervised their daily growth. Every morning, as they were led out, he examined each foal, feeling their ankles for heat, tending meticulously the inevitable scars and bruises. Often, he would be called out at night to see to a foal suffering from colic or running a fever.

So Manford Manor began to live again. Whitney had hired a maintenance crew to begin repairing the fences, refurbishing the barns, the mansion itself, with fresh paint and careful repairs. Mowers kept the grass in the paddocks and pastures cut to the proper height for maximum growth and richness; the fence lines were cleaned of undergrowth.

The gray stallion, linchpin of the operation, would not be put to his task of servicing mares until the spring; meanwhile, he occupied the stone barn alone, for the near presence of broodmares would have agitated him unduly. He ranged his private paddock in solitary splendor; he would have killed any foal, fought any stallion, harassed any broodmare.

Despite the deeply felt peacefulness of the time, however, there were also adumbrations and portents.

Late one afternoon, nearly sundown, Leslie was returning from the long walk she had adopted as a means to loosen her saddlesore body.

Aside from the physical pleasure of stretching her muscles, it was lovely, these warm and sultry nights, to stroll in the growing Kentucky twilight. She could choose at caprice any one of a dozen farm roads and know she would be undisturbed in her solitude. On returning, often, whisper-winged owls flew in the dusk, there came softly the calls of whippoorwills, she could gaze at a contrail high in the sky, illuminated brilliantly by the last rays of the already set sun.

Tonight, as had also become her custom, Leslie detoured by the stone barn to visit with King's Man. He had come to recognize her; she had the feeling he waited for her daily visit to his ample quarters.

He whuffed a soft greeting at the sound of her step. When she opened the stall door, removing the barrier between, he nodded his head vigorously, rattling the rings of his halter.

"Hello, King's Man," she said. "Have a good day?"

He tilted his head to one side, showing his teeth as he made a feint. She laughed, slapping a flat palm against the side of his muzzle. He shook his head again in vigorous, playful protest, then, stubbornly, made another feint. This time she felt his soft lips nibbling the flesh of her arm.

Satisfied with the game, he pushed his nostrils into the palm of her hand in an affectionate caress. Leslie laid her other hand strokingly against the side of his head.

"You big baby," she said, crooning. "How could you have anything *but* a good day? The finest oats, a beautiful paddock to graze in, and, next spring, all the mares a stallion could wish."

He made a sound so much like conversation that she distinctly felt he was agreeing with her.

Leslie was enthralled by the great gray stallion. Not simply his handsome physical presence, but the *idea* of King's Man as a progenitor of race horses. Such a perfect embodiment of combined power and grace; he would *have* to get great runners.

And, withal, such intelligence, showing plainly in his eyes, in the shape of his head. Such gentleness of affection, as demonstrative as one could wish without speech. Even now he was rubbing his forehead against her shoulder. So many Thoroughbreds are head-shy, but it was King's Man's particular pleasure to have Leslie play with his ears.

In an excess of emotion, Leslie ducked under his chin and clasped both arms around his neck. Her face pressed against him, she could feel on her cheek the coarse hairs, smell his strong odor. She was, suddenly, on the verge of weeping. And she did not know why.

A harsh voice spoke behind her.

"Keep on like that, one of these days that stallion's going to take your arm off."

She whirled, her startled eyes finding Tom Musgrove standing close—too close—a flashlight in one hand. As she stared, he flicked on the beam, brushed past her, forcing her to move out of the way, and closed the stall door. King's Man made a sound of protest.

"But . . . but we've become great friends," Leslie said uncertainly. She had known that Musgrove was hostile to her presence at Manford Manor, but now there had been in the angry tone of his voice much more than mere dislike. She felt bruised by the whiplash of his words.

"Ain't nobody's pet," Tom declared. "Never was, never will be. Ain't no Thoroughbred stallion nobody's pet."

"But he's so affectionate. He waits for me to come to him, I swear he does."

Though his face was shadowed in the growing darkness, the whites of Musgrove's eyes gleamed in the back-flare of the flashlight. It *is* dark, Leslie thought irrelevantly. They'll be waiting dinner. Dark enough to make the inimical man seem sinister, almost evil, here in the deserted stone barn.

"Sure, he's been hand-raised from a foal." Tom's voice was relentless. "But you better not forget that he's an animal. He can be playing a nice, friendly game one minute, and the next minute he'll savage you." He jerked his head. "Them jaws, they're strong enough to break a bone. You'd do best to remember that, and leave this stallion alone."

Such intensity in the words! He's been forever at Manford Manor, Leslie reminded herself silently. Having known her as a child, he's probably fond of Mary Ben. It occurred to her she had no idea of Tom Musgrove's attitude toward Whitney Ashe. Speaking with him, Musgrove's demeanor was neutral, bland, though properly respectful.

"Are you *forbidding* me to visit King's Man?"

He regarded her. "Ain't my place to say you nay. But I aim to let Mr. Whitney know the risk you're running."

Holding his head to one side in his typical wry-necked fashion, he was turning away. Leslie, until she heard herself speaking, had not known she was going to ask the question. She had not even known that, all these days since coming to Manford Manor, it had been pressing against the edge of her mind.

"Tom. What happened to make Mary Ben a cripple?"

He whirled, the long-bodied flashlight swinging also, pinning her in the beam. Behind her, King's Man made a startled movement.

"He tried to kill her. That's what happened." His voice snapped like a whiplash, sudden and vicious. Such anger, such hatred, bottled up in this little man. Not simply anger at what life had done to him, racking his body with twisted pain; more focused than that, directed. Directed, in part at least, toward Leslie Tallant, her presence at Manford Manor.

Her voice came strongly. "*Who* tried to kill her?"

From behind the strong light, he studied her. He was only a darkened figure, shielded so, and his words seemed to be issuing from an immense blackness.

"Ain't they told you?"

She faltered. "One could scarcely ask. Perhaps Mary Ben *can't* talk about it. It would help me to help *her*, you know, if I understood these things."

"Ain't my place to tell you anything they ain't seen fit to let you know about."

The words were irrefutable; without protest from her, he walked away.

The next disturbing event followed so closely on the heels of her confrontation with Tom Musgrove, Leslie could not help but wonder if it were mere coincidence. She had a strange feeling that, as she arrived late and apologetic for dinner, as she sat over Russian bank later with Mary Ben, the unanswered question she had addressed to Musgrove lay so heavy in her mind it actually triggered the aftermath.

As she observed Mary Ben, so competitively intent upon the cards, she knew she must begin to seek answers. If she were to fulfill her duties as companion and guardian, it was not enough to drift from day to day like a chartless voyager. She must arm herself with knowledge.

Mary Ben was nervous tonight, more so than at any time since Leslie had been with her. Perhaps it was the oppressive sense of violent weather in the offing; all afternoon the air had been sultry, hushed, and now, after a beautiful sunset, the rumble of thunder, stalking in black clouds over the horizon, could be heard in the distance. It would surely storm before the night was done.

With each rumble of thunder, Mary Ben would lift her head alertly. Her face was drawn, harried, and often, as she dealt the cards, her hands would tremble. Once Leslie suggested that, since Mary Ben seemed distraught tonight, perhaps she should retire. Mary Ben vehemently rejected the idea, saying she wouldn't be able to sleep, anyway, until the storm had passed.

As the thunder rolled closer, Leslie observed something she had not noticed before. Every time Mary Ben lifted her head, pausing in the play of the cards to listen, she ended by glancing furtively at the portrait over the mantel. As she did so, a strange expression crept fugitive across her face.

Finally, Leslie remarked with careful lightness, "Mary Ben, you don't care for that portrait of your great-grandmother at all, do you?"

There was sudden passion in Mary Ben's voice. "I hate it! I can't stand it!"

Leslie laughed. "Then why don't you have Martin take it down?"

"It has always hung there."

Leslie shook her head in protest. "Mary Ben, I'm a great lover of tradition, too. But, as much as you dislike it, there's no reason you have to live with it. Tell Martin to remove it, stow it in the attic safely out of sight and out of mind."

"I couldn't do that," Mary Ben protested.

"You're the mistress of the house, aren't you? You can do anything you like." She grinned at her friend. "Come on, Mary Ben, call Martin. This minute. Tell him to bring a stepladder and take the damned thing down."

Mary Ben, refusing to respond in like manner, showed a face as brooding and potent as her words. "No, Leslie. I don't own Manford Manor. Manford Manor owns me. It always has. It always will."

Her tone so fatefully morbid, Leslie put out a hand to touch her arm. "Mary Ben, it may require courage to assert your command of ownership. But you have that courage. I know it."

Mary Ben looked straight into her eyes. "You know, of course, that Whitney married me only because of Manford Manor."

Leslie was shocked by the calm, almost casual, statement. "You can't believe that, Mary Ben. Why, the man absolutely cherishes you."

Mary Ben nodded. "Yes. It's true." She lifted her chin. "But I don't care. I didn't care then, and I don't care now. Whitney Ashe is worth a dozen Manford Manors."

"You mustn't think it of Whitney. If you can't see it, I certainly do. Any woman would be proud . . ."

Mary Ben nodded solemnly. "Yes, I think he loves me. Now. You know, when I was crippled, I was sure he'd leave me in short order. No one who knows Whitney Ashe could believe him the sort of man to devote himself to a helpless wife." She leaned forward confidentially. "But, Leslie, I'm as sure as sure can be that Whitney has not looked at another woman." She smiled almost smugly. "He's never been far enough from my side to have an affair."

"You see?" Leslie exclaimed. "So how can you say . . . ?"

"It wasn't like that in the beginning. He loved Manford Manor, not Mary Ben Manford. I knew it all the time. I just didn't care." She laughed self-indulgently. "I fell madly in love with Whitney, you see, the day he arrived to take over as farm manager. He thought of me only as a child, not a woman. After all, I was only seventeen."

She sat thoughtfully for a moment. Remembering.

"He'd never have looked at me if I hadn't made the first move." She glanced slyly at Leslie. "I was brazen, Leslie, as only a girl madly and passionately and hopelessly in love can be brazen. I simply looked him straight in the eye one day and told him, 'You know, Mr. Ashe, that in time I shall be mistress of Manford Manor. I'll need a very good man to own it with me, don't you think? Perhaps you'd care to apply for the job.'"

Leslie was fascinated. "What did he say?"

Mary Ben, laughing, shook her head. "Oh, he was very gentlemanly about making it all a great big joke. Absolutely refused to recognize how serious I was."

She smiled a small, half-secret smile. "A week later, early one morning, I caught him in the hayloft over the breeding shed, counting up how many bales remained. Climbing the ladder, I stood close behind him. He didn't know I was there until I said, 'Whitney. Will you make love to me?'

"He turned. He was wearing khaki pants and a khaki shirt, I remember, and there was a sweaty smudge on one cheek." She paused, reminiscent.

"Well?" Leslie said impatiently, half wondering, at the same time, if it were a made-up story. But it was not easy to doubt the truth of Mary Ben's expression as she recalled that past moment.

"He said, 'We must be married first, Mary Ben.'" She shuddered, suddenly, a long, delicious shudder. "And then . . . he put his arms around me. He kissed me."

She looked defiantly at Leslie. "We made a bargain, Whitney and I. Struck openly, well understood on both sides. I gave him Manford Manor. He gave me . . . Whitney Ashe."

"He must have decided that he did love you, after all," Leslie protested. "Be fair, Mary Ben. Don't you think that might have been what happened?"

"No," Mary Ben said matter-of-factly. "We understood each other perfectly. And it was wonderful, you can't believe how wonderful, until . . ."

The shudder, this time, had a different texture. The horror again, come suddenly upon her like the black storm cloud that was advancing, a rumbling threat, through the Kentucky night.

"You see," Mary Ben whispered. "I hadn't told him. I didn't give him any warning at all. Because I knew he wouldn't marry me if he understood that he must immediately take me away from Manford Manor. And so . . . it happened."

The meaning of the words was obscure. Nevertheless, they thrilled through Leslie's soul. She leaned tensely forward.

"*What* didn't you tell him?"

Mary Ben's eyes became evasive. "You know, it's not my great-grandmother's portrait I don't like. It's the stallion. Black Prince." Her voice turned vicious. "I ought to cut him out of the canvas. Just take a knife and rip him right out. Even if it left only a fragment."

Leslie, keeping a tight grip on her sanity against the mad whirl of words, refused to be diverted. "What should you have told Whitney that you kept from him? Don't you think I ought to know, too?"

"Oh, Leslie, you're not paying attention, you're simply allowing me to beat you again," Mary Ben said pettishly. "Come on, now, play good. It's no fun if you won't give me any competition."

And Mary Ben, capriciously, playfully, obstinately, refused further communication beyond the play of the cards.

It was after midnight when the storm, after long rumbling in the prologue, burst finally upon them. Mary Ben, despite visible fatigue, at the end of each game had refused to go upstairs, dealing the cards without asking whether Leslie wished to continue. Leslie, tired also—not so much from physical exhaustion as from the emotional stresses of the day—found herself wishing that Whitney would look in upon them and, noting Mary Ben's fatigue, insist that she go to bed. But he remained cloistered in the library.

For some time now there had been a stillness. It lasted so long Leslie began to hope the storm had by-passed Manford Manor. Apparently, however, the pause had served only to gather the atmospheric forces for an ultimate effort.

There came suddenly a stroke of lightning, so brilliantly dazzling it blinded Leslie's vision. It was followed so immediately by the crack of thunder the electrical energy must have seared its way through the air directly over the mansion.

Leslie, startled, sprang to her feet. Mary Ben, clasping her hands over her head, cowered, screaming in wordless shock. Her voice was piercing, unbearable. Leslie, galvanized by the woman's terror, put her arms around Mary Ben, holding her close.

"It's all right, it's all right," she kept saying. "Just thunder and lightning, that's all it is."

Immediately another stroke flared. Leslie recoiled. Mary Ben screamed again, her head burrowing against Leslie, suddenly babbling senseless words, "He's going to kill me, save me, Leslie, he wants to kill me all over again!"

A strong wind, rushing against the old house, made shutters slap loudly. The ancient, settled structure creaked and groaned in protest. The rain came, a sudden downpour that was a veritable deluge.

Mary Ben's body was shaking. "He's coming, Leslie. He tried to kill me once. This time . . ."

"Who's trying to kill you?" Leslie demanded, the back of her mind occupied by the continued absence of Whitney Ashe. Surely he must have heard the screams.

"*Who's* trying to kill you?" she repeated.

Mary Ben had merged into incoherence, her throat torn by sobs. Trembling, she struggled to rise from the wheelchair.

Leslie held her strongly, restraining her violence while at the same time soothing her with hand and voice.

"There now, it's over now, see, it's raining, the rain will wash all the turbulence out of the air."

"He's coming. I can *feel* him coming," Mary Ben whispered.

Her eyes showed white rims, her face was crumpled, she was suddenly ugly with the fear.

It came.

The deluge had diminished to a steady downpour. The thunder marched off on the leading edge of the storm, as to the sound of distant drums. The wind had slackened into a steady pressure against the house.

Suddenly, there was added a new element: the piercing neigh of a stallion, a tumult of racing hoofs. The high, piercing trumpet call again, then again.

Mary Ben's scream, so harshly agonizing, must have ripped the lining of her throat. Bursting free from Leslie's restraint, she whirled the chair across the room, spinning into a corner, where she sat whimpering, her face hidden in her hands.

A door slammed. Whitney was suddenly with them. Leslie, grateful for his presence, turned to him. His face, savage with shock, was flushed with what must have been an indiscreet portion of after-dinner port. He had obviously been snatched out of sleep.

"What the hell?" he shouted, his voice rising as he sought to orient himself in time and space.

Before Leslie could reply, the stallion trumpeted, and again there sounded a thunder of hoofs, nearer this time, as though the great beast was charging the house.

"My God!" Whitney exclaimed.

He stood frozen, unbelieving. His mouth was set in harsh lines, the thin lips bloodless.

He remained unmoving for a minute that lasted forever. Then, snatching a flashlight from the telephone table near the archway, he began to run.

"Mary Ben!" Leslie called. "She's . . ."

"Get the nurse," he yelled over his shoulder. "Double quick. I've got to . . ."

Leslie was grateful for something to do. Hastening to the telephone, she pressed the button that communicated to Nurse Nunn's quarters. She spoke briefly, urging hurry, hung up, and went to Mary Ben.

Mary Ben suddenly propelled the wheelchair out of reach. "Stay away from me," she said. "Stay away!"

Her eyes were glittering. She had retreated into the sheer animal instinct of survival.

"It's all right now," Leslie said cajolingly. "Whitney's gone to see."

"Whitney!" Her voice curled with scorn. "What can *Whitney* do?" She propelled the wheelchair toward the archway. "I have to go. He's . . ."

"You can't go out into the storm," Leslie protested.

Mary Ben turned the chair to look at her. The terror remained, but crystallized into something more, a fatedness, a yielding to fate . . . even a *desire* to yield.

"He's calling me. I've got to go. You can't stop me."

The crippled woman must be restrained from exposing herself to the storm. Leslie ran across the room, hoping to arrest the wheelchair before she could escape. Mary Ben was at the outside door, struggling with both hands to open it. Leslie, grasping the handles, pulled the chair backward. Mary Ben almost toppled to the floor as she clung desperately to the doorknob.

Nurse Nunn came hurrying. "What's the matter?" Her voice was agitated.

"Mary Ben's hysterical," Leslie told her as calmly as she could. "She became frightened by the thunder and the lightning, by . . ." She realized, then, that she did not know how to name the other terror which had visited Manford Manor tonight.

"She's determined to go out into the storm," she continued. "Have you got something . . . ?"

"Keep her quiet, if you can," Nurse Nunn said. "I'll only be a minute."

She hurried up the stairs. Leslie kept hold of the wheelchair, though there was no immediate need; Mary Ben had collapsed, weeping now, a tearing, ragged sound that had in it nothing of easeful grief. A fresh gust of wind shook the house, the downpour came strongly for a moment, then slackened.

Nurse Nunn came hurrying, hypodermic syringe held high in one hand. Mary Ben cast one frantic glance and cowered away, saying, "No, no, no, no, no," on a rising note of protest.

"It'll do you good," Nurse Nunn said, advancing steadily. "Calm you down, let you sleep . . ."

Mary Ben made no physical struggle, though her voice continued its hopeless protest as the nurse swabbed at her arm, then grasped the muscle with one strong hand while with the other she plunged in the needle.

It must have been a powerful, quick-acting sedative . . . or perhaps the idea had as much effect as the substance. Mary Ben turned quiescent, except for an occasional whimper, a tremor of the flesh. Leslie took her hand, holding it warmly. But the crippled woman remained remote, still caught in whatever were those traps in her mind.

The front door slammed open. Whitney. He was soaked from the downpour, hair plastered to his forehead, the flashlight still aglow. He stood so for a fraught moment, gazing at his wife. Swiftly he went down on one knee to take her into his arms.

"There's nothing to be afraid of, my love," he said in a strong voice. "Nothing at all."

She laid her face against his shoulder, clinging. "Are you sure, Whitney? Are you *sure?*"

His arms were about her, his hands patting her back as he held her close and secure.

"Absolutely nothing," he repeated. "Somehow or other, King's Man's stall door was blown open by the wind, and he got out. That's all, love. King's Man, excited by running free in the storm."

"Thank God," Mary Ben breathed. "*Oh, thank God.* I thought it was . . ."

"Tom Musgrove is rubbing him down now," Whitney said. "I'll have that latch looked to tomorrow."

He held his wife, weeping now in relief, calmed by the twin influences of the sedative and the presence of her husband.

He stood up. "Just King's Man, loose in the storm," he repeated. "Now weren't you being rather silly, my dear?"

He glanced at Leslie over the top of Mary Ben's head, as quickly looked away. And Leslie knew. His eyes had told her, as truly as words: He had spoken a lie.

Whatever it might have been, out there in the storm, it was not the great gray stallion, King's Man.

And Leslie knew, as well as if Whitney had warned her, that Mary Ben must never learn the truth of the soothing falsehood.

CHAPTER SIX

It felt astonishingly good, this escape from the brooding atmosphere of Manford Manor. An exhilaration had started to build in Leslie the moment she had stepped on the accelerator of the Mercedes-Benz roadster and swept through the curves of the driveway, to halt briefly at the gates to check the traffic before pulling out into Paris Pike.

The expensive little car responded magnificently; it gave her a feeling of elegant adventure to drive such a sporting machine. It was white, low-slung, and the detachable hardtop was removed, so that her hair could blow in the wind of passage.

She had, until now, been reluctant to leave the confines of Manford Manor. Though entitled to one day off a week, today was the first time she had taken advantage of it. There had been the matter of the macramé supplies, but she had resisted being driven into town behind surly Tom Musgrove.

Yet more; something within her, quite actively, did not wish to breach the hermetic circle of Manford Manor. It was as though, in arriving, she had arrived also into a dark home of her soul. Something within her responded to this old mansion, these magnificent acres. Now she was happy she had forced herself to it; wheeling into the Paris Pike, it was as though a black cloud had floated out of her mind.

With a luxuriant sense of idleness, she used up most of the morning in shopping. She didn't need many things: cosmetics, an emery board, personal supplies . . . including the impulse purchase of a luxurious bottle of Vitabath All Over Body Cologne. She lingered especially over the macramé materials, chatting with the shop owner, admiring the samples on exhibit.

Finished, she drove to the Campbell House for a leisurely lunch, graced by two extravagantly dry martinis. But then, faced with an arid afternoon, she stood uncertainly in the parking lot, car keys in hand. It would never do to admit defeat by returning early to Manford Manor. There was the prospect of an afternoon movie, but she did not relish the thought of sitting alone in darkness watching the flickering, unreal images. To do so would be to admit an undoubted future pattern of free days; leisurely shopping, an excellent lunch . . . then another film.

No, Leslie, she told herself sternly. Surely you can find something better. It was then that she remembered passing tennis courts somewhere along the way to town. She wasn't sure just where; it had been only a flicker, caught in the corner of an eye, of white-clad figures moving in graceful patterns.

With brisk decision, she got into the car and, after a couple of false starts in finding her way through the maze of one-way streets in the downtown section, she found the Paris Pike, and the tennis courts. A private club; her heart sank.

I can watch, anyway, she told herself defensively. No one, surely, will mind if I watch.

She parked the white Mercedes, got out to look around. An old and graceful clubhouse, figures in golf carts moving over fairways, tennis courts filled with players in crisp white uniforms—it was a pleasant, peaceful scene. Strolling to a bench, she sat down to watch. Though it would be impossible to fill the entire afternoon as spectator, it was better than nothing.

Most of the courts were taken up with doubles matches. Young people in the main, agile and quick and laughing. Watching, Leslie felt the very muscles of her body aching enviously. She yearned to experience the stretching runs, the good flow of sweat, the thrill of an aced serve or a well-placed return. This, at least, she had had in New York.

Her attention focused on the near court, where a girl was taking a lesson. Very much the beginner, she moved with awkward self-consciousness, laughing when she missed, seriously attentive as the instructor demonstrated patiently, all over again, the mechanics of the grip.

Working too hard, like all beginners, she was panting and disheveled when the lesson had ended. The teaching pro, a lean young blond man with long legs, put an arm around her shoulders as they walked to the gate, talking earnestly. The girl gazed up into his face with absorbed eyes. Leslie watched, amused; she thought she understood why she had decided to take up tennis.

Picking up a towel, the girl departed toward the clubhouse. Leslie turned her head to watch, noting the assurance, the grace, with which she walked. Undoubtedly she would become a good player; if she could keep her mind on the lessons.

"New around here, aren't you?"

She turned to the sound of the teaching pro's voice. He was smiling, casual; but his eyes were lighted with more than casual interest.

Leslie smiled in return. "Not even a member, I'm afraid . . . just dropped by to watch. Hope you don't mind."

He sat beside her, wiping his face with a towel. "Do you play?"

"Haven't since I came to Lexington," Leslie confessed. "It's a shame they're not open courts. I'd love to have a place to play."

He nodded. His face was serious, his tone careful. "I'll give you a game, if you'd like. You can be my guest." He glanced at his watch. "I don't have another lesson this afternoon, anyway."

"Oh, I couldn't impose," Leslie protested. "Besides, I don't have clothes with me, a racket . . ."

"I can loan you a racket." He gave her a dazzlingly persuasive smile. "As for clothes and shoes, you can always use a new outfit, can't you?"

Leslie was tempted. She glanced at the players on the courts, aching to join them. She had always preferred playing with someone better; only in that way, she felt, could she improve her game.

"Come on," he said. "Maybe I can persuade you to join the club. We happen to have a few openings the management would like to see filled."

"All right," Leslie heard herself saying. "Should be fun. I'll do it." She laughed tentatively. "But I don't know about joining . . . it looks rather expensive."

"Not all that bad," he said casually. "Of course, you'd have to be sponsored. Do you know anyone . . . ?"

"I work at Manford Manor," Leslie said.

A flicker of . . . something . . . crossed his face. A quick frown, perhaps a heightened curiosity.

It went away as quickly as it had appeared. He said casually, "Then of course you know Mary Ben."

Leslie quickened. "Oh, do *you* know her? I'm her companion, as well as private secretary and office manager."

Was there a cool note in his voice? "Yes, I *used* to know Mary Ben. Before she was married. Our families . . ." He stopped, as though brushing it away. "Certainly Mary Ben can sponsor you. The Manfords were founding members of the club, of course." He rose. "Come, let's get you outfitted, find out how good you are." He laughed at her. "Maybe, for all I know, we've got a new club champion."

"Oh, I'm not nearly that good," Leslie said, laughing.

As they walked to the clubhouse, the man said, "By the way, my name is Bob Berry. And yours?"

When she told him, his eyes lighted. "Lovely name. Lovely girl." There was that in his tone of voice which let Leslie know he was interested far beyond a good game of tennis.

It was indeed a good game. After Leslie had bought clothes in the pro shop and changed in the locker room, they went swiftly into action. Bob was, of course, an excellent player, stretching Leslie to the utmost to give him any sort of a game. What she liked most of all, he did not coddle her, did not drop easy points, but made her play to the hilt.

Leslie felt gloriously alive. The strenuous exercise had cleared the cobwebs out of her head. Not cobwebs . . . stray wisps of the dark atmosphere of Manford Manor. As she had needed friendly male companionship to push Whitney Ashe out of her mind.

The game over, Bob Berry draped a companionable arm over her shoulder as they walked from the court. She was not surprised when he said lightly, yet with a serious undertone, "After a good set like that, Leslie, you must let me buy dinner. Agreed?"

She hesitated. "I really must get back, Bob. Mary Ben . . ."

"But it's your day off! Surely they won't expect you back so early."

Leslie had anticipated returning in time for dinner, for the usual evening of Russian bank and Kipling with Mary Ben.

"I . . . I'd have to telephone . . ."

"Then phone," he urged. He grinned unabashedly. "I have absolutely no intention of allowing a great girl *and* a good tennis player like you get away."

Leslie, showering and changing, thought it over more seriously, really, than the situation called for. There was a choice. She could fake the call, tell Bob that Mary Ben really did expect her for the evening. Or she could simply inform her employer she was invited out to dinner.

Bob Berry. Tennis pro he might be, but obviously of a good family; the aura was unmistakable. Leslie could only feel complimented that he, transparently attractive to the girls who frequented the tennis courts, had so quickly shown an interest.

She emerged to find Bob waiting, wearing blue slacks and a blue turtleneck sweater under a light sports coat. The clothes hung well on his tennis-conditioned body; they were obviously more expensive than the average teaching pro could have afforded.

He handed her a dime and a grin. "Here's your phone call. Don't let me down, now, I've got an investment."

She took the dime, went to a pay phone, dialed the number. "Martin. May I speak to Mary Ben?"

Mary Ben came on the line. "Yes?"

"Leslie. Listen, I've been playing tennis with an old friend of yours, a fellow named Bob Berry . . ."

"Oh, yes, Bob," Mary Ben said. Leslie listened critically, searching her voice for overtones. She would not, she decided, upset Mary Ben for anything. Not even dinner with an attractive man.

"He's asked me for a dinner date," Leslie said carefully. "I thought I'd accept unless you expected me back."

No overtones. Indeed her voice was light, gay . . . even envious. "Oh, Leslie, I wouldn't *think* of allowing you to turn down a date with Bob. You have, my dear, in case you didn't know, latched onto the most eligible man in town. He always *has* been." She laughed. "But, I warn you, most elusive. With much practice at it. After all, he's *my* age."

Leslie looked at Bob, waiting carefully beyond earshot. She smiled at him, saying, "We're only having dinner, Mary Ben.

After a lovely set of tennis." She chuckled. "I think he's trying to sell me on the idea of joining the club. Will you sponsor me if I decide to do so?"

"Of course." Mary Ben laughed again, a merry peal. "But only on condition you tell me all about your evening. I had a *terrible* crush on Bob at one time, you know. Like every other girl in town."

"I promise," Leslie said mendaciously. "Now I must go."

"Have a lovely evening, dear," Mary Ben said affectionately. "I just . . ." Her voice trembled suddenly. "I just wish I could be with you. It's been so long since . . ."

"Now, Mary Ben, if you're going to feel that way, I'm coming right home," Leslie said. "I don't want to spend the time worrying."

"Oh, no, you're not!" Mary Ben said indignantly. "You're going to have your evening out."

"Thank you," Leslie said quietly. "You're a lovely friend."

"And so are you," Mary Ben said quickly.

Turning away from the phone, Leslie thought soberly: She *is* pleased to see me interested in Bob Berry. Extraordinarily pleased. Because of Whitney?

She pushed away the thought, saying to Bob, "It's all set. And I'm starving!"

Bob escorted her to a Mustang II, fire-engine red, and drove her swiftly to the Campbell House. Though Leslie had had lunch here, she enjoyed the dinner atmosphere even more. There was a trio to play for dancing, spelled by a young man on a guitar singing country music. Even before they had finished the first drink, Bob took her to the dance floor.

He danced as well as he played tennis, his arms hard and sure about her in the slow numbers, his tireless body moving before her in the intricate patterns of the modern dances. He was openly delighted that she could match him step for step.

As they returned to their table, Leslie intercepted curious glances; she had already noted, on their entrance, that Bob was known and liked, several people waving or speaking as they passed. There had been, also, a jealous female appraisal or two; which didn't do her womanly ego a bit of harm.

Only over dinner did they talk. Leslie began by asking about the initiation fee and monthly dues for a tennis membership. When he told her, she frowned.

"That's pretty steep for a working girl."

He shot her a quick glance. "Any chance of the Manfords—the Ashes, I mean—taking up their old membership? You could play on that, you know."

"I doubt Whitney, so busy getting the farm going again, would be interested," she said slowly. "And of course Mary Ben . . ."

"So he intends to establish Manford Manor as a Thoroughbred nursery again, does he?"

Leslie brightened. "Oh yes, indeed. He has just imported a magnificent gray stallion, King's Man, from England." She reverted to the previous topic. "I really do need a place to go, my days off, and it's the only way I can keep up my game. There are no courts at Manford Manor." She paused. "Could you . . . would it be possible to pay by installment?"

"Of course," he said. "No problem." He frowned. "We *will* have to find a sponsor. I could put your name up, but . . ."

"I've already spoken to Mary Ben," Leslie said happily. "So that's taken care of."

"Wonderful." In a spontaneous gesture, he put his hand over hers. "I'm delighted, Leslie. Now I *know* I'll see a lot of you." His voice was warm. "At least, I hope so."

"I hope so, too," Leslie responded honestly. "Of course, I'll only be able to come on Thursdays, for sure. I'd like to get in more tennis than that, but . . ."

"Then it's a date for next Thursday?" Bob urged. "I may not be able to play with you, don't remember offhand my teaching schedule for next week. If not, I'll line you up a partner, maybe fix it so you can fill in on a doubles match." He grinned. "You can rest assured your partner will be the ugliest member of the club. Afterward, at least, we can have dinner together. All right?"

"You rush a girl right off her feet," Leslie protested, but with a delightful feeling down her spine all the same.

He leaned urgently over the table, holding her hand. "I mean to tie up *all* your Thursday nights before anybody else at the club gets a look at you." He laughed. "After all, I'm only the teaching pro."

"I don't think you have to worry," Leslie said lightly. "I hear you're Lexington's most eligible bachelor. Mary Ben told me."

"How *is* Mary Ben these days, anyway?" Bob asked, so deftly turning the conversation away from himself that, amused, Leslie allowed the gambit to succeed.

"She's . . . well, it's hard to say," she said carefully. "She has her good days and her bad days." She hesitated. "I don't think . . . she really wanted to come home to Manford Manor."

"I wouldn't have thought she would," Bob said, his voice reserved. "Not after what happened. I suppose that husband of hers insisted. He is, at least, a horseman."

The phrases resonated in Leslie's mind: *That husband of hers*, and *At least he's a horseman.*

"Have you known Mary Ben long?"

He smiled reminiscently. "Grew up together. My family is in the horse business, too, you know. Our place is The Berry Patch . . . isn't that awful?" They laughed together, then, charmingly, he added, "Personally, I couldn't care less if a Kentucky horse never won another race. All my life that's all I've heard: talk, talk, talk of horses. I suppose that's what made a tennis player of me."

"I *love* horses," Leslie said. "You'll never persuade me otherwise."

He threw back his head. "Then you've come to the right town. By the way, where *is* the wrong place you came from?"

Leslie told him about New York and Maryland, then reverted to Mary Ben.

"She's rather nervous now. Was she always that way? Or is it the result of her accident?"

"Nervous?" Bob looked puzzled. "She was always the most carefree girl I've ever known. Made you feel good just to be around her. I was fond of Mary Ben, you know. I never could understand what she saw in . . ."

He stopped abruptly, pushing back his plate. Leslie had already finished. "How about an after-dinner drink?"

Leslie, wishing to hear about Mary Ben, ordered a crème de menthe frappé, while he took a brandy.

"You see, it's my job—part of my job—to provide companionship, a sense of security, for Mary Ben," she explained. "The more I know about her, the better." She paused, looking at her escort. "I gather you don't care for Whit . . . Mr. Ashe."

Deliberately he inhaled the aroma of the brandy, warming the snifter in the palms of his hands. He looked at her. "My dear, their marriage was the scandal of the county. Didn't you know that?"

"No," Leslie said uncertainly. "Why should it have been? I mean, after all . . ."

"Why shouldn't it?" Bob said bluntly. "He was an English upstart, a *gentleman jockey*, he called himself, imported to manage the horse farm. Mary Ben, well, she's not only the daughter of one of the oldest families in Kentucky, she was, for God's sake, barely eighteen years old." He laughed shortly. "He had his eye on the main chance, no doubt about that." He shrugged. "Whitney Ashe took one look at that estate, another look at Mary Ben, and . . ." He paused, somberly. "One can imagine just how he went about it, a young, impressionable girl like that. And once he'd . . ."

Leslie thought of the story Mary Ben had told, how *she* had trapped Whitney. Rebelliously, silently, she was rejecting this cynical analysis of the man's motivations.

"God knows what she ever saw in him," Bob continued. "He's just about the strangest thing that ever came down Paris Pike. Always that black look to him, and when his eyes light on you, it's as though they were cutting right through. I've . . . a lot of people have wondered what his *real* history is. Of course, you have to give him one thing: he's a hell of a horseman."

Leslie was moved to defend Whitney Ashe; even as she remembered that Mary Ben herself had maintained that Whitney had married her for exactly the reasons Bob Berry believed.

"You have to grant him one other thing, Bob," she said quietly. "An important consideration. After Mary Ben became crippled, he stayed with her. You should see them together."

"Why not? The land is still in her name," Bob said brutally. He shook his head. "He'll undoubtedly build Manford Manor again into a great breeding farm. But it will be *his*. Not hers."

Leslie felt depressed. For the moment, charming though he was, she disliked Bob Berry. But certainly, she told herself, he means no harm, he's simply repeating old gossip.

"As a matter of fact, Leslie, there was . . . talk . . . of an official investigation when Mary Ben was hurt. It happened right after she had inherited the place, you know. The idea seemed to be floating around that maybe, just maybe, Whitney Ashe had had something to do with it."

Leslie drew back. "I don't believe for a minute that Whitney would do such a thing."

Bob looked sharply into her face.

"Are *you* taken by the man, too?"

Leslie fended off the implication with a laugh. "Of course not. It's just that . . . well, he's my boss." She tossed her head. "And, I must say, we get along. He's a perfect gentleman, Bob, whether you think he's an 'English upstart' or not!"

"Well!" Bob said. "Looks like I've stirred up a tiger." He did not attempt to sustain the levity. "The fact is, Leslie, Mary Ben refused to return to Manford Manor when she came out of the hospital. They moved directly to Europe." He paused. "And now he's brought her home, and a lot of people are wondering just why. She hasn't seen any of her old friends, you know, no one's been invited to the house."

"They returned because he intends to re-establish Manford Manor, that's why," Leslie said resolutely. "And he told me that Mary Ben *needed* to come home. For her mental health."

"Yeah," Bob said skeptically. He was aware now of her resistance. "Well, I shouldn't be telling tales out of school. None of my business, really."

"No, it isn't!" she said with spirit.

He held up both hands in mock surrender. "I'm through talking. Not another word about Mary Ben or Whitney Ashe will you hear from me." Winningly, he reached across the table. "Truce?"

Leslie did not take his hand. She was far too seriously engaged in the unfinished conversation. "What *was* the accident, anyway? Mary Ben has never volunteered, and I didn't like to ask."

He looked at her curiously. "You didn't know? A Thoroughbred stallion nearly killed her."

"But how? I mean, they're always so careful around the stallions. Mary Ben herself told me . . ."

"Exactly what caused a lot of people to wonder. Mary Ben was *raised* on a horse farm, for God's sake. But somehow she was in the stallion paddock, one night, and the stallion was out of the barn. He attacked her. Whitney himself found her." He paused, bodingly. "At least, that was *his* tale."

A shiver ran the length of Leslie's spine. No wonder Mary Ben had been afraid to return to the scene of such an experience. No wonder the neighing of King's Man, the other night in the storm . . . Then she remembered, as vividly as seeing it all over again, the expression in Whitney Ashe's eyes which had betrayed his lie.

"It's strange," she said. She could feel the quiver in her voice. "It *is* strange, isn't it?" She looked across the table. "Bob, tell me . . ."

"Not another word," he said firmly. "Remember, I promised. My lips are sealed."

Obviously he did not wish to alarm her further. And, suddenly, Leslie didn't want to hear any more. The burden of what she had learned tonight was more than enough.

And . . . she had no wish to dislike this charming, older—not *too* much older—man. A window of sanity upon the world, he was her escape from the oppressive atmosphere of Manford Manor.

His hand lay open between them. Putting her palm into his, Leslie said quietly, "We have time for just one more dance before I must go."

Determined to put the conversation behind them, they succeeded in doing so. The one dance turned into three before Bob would consent to return to the table, pay the check, and depart. He drove to the club, where the Mercedes sat alone in the parking lot. Leslie looked at it, feeling that the beautiful little car, waiting so gallantly to transport her home to Manford Manor, was somehow a symbol of Leslie Tallant in Kentucky.

They stood together between the two cars. Bob, taking her keys, unlocked the door. As he returned them, he said seriously, "I *will* see you again on Thursday? I hope I didn't turn you off with all that talk about your boss."

"Of course not," Leslie scolded gently. She smiled across the darkness. "And of course I'll see you next week."

He did not touch her, only leaned his blond tallness to brush his lips lightly against her mouth. "Good-by, Leslie," he whispered. "Until then."

Only when she turned into the curving driveway did Leslie

remember she did not have a key to the front door. She had, after all, expected to get back in time for dinner. It would be necessary to arouse Martin to let her in.

She put the Mercedes into the garage alongside the Lincoln Continental. Walking around the house, she saw that all was dark upstairs, only one light, in the library, showing downstairs.

She moved thoughtfully, reflecting on tonight's conversation. It explained so many things. It also created deeper mysteries. Did people really believe that Whitney Ashe could have—would have —staged the accident? She shuddered. There were deep places in him, dark; no knowing what the man was capable of.

A light over the door had been left on. Perhaps . . . She tried the knob. No. She rang the bell, waited, heard footsteps coming.

The apologetic words were ready on her lips. "I'm sorry to wake you, Martin. I simply didn't think about a key when I left . . ."

Her voice stopped. Whitney stood in the open doorway.

She faltered. "Oh. I'm sorry I disturbed you."

"Martin's gone to bed," Whitney said, standing aside for her entrance. "So has Mary Ben, for that matter."

He was wearing his smoking jacket, there was a glass of port in one hand. Evidently it was one of his working nights, not a time for addressing himself to the port alone.

He was looking at her with steady eyes. "Have a good time?"

"Marvelous," Leslie said. "Played tennis, then went to dinner."

"Yes. It's good, I'm sure, for you to get away," he said remotely. "I'm glad you enjoyed yourself."

She could sense a strangeness in his attitude. Perhaps it emanated from her, from the things about him she had learned tonight. Not that she counted them true, she told herself resolutely; only now I understand how Whitney Ashe is viewed by the Bluegrass people.

"Thank you," she said, walking past him. She paused, turned. "Mary Ben . . . is she all right?"

"Just fine, she was quite pleased you were invited to dinner. I'm sure she'll want to know all about it tomorrow."

Leslie, feeling pleasurably tired, started up the stairs, saying, "Good night," over her shoulder.

His voice stopped her. "She told me you were out with a fellow named Bob Berry."

She turned. The expression on his face, in his eyes; she did not want to read the meaning. At this time of night, with this tiredness, she *refused* to read the meaning.

"Yes," she said. "He's the tennis pro at the country club. I . . . I'm thinking of joining, to have a place to play on my day off. I do like tennis, you know. I've missed it here."

He was not listening, she knew suddenly. Only waiting until she had finished. So she stopped.

"Yes," he said. "Mary Ben was quite pleased. Berry, you know, was Mary Ben's favorite beau. Everyone in the county expected them to be married at the proper time, in the proper way." A savage grin appeared startlingly on his face. "Until I came along, that is, to upset the romantic, dynastic apple cart."

As she stood nonplused, staring, he walked past her and disappeared into the library.

CHAPTER SEVEN

Leslie resumed her duties, the morning after her day of freedom, in far more of a quandary than before. Rising early enough to breakfast alone—for an unexplored reason, after last night, she did not wish to face Whitney Ashe just yet—she went at sunrise to the office.

She had thought to immerse herself in work; and there was much work waiting to be done. Already, as a result of the publicity about the arrival of King's Man to stand at stud in Kentucky, there were calls every day with requests to view the stallion, with an eye toward booking a season next spring.

So early in the morning, of course, one did not expect the phone to ring, so Leslie could concentrate on the tasks at hand. Yet in the back of her mind dwelled heavy the web of last night's meanings and implications.

It did seem as though a different order of reality prevailed at Manford Manor. Things unseen, unspoken—only sensed, felt, perceived—were the *real* truth, while the ancient mansion, the cavorting foals, the broodmares, the beautiful land, the great stallion himself, were only ephemeral ghosts.

She had cherished Bob Berry as a window of sanity upon the real world. But Bob, she realized, had lied . . . by omission, at least. He had implied that he and Mary Ben were only good growing-up-together friends, not, as Whitney had revealed, a recognized pairing that had been expected to bring about through marriage the merging of two great Kentucky families.

Perhaps his lying-by-omission was without ulterior motive, nothing more than the evasiveness habitual in an eligible but elusive bachelor. But, thinking back on their dinner conversation, Leslie had a feeling he had not been at all reluctant to reveal Whitney Ashe's unsavory reputation.

Could *that*, too, have been without ulterior motivation? Or was he paying Whitney for having captured the ardor of the girl Bob Berry had loved, had expected to marry?

Leslie shook her head in bewilderment. Such a tangled web of meanings and non-meanings, of hints and allusions and old secrets, reaching so far backward into time they were indelibly etched into the characters of the people about her. How could she hope to cut through the web, seemingly as fragile as the web of a spider, but in reality made up of cables so strong they held in thrall generation after generation.

One thing for sure, Leslie told herself. Meeting Bob was sheer accident. He had not the faintest idea, until I told him, that I had any connection with Manford Manor. She was, at least, grateful for that much. For, she acknowledged quite frankly, she wanted to continue seeing Bob. Not only because he was a charming, gallant, good companion, but as a bulwark against the impact of Whitney Ashe upon her sensibilities.

Once she had allowed that thought into the domain of her mind, Leslie arose and busied herself making a pot of coffee. As she went through the familiar motions of placing a fresh filter on the automatic drip pot, pouring water, measuring out the spoonfuls of Maxwell House, she kept her mind carefully blank. Only after she had returned to her desk, cup in hand, did she allow her thoughts to go the rest of the way.

All right, girl, let's face it. You are attracted by the man. Attracted, hell. Enthralled!

For the first time Leslie allowed Whitney Ashe, with all his strength and charm, in all his dark power, fully into her being.

Leslie, as any other woman, had an adequately self-protective capacity for not allowing herself to know that which she was not yet ready to deal with. Yet, all along, a part of her *did* know. It was that part of her nature which now ruled.

Leslie Tallant loved Whitney Ashe with a love deep and true

and irrevocable, as she had not loved any man. Not even in her unrequited attachment to Michael Rennick.

The texture of this love was not innocent. The potentiality of Whitney Ashe dwelled in her flesh as in her mind and in her heart. She knew that she could surrender herself to him as she could never have, until now, given herself to any man. Body and soul.

As simple as that, girl, she told herself. And so . . . what are you going to do about it?

Her mind flitted into irrelevance. *I suppose this means Bob Berry isn't going to count.*

She was, strangely enough, saddened by the thought. A love with Bob could have been lighthearted, delightfully fulfilling. Quite in contrast to this murky, black-and-red passion she felt for Whitney. She was almost regretful that the easier, more pleasant adventure was not to be.

Whitney could be expected at any moment, she realized. How could she speak casual morning words, now that she had admitted his vibrant presence into her heart? With a sense of dread she began to anticipate his appearance.

Yes. Dread. She was afraid to be vulnerable to Whitney. Afraid of *him,* for the same reasons which gave him a fatal attraction: the moodiness, the darkness of soul, the intense strength that dwelled within him as it dwelled within the great gray stallion.

Her thoughts veered again. *Manford Manor is not, has never been, a place for women.* For the very reason that it had been established originally, in all its glory, *by a woman*—Mary Ben's great-grandmother, Brooke Manford—the old house, the very land, was uncompromisingly masculine. What had they called Kentucky in the beginning? The dark and bloody ground. Yes.

No woman, she thought fatefully, has ever felt at home here. Her very sense of herself is assaulted, outraged, by the environment of this place.

She tasted the coffee again. It had gone cold. She did not rise to pour another cup.

She could not feel within herself a moral bulwark against the idea of a liaison with Whitney Ashe. She had never before admitted the possibility of an affair with a married man. Not even Michael Rennick. Indeed, she realized suddenly, her unrequited love had endured only because it was impossible of consummation. The slightest hint on his part toward such a denouement would have shattered instantly the fragile crystalline structure.

This, now, with Whitney, was different. She would, she knew, be taking nothing away from Mary Ben. Indeed, she could rationally see herself as *preserving* the marriage, insuring Whitney's continued devotion to Mary Ben's well-being. She could see with clear eyes that, if she did undertake this adventure, it could be only with the soul-deep conviction that she would never allow the marriage to be destroyed.

Another, even stronger, factor prevailed; she understood it so deeply the knowledge was beyond truth. Leslie Tallant was not in control. If ever he came to her, she would not have the strength of will to send him away.

Such lack of will cannot make one innocent, she told herself. If it happens, it will be your fault as much as his. But that is how it is; he need only touch me, to have me.

One part of her, the primordial female, accepted—even gloried—in this knowledge. Another part, the clear-eyed, sensible woman-of-the-times, rejected utterly such submission. But, she knew quite well, it was the primitive woman within her which, fastening upon the dark masculinity of Whitney Ashe, yearned to be swept away on endless, rolling surges of darkly fulfilling passion.

It was, she knew, the place as much as the man. She was caught, here at Manford Manor, by a concentration of masculinity that was not only tender, loving, but also strong and cruel, remorseless in its appetite. That was the reason Whitney Ashe fitted Manford Manor so well . . . the land was an extension of him, as he was an extension of the land.

She could, she saw quite clearly, deny it all by a simple decision; packing her bags and catching the next plane, going anywhere. She realized, however, with equal clarity, that in denying this man she would be denying, most profoundly of all, her total self. It would be so easy—too easy—to leave. But she did not want to go. And, she knew without the necessity of thinking about it, she would not go.

So now, she reflected almost lightly, I have discovered the curse of Manford Manor. It is this which Mary Ben fears so deeply.

Not consciously, of course; but her unconscious knows, exactly and truly, the peril in which she dwells.

And so do I.

Absorbed in these self-revelations, Leslie was aroused belatedly by the ringing of the telephone. She looked at the clock on the wall; too early for the business of the day to begin.

She picked up the instrument, to hear Mary Ben's voice, brightly cheerful. "Come along, Leslie, share breakfast with me."

"You're up early!"

"I'm *dying* to hear all about your evening," Mary Ben said. "So hurry, and I'll have Martin put another plate on the tray."

"I've already had breakfast, and there's work to do," Leslie protested.

"Oh, hang that old work. Your *important* job is with me." She chuckled. "This morning I am in dire need of female companionship and conspiracy. So just you come along. Right now."

Mary Ben hung up, cutting off her sweetly imperious voice. Leslie laughed, shrugged, began clearing her desk for departure.

Even as she closed the door behind her, Leslie wondered why Whitney had avoided coming into the office this morning.

Mary Ben was wearing a flowered robe over gay pajamas, her hair was pulled back tightly. Without make-up, the delicate facial bones showed even prettier. Nurse Nunn discreetly departed, leaving them alone.

Mary Ben greeted Leslie with delight. "Come, sit beside me, tell me all about it," she cried. "How is old Bob these days, anyway? Did you have an absolutely great evening?"

Leslie sat down, accepting the cup of coffee Mary Ben had poured for her. "I had a good time," she admitted.

Mary Ben cut a sly eye. "I suppose . . . he came on rather strong?" She giggled. "Used to be all hands, you know. I called him 'Octopus' when he'd get that way. It'd make him so *mad!*"

"I imagine he's become rather more sophisticated," Leslie said dryly. "He scarcely kissed me good night, to tell you the truth."

"Oh, Leslie, you don't mean it!" Mary Ben said, her face disappointed. "I was sure that by now a great romance was flourishing."

Leslie laughed at her. "Bob is a very nice gentleman. We had a lovely dinner, we danced, and we talked . . . about you, I might add. That's all there was to it."

Mary Ben brightened. "About me? What did he say?"

Leslie regarded her. "He *didn't* tell me he was your favorite beau," she said. "Whitney gave me that news when I got home."

Mary Ben put down her fork. "Aren't you going to eat? Your eggs will get cold."

"I don't need a second breakfast," Leslie protested. "Coffee is enough."

Mary Ben, for the moment, regarded her stilly. "Did it *bother* you to learn about me and Bob?" She grinned slyly. "Did it make you just a wee bit jealous?"

Leslie laughed. "I couldn't be jealous of you, Mary Ben. No. I just wondered why he . . . implied . . . you were only childhood friends."

"He did, did he? That rascal!" She smiled reminiscently. "He was *frantic* when I told him about Whitney. Why, the night before the wedding, he spent *hours* on the phone, begging me to run away with him instead. Then, after I'd hung up on him for the umpteenth time, and left the phone off the hook so I could get *some* sleep, he raced his car up and down Paris Pike until dawn. She chuckled. "I'll bet I was yawning all through the ceremony, I was so tired."

"Then he really did care for you," Leslie said steadily.

Mary Ben looked to make sure the nurse had gone. "Bob was my first lover," she said frankly. "And I was his . . . at least, he swore I was. We were always going to be married, of course. But . . ." She moved her shoulders. "Bob was a *boy*, while Whitney was a *man*." She looked at Leslie. "Do you understand?"

"Yes," Leslie said. "I understand."

And that, she thought, *is the understatement of the year.*

Mary Ben began eating again. "The first minute I laid eyes on Whitney Ashe, Bob was right out the window as far as I was concerned." She smiled at Leslie. "I do hope you two will get along. Bob, you know, comes from a very good family."

Something rebelliously vital in Leslie said, Why should I settle for the boy?

"We have a date for next Thursday," she said easily.

"So Bob talked about me," Mary Ben said. "I hope he had nice things to say."

Leslie responded to the transparent gambit. "He told me he was very fond of you, still." She paused, looking at Mary Ben. "He also told me how you got hurt. No wonder you were so frightened, the night King's Man got out into the storm. It must have . . . brought it all back."

Perhaps it was cruel. But Mary Ben had been practicing unconscious cruelty on her. Perhaps, not totally unconscious. Maybe she knew, at least sensed, something of Leslie's feeling for her husband. With an acute, self-guarding perception, perhaps Mary Ben was warding off Whitney–Leslie with Leslie–Bob.

Mary Ben's face was frozen. "So you heard all about it. I . . . I didn't want you to know about Great-Grandmother Brooke. I was afraid, if you found out, you'd leave me."

Her hands were gripped so tightly they were white at the knuckles.

Leslie, astonished at the intense reaction, said, "Why, no, he only told me you were attacked by a stallion. He didn't mention your great-grandmother." She straightened. "What about her?"

Mary Ben, realizing she had betrayed herself, spoke sullenly. "I don't want to talk about it."

Leslie took Mary Ben's hand. Feeling it trembling, she gripped it, hard. "How can I help you, Mary Ben, if you won't trust me?"

Mary Ben's eyes clung to hers, then drifted evasively away. "I do trust you, Leslie. It's just that . . ." She stopped. Her face twisted. Frantically, she blurted, "I can't run the risk of losing you, Leslie. I can't!"

Leslie remembered her own thoughts, this morning, about the pervasive, rapacious *masculinity* of Manford Manor. Mary Ben was in thrall to it, far more than Leslie, because she had been born into it.

"Mary Ben," Leslie said steadily, "there is *nothing* you and I can't talk about." She covered Mary Ben's hand, clasped in her own, with her other hand. "Nothing in this world that can't be faced, if one has the courage and the common sense to look directly at it."

She stopped. Mary Ben, thank God, was listening. Leslie,

moved beyond herself into a certainty she had not, until now, felt capable of sustaining, continued.

"You're going to tell me," she said. "All of it. Right now. Then it will be out in the open."

Mary Ben shrank back. "It's evil. *True* evil, I mean, like the devil used to be real."

"That's all right," Leslie said steadily. "Let's take a hard look. All right?"

Mary Ben drew a shaky breath. Leslie watched anxiously, wondering if she had succeeded in instilling enough courage. They, two women in league against this ancient house—against, she suddenly realized, Whitney Ashe, for he was wedded to Manford Manor as he would never be wedded to his wife—must either go forward together, sharing all that must be shared, or their alliance would shatter into ineffectuality, incapable of defending this fragile woman against the forces menacing her.

Mary Ben looked into Leslie's eyes. Her voice was shaky. But the words came clearly.

"I was crippled by the ghost of the stallion which killed my great-grandmother. Now that I have been forced to come home, Black Prince has returned, too, determined to finish the job."

It was an incredible tale. But, deep down in the bone, Mary Ben obviously believed every word of it.

She told Leslie that Brooke Manford, her great-grandmother, had not only been a beautiful, vital woman—as Leslie already knew from the striking portrait that hung over the fireplace—but also one of the world's great horsewomen. She had ridden before kings and queens, had won so many cups and trophies most had long since been donated to the state's archives for lack of room to display them.

Manford Manor had been in existence as a Thoroughbred breeding farm before the Civil War. During Reconstruction the estate, like Kentucky itself, had fallen upon parlous times, so that, when Brooke Manford was growing up, there had been scarcely any horses—none of consequence—in the barns.

A woman of will and determination, Brooke had set out to restore the family fortune. She had converted heirloom jewelry into a spectacular wardrobe and, chaperoned by the massive black woman who had raised her, set out for Saratoga Springs. Within the year she returned triumphantly to Kentucky wedded to an up-start North Carolina tobacco magnate. So enthralled was he by her beauty, awed by her august lineage, he had even allowed her to retain the family name.

While her uncouth husband, in conspiracy with Dukes and Reynoldses and Lorillards, had pursued more millions, Brooke devoted her attention to Manford Manor. Spending with a lavish hand, she restored the old place to far more than its former magnificence.

With such great wealth to back her efforts, Brooke disdained the commercial breeding of flat racers, concentrating instead on steeplechasers and hunters, her first and greatest love. She contin-ued to ride, of course, waiting impatiently through her single preg-nancy—a daughter who promised in time to be as beautiful and headstrong as she—to resume her riding activities.

Only when, in a sudden debacle, her husband lost his fortune almost overnight, did she resolutely turn her attention to making Manford Manor pay its way. Widowed now—the husband, much older than she, died within six months after being wiped out financially—she sold off the breeding stock and began to rebuild on a commercial basis.

Her first move, reminiscent of her foray to Saratoga, was a trip to England, where she purchased a leading sire. Black Prince had been a great racer in his time, though he had broken down on the eve of the Derby and so, forced to retire to stud, had missed the ultimate accolade.

So great were his bloodlines, and hence his sire prospects, she had been enabled to buy him for only one reason: always of difficult temperament, in his retirement Black Prince had become vicious. He had savaged so many grooms it was almost impossible to find a stable lad willing to take on the job. Indeed, unlike most Thoroughbreds, because he could not be handled in the breeding shed, he had covered his mares by being turned loose in a pad-dock.

Legend had it that when Brooke Manford arrived to view Black Prince, she had stood looking at him for a full three minutes. Then, moving quietly, speaking to the savage beast, she came for-ward, reaching out a hand to touch his muzzle. While the owners stood aghast at such temerity, the noble stallion actually permitted a human hand to caress him.

She had turned to the owners. She had smiled. "How much will you pay me to take him off your hands?"

A tough bargainer—and well aware of her hole card—she had bought him at a price unreasonably low for a stallion whose first three crops had each contained at least one stakes winner.

In those days, it had been necessary to transport horses by ship. During the long voyage, Brooke Manford, though she had hired two brave grooms to accompany Black Prince to America, spent her entire time, except for sleeping and eating, with the great black stallion. When the ship docked, she led him down the gangplank, the stallion, besotted with love, nuzzling insistently at her shoulder.

The love between the beautiful, spirited woman and the savage stallion, it was said, had been as intense and fated as a storied love between a god and a goddess. They were inextricably linked, heart to heart; she had to stand by, speaking to him, when his groom entered the stall to fill his water bucket or ration out his oats. Brooke, with a necessary defiance of the unbreakable rule that no woman could be present at the mating of a stallion, had to lead him to the breeding shed, stay with him while he performed his service, return him to his stall. Free in the paddock, he paced the fence nearest the mansion until a rutted path had been worn, hoping only to catch a far glimpse of his mistress. Remaining always viciously unpredictable with anyone else, with her he was as tractable as a cosset lamb.

After some years, during which Manford Manor became a highly profitable operation, Brooke Manford took unto herself a second husband, a tall, fair, indolent man of good family some years younger than she.

The first, and only, time the new husband accompanied Brooke to visit the stallion in his paddock, Black Prince, in a fit of rage, laid back his ears and charged the fence. He almost crashed through, splintering the boards, one of the splinters gouging a bloody hole deep into his shoulder. Oblivious of the pain, he continued rearing and neighing until Brooke had hastily sent away the interloper. Only then would he consent to the soothing touch of her hand, though sullenly still, his ears laid back viciously.

At evening, she came late to lead him to his stall. It was nearly dark when she called from the gate. Still sulking, unresponsive to cajolery, he refused to come to her. At last, with impatient haste because her new husband was waiting, she opened the gate and went in to get him.

She was not afraid; many times over, she had done the same. With confidence in the stallion's love, she approached him, chain shank in hand, speaking chidingly of his stubborn willfulness.

She had not reckoned with the jealousy eating at his savage heart. Rearing until he towered over her, sharp-edged hoofs flashing, he threatened his dearest love. Still unafraid, she spoke sharply, demanding obedience.

He did not obey. Instead, he reared again, gone wild this time, and her slender body crumpled suddenly under his assault. After she was down, it was said, he reared and stamped on the lifeless body again and again, while her blood soaked into the earth she had loved so dearly.

Brooke Manford, in her intensely directed life, had not lived by love, but by wits and courage. She died by love.

The stallion groom, waiting with the bucket of oats, had seen the whole thing. He attempted to go to her rescue, but the stallion drove him from the paddock. Only when the new young husband came with a rifle, steadying it over the paneled fence to drill a bullet through the stallion's brain, could the body be recovered.

So Black Prince had fallen beside the woman he had so greatly loved, and the two, the woman and the horse, lay dead together upon the Kentucky earth.

"That's not all of it. It's only the beginning," Mary Ben said.

Her voice was steady, having firmed itself into a monotone at the beginning, as though only in this manner could she bear to tell the tale. It had somehow made the story more real, more believable.

"But surely . . ." Leslie began.

Mary Ben lifted a hand. "That's what everyone thought. A tragedy, of course. Such a great love between the woman and the horse, to end so, dead side by side out there in the paddock." She lifted her head. "It's the same paddock, you know. The fencing has been replaced, a number of times. But it's the same piece of earth."

Mary Ben looked down at her hands. "Another horse story, to go with all the legends of horses down through the ages. But . . ."

She looked up, directly into Leslie's face. "When it happened again, to my grandmother . . ."

"*Again?*" Leslie said.

Mary Ben's voice sank once more into the monotone. "When my grandmother was twenty-two, she was married, with a great reception at Manford Manor. Everybody in Kentucky who *was* anybody assisted, because Manford Manor was still great in those days. They departed that night for a year's honeymoon in Europe —that sort of thing was done then—and when they came home she was carrying in her arms a newborn daughter."

Mary Ben smiled faintly. "Maybe there was a reason for the year-long honeymoon; maybe that girl baby got started a bit early.

"The night of their return, there was a tremendous storm. In the morning . . . my grandmother was found crumpled in the paddock. No one, not even her husband, ever knew why she went out into the storm, or what killed her. Except . . ."

A white line showed suddenly around her lips. "The farm hands swore that, during the worst of the storm, they could hear trumpeting and galloping. One old black man made his oath that, as he was hurrying alongside the paddock fence toward shelter, the ghost stallion rushed out of the storm, sailed over him and the fence, and . . . and then he ran, afraid of seeing anything more."

I can't think about it yet, Leslie thought. "And your mother?" she said.

"My mother believed in the ghost stallion," Mary Ben said. "My father, too. They were cousins—that's why I still have the old family name—so they both grew up on the legend of the Manford curse. From her wedding day, my mother never set foot to the earth of Manford Manor. She lived in town, while my father ran the place. We moved here only after my mother died . . . of natural causes."

Mary Ben sat quietly for a moment.

"She believed it. She made me believe it. The ghost stallion is real, Leslie. As real as you and I. And he will not allow a married woman to own Manford Manor."

Her face quivered. Quickly, she tightened herself. "I knew the risk I was running when I married Whitney. I didn't dare tell him we would have to leave Manford Manor on the wedding night." Her hands twisted. "Can't you understand, Leslie? I loved him so. But he loved Manford Manor far more than he loved me. If he had known that marrying me meant losing the opportunity to live here, master of these acres . . ."

"But now . . . Couldn't you take a house in town, like your mother and father?" Leslie asked sensibly.

"When Whitney began talking about coming home, I begged him to do just that." Mary Ben shuddered suddenly. "He refused. He said I must face it, live with it, learn that it's all in my head."

She crumpled suddenly, putting her face into her hands, wailing, "I'm frightened, Leslie, so frightened. I . . ."

Leslie's brain was in a whirl. She had listened to the tale with something of a willing suspension of disbelief. But now that it had been told . . . She lifted her head. This is Kentucky, she told herself. A state in the middle of the United States of America. America is in the western hemisphere, on this planet Earth. In the garage, beside the Lincoln Continental, is the beautiful little Mercedes-Benz sports car, in which I can drive to a McDonald's for a hamburger, to the Campbell House for a meal and a drink, to the club to play tennis with my new male friend.

This is the real world. In the real world, there cannot be a piece of the earth which a black ghost stallion will not permit to be owned by a woman married to a mere human male. That kind of active, malevolent evil does not live, *cannot* live, in the world of reality.

She rose, went to enfold Mary Ben's shaking body in her strong arms. "You must have faith in your husband, Mary Ben. You must believe Whitney when he says the ghost stallion is only an old legend you were frightened with as a child."

"I want to believe him," Mary Ben moaned. "I *want* to, Leslie, you know I do."

"Do you love him?" Leslie said steadily.

"Yes. I loved him enough to risk being killed, didn't I? I can't understand to this day why I was only crippled. I think, sometimes, I was spared because I am the last of the Manford women." Her face became sad. "At the same time, Black Prince made sure I *was* the last. But now that I have dared to return into his domain, he has determined to finish the job."

"*Believe* in Whitney," Leslie said, refusing to be diverted by the whirling words. "*Know* he's telling the truth."

Mary Ben straightened. Suddenly her face wore the sly look of a wise child.

"But what if he believes it's true, too? What if he *knows* it's true; *and he's making me live at Manford Manor because he wants the ghost stallion to finish killing me?*"

CHAPTER EIGHT

Leslie Tallant walked rapidly away from the mansion. One would have thought she had a long way to go, a distant but fixed destination; she moved vigorously, with long strides, and she did not pause to look back as the great, ancient house receded into perspective behind her.

In her troubled mind, she was not going toward, but fleeing from. The moment she had escaped from Mary Ben, she had felt the need to escape Manford Manor as well. The story so recently told within its legendary walls was oppressive upon her soul. It was necessary to get away, temporarily at least, if she hoped to recover the person she knew herself to be. Only then could she begin to cope.

She had been caught by the magic of the telling; yet all the while, like any sane person, her practical, rational mind had been busy sorting it out. Those rational considerations had been shattered by Mary Ben's last words.

Leslie slowed her pace, then came to a standstill, hands in the pockets of her skirt, as she soberly contemplated that last fateful sentence.

He's making me live at Manford Manor because he wants the ghost stallion to finish killing me.

That incredible statement, issuing so matter-of-factly from Mary Ben's mouth, placed another, far more sinister, mask on the face of the matter. Not that Leslie believed it. She shuddered inside. How *could* she believe it, when only this morning she had acknowledged a consuming passion for Whitney Ashe?

Leslie, by now, had reached the most distant barn, where the newest foals were kept. So deep in thought, she had not realized she had come so far. She leaned against the paddock fence, looking back over the road she had traveled. In the distance, a pickup truck whirled rapidly across the span of her vision. She wondered if it were Whitney. He had seemingly avoided her today; he had not come to the office while she was there, he had not been in the house when she had returned in answer to Mary Ben's summons.

Two foals approached the fence inquisitively. Their legs, far too long for their bodies at this stage of growth, were as comical as their vestigial tails. They thrust forth their noses to be rubbed, making soft sounds of gratification as she did so, and immediately began to vie with each other for the lion's share of attention. Their dams watched in placid content.

So trusting, so affectionate, Leslie thought. Of course; in their short lives they had met with nothing but kindness. Just as they would always receive devoted attention, the best care veterinary science could offer, the oats and hay provided for their nutrition only of the highest quality.

Yet, Leslie reflected, these pampered animals often become nervous, at times so unmanageable they must be barred from the starting gate. The bloodlines so terribly inbred, they are too highly specialized in their dedication to speed and more speed.

Mary Ben, like a Thoroughbred, had been pampered from birth. Just as some two-year-olds cannot endure the rigors of race-track life, so Mary Ben had been unable to withstand these assaults upon her being. Her mind, her very self, undergoing a sea change, she viewed the world from a twisted perspective that turned love into hate, turned . . .

Leslie stood suddenly erect, ignoring the importunities of the abandoned foals.

Insanity—paranoia especially—can mask itself so cleverly, Leslie thought. From the first moment, she had instinctively liked Mary Ben Manford Ashe. Charming, at times childlike, she evoked one's sense of protectiveness. But suppose, behind that all too plausible façade . . .

Certainly Mary Ben, in her short life, had endured trauma enough to have become deranged. Reared in an atmosphere of dark family legends, generated by a mother so fearful she could not endure to live within the walls of the ancestral home, they had been imbued into the very convolutions of her brain. This assiduous brainwashing had been acquiesced in by her father, himself a Manford though of a collateral branch; so that the malignant legend, proliferating through the structure of her psyche as a cancer metastasizes itself through healthy bodily tissue, had been reinforced beyond rational assessment.

The signs—what could be interpreted as signs—had manifested themselves early in Mary Ben's girlish passion for a glamorous stranger. Willfully, oblivious to every consideration that militated against such an alliance, she had pursued Whitney with single-minded intent. Braving the scandalized eyes of the community in which she had been reared, she had rejected a charming and entirely acceptable suitor; even, with an irrationality that doubled in upon itself, finding the courage to defy the legend simply because she feared that Whitney, if they could not live at Manford Manor, would not condescend to accept her importunities.

Of course, the attack of a stallion—however that had come about—immediately following her wedding, had awakened the old fears with an irrefutable reinforcement of the legend.

After all, Leslie told herself, simply the fact of being crippled for life would be enough to warp anyone. Especially a young and beautiful woman like Mary Ben.

Ample structure to support a hypothesis of paranoia, she thought. An insanity so deeply ingrained, so strongly reinforced by all the events and meanings of her young life: it was the best and plainest explanation for Mary Ben's startling accusation.

The perception of conspiracy is an inescapable facet of the paranoid mind, as Leslie knew from her college readings in psychology. With Mary Ben, it was focused upon her husband.

The fact remained, however: Whitney *had* insisted on returning from Europe, he *had* insisted that Mary Ben take up residence at Manford Manor instead of living in town. It could only have added fuel to the flames burning so hotly in her twisted mind.

If something is not done, Leslie thought clearly, Mary Ben will destroy herself; perhaps, in the process, destroying everything and everyone about her. For, as she also understood, the paranoid personality can be terribly destructive. *And* utterly ruthless. Something must be done. Done quickly. But . . . Wait now. Wait. Think it through.

Perhaps Whitney knew Mary Ben was insane. Despairing of a cure being effected by the psychiatrists who had treated her in Europe, he had decided on the drastic remedy of forcing Mary Ben, by coming home, to face her old fears, and conquer them . . . or be conquered.

Decision came to Leslie. She and Whitney must talk. *Really* talk this time. If they were to be allies in the care of Mary Ben— as they had to be—they must understand each other clearly, without evasion. She must know not only what Whitney knew, but what he believed. And Whitney must know also her mind.

Sure of herself now, she began walking rapidly toward the stone barn.

She found him standing on the small knoll, Dragon sitting beside him. The white dog stood, looking toward her, but Whitney, brooding over these acres that he managed but did not own, remained oblivious to her approach, affording Leslie an opportunity to study him unseen.

Dressed in riding clothes and bearing a residual tenseness, he had, she knew, been schooling the intractable Tara Boy. He stood in profile, both hands grasping the riding crop. When she spoke, Leslie thought he had not heard, so slow was he to respond. Then, in a startled movement, he turned his head.

Leslie continued to approach. "Whitney. I must talk to you."

"What do you want to talk about?" His voice was cold.

She forced herself to look into his face. Though he gazed upon her as a stranger, she would not allow herself to flinch.

"Mary Ben."

The words seemed to make for an alteration in his demeanor. Relaxing somewhat, he took a step toward her. Then, as though afraid to come too close, he stopped.

"Yes?"

Leslie kept her eyes on his face. "Mary Ben has told me the story of the curse on the women of this house."

He was very still. "Do you . . . believe it?"

Leslie moved her shoulders impatiently. "Doesn't matter whether I believe it or not. The point is, Mary Ben believes it.

Whitney, she was raised on it, it's in her blood." Her voice slowed, leveling in tone as she made herself speak the words. "It's in her mind."

She had hoped, watching him absorb her meaning, to determine whether he, too, believed Mary Ben to be insane. But his unrevealing countenance had closed against her.

"Yes. I know," he said. "If it can't be got out of her mind, it will destroy her. Do you think I don't understand that?"

"You're asking more than she can give, Whitney," she said desperately. "The strength is not in her."

She looked at the man with clear eyes. It was a test for Whitney Ashe.

"I can find a house in town," she said. "There'll surely be one where she can feel at home. Where . . ." She hesitated. "Where she can see her old friends, perhaps entertain a bit, become once more a part of the society in which she grew up."

His voice snapped. "Old friends like Bob Berry?"

She refused to be deterred. "I'll find it. I promise. If you will agree to let her go there to live."

He did not hesitate. "No."

A cold, watchful part of herself had its eye on him. "Isn't it worth a try? You'd still have Manford Manor. She would have . . . peace."

"Mary Ben belongs to Manford Manor. As Manford Manor belongs to her. She can't escape that simple fact of her life."

"The place terrifies her. Can't you see that?"

His words drove at her with angry impatience. "It's all in her mind. Leslie, can you possibly believe all that nonsense she's been filling you with? Old wives' tales, that's all they are. It's childish for her to cling to them."

"Whitney."

The sound of his name in her voice stopped him. Embattled, they regarded each other.

"Mary Ben believes you mean to . . ." Her voice faltered, then drove on, ". . . to kill her. That's why, she says, you insist on her living in the mansion. Did you know that?"

His voice came low, but steady. "She has accused me of it to my face."

"How can you bear it?" Leslie cried.

"Mary Ben's mind has been twisted out of shape by these old tales," he said. "She is willful and passionate . . . and strong where her will, her passion, reigns. But she loves me still. If I can sustain her—if *you* can sustain her—she'll work her way through it. You must believe that. As I believe it."

Her reaction surprised even Leslie. "I think *you* believe in the curse." He made a move to speak, but a quick gesture of her hand forestalled him. "There can be strange things in this world, as you know; events generated by inimical forces, pressing in upon that small, lighted area of human consciousness." She stopped, took a deep breath.

"The other night, during the storm . . . Whitney, what did you see when you went outside with the flashlight?"

She forestalled him again. "I know, you told Mary Ben it was only King's Man, loose in the paddock." She regarded him. "But *I* knew you were lying." Her voice hastened. "Oh, I understood the necessity, I couldn't blame you, I'd have probably done the same. But . . . what *did* you see?"

"I wondered how long it'd be before you asked that question." A grim smile touched his lips. "You want the truth? I didn't see anything."

He hesitated, went on. "It could have been King's Man. His stall door *had* been left unlatched. That's what gave me the idea."

"But he was in his stall?"

"He was in his stall."

"Was he . . . wet from the rain?"

A perceptible hesitation. "I . . . didn't go in to find out."

"You were afraid of what you'd discover," Leslie cried. "You didn't dare risk knowing, did you, that King's Man had never left the barn that night?"

"It was a wild time," Whitney said harshly. "I'd had too much to drink, I was jarred awake out of a sound sleep. I didn't dare trust my own senses."

It was the first sign in him of vacillating doubt. It warmed Leslie, made her vulnerable all over again.

"Whitney," she said, "wouldn't it be better to accept what cannot be changed? Give Mary Ben your permission to live away from this terrible place. She can be happy, then. Once she's happy, you can be happy, also. It was the solution for her mother. Why can't it be for her? And for you?"

His voice came strongly. "Whatever it was, out there in the storm, I know one thing. It wasn't the ghost of a vicious black stallion, carrying his evil jealousy beyond his own grave. You'll never convince me such things can be."

"So many things cannot be understood," Leslie said softly. "Sometimes it's necessary to accept them as unassailable fact. It wouldn't be surrender to allow Mary · Ben to leave Manford Manor. It could be a victory of sorts. Can't you see that?"

The words were bitter in his mouth. "A *victory of sorts*." He regarded her narrowly. "Mary Ben is right, you know. I did marry her for the sake of Manford Manor."

His tone became fierce. "I'm not ashamed of it. Who else was there to save the estate? Her brother, Howard? So greedy for ready money, he would have sold Manford Manor for a housing development. Mary Ben's father understood that, which is why Howard was left out of the will."

"Is it worth it, Whitney?" Leslie said. "Manford Manor, I mean, the estate, the land. To marry a woman you didn't love, to . . ."

He came a step closer. "Yes." Visibly, he shook himself. "Love, to my mind, has never counted. I didn't look for love; a woman, to me, was only a vessel, not a being." His hand was on her arm now, gripping hard. "When I saw this lovely piece of land, destined to come into the careless hands of a child-woman like Mary Ben . . . well, why not? I was quickly fond of her, you know, and her passion was passion enough for both. So we struck our bargain. And I kept my side of it, Leslie, even after she became crippled, even after I had to abandon Manford Manor in order to protect her from herself."

They stood facing each other. His hand was on her arm, the palm moist and warm. She could smell the horsy odors on his skin, in his clothing. Her knees were so weak she was afraid she would fall against him.

He shook his head. "No. Love couldn't measure up, not for me." He stopped the talking, as though willing his tongue to be silent. The words came, however; irrevocably, they came.

"Until now," he said.

His arm slid around her waist, bringing her close. She had to lift her chin to keep on seeing his face, so that, when he bent his head, their mouths met almost involuntarily. At first his lips had a hard edge, as though the kiss were against his will also, but when her mouth softened, warmed, so did his, and suddenly, not knowing how it happened, her body surged strongly against him.

The arguments, the antagonism, were forgotten. There remained only the man and the woman, clinging to each other in unquenchable passion. His other arm taking also her waist, he held her in a hard circle of bone and sinew. This time he did not kiss her, only put his head beside her head, holding her so close and hard she felt the single harsh tremor flowing through his body.

"Tonight?" His tone was harsh, hurting, urgent. "Tonight?"

She put both hands against his chest, pushing him away with all her strength, all her will. "Not tonight. Not ever!"

Before she could fight free, he let her go. From the distance between them—so near, yet so far—he regarded her with an inscrutable gaze. A thousand belying words scrambled in Leslie's brain. *He, she, they, could not betray Mary Ben, their passion could only be evil, now and forever . . .*

Leslie could not speak a word of all the words within her which sought to deny the kiss.

Whitney spoke. One word.

"Tonight," he said.

He walked away, the dog following, leaving her standing, as he had done once before, on the little hill.

This time she was not alone. She would never again be alone. For the knowledge of Whitney Ashe's love lived brightly within her.

CHAPTER NINE

Leslie had been infected more than she realized by the black magic of the Manford Manor legend. Though she could substitute no ready explanation, she had not believed Mary Ben's superstitious interpretation of the events of that turbulent night. Yet the two mild storms that had occurred since had been periods of tense waiting for the inexplicable phenomenon to repeat itself.

Leslie had, of course, interpreted her reaction as concern for Mary Ben, who invariably went into a panic at the sound of distant thunder. Leslie had come to dread the prediction of a weather front; she had the definite feeling that the evil which dwelled at Manford Manor became more actively malevolent during a storm.

Tonight, however, she was at peace as she walked up from her twilight visit with King's Man. The soft, warm Kentucky evening was a blessing to soothe her ragged nerves. A full moon edged over the horizon line of trees, refulgent with the promise of a tranquil time.

Leslie's soul required tranquillity as an overexerted body needs cool water; for, though the quiet moonscape made for serenity, there yet remained the troubling matter of Whitney Ashe. Every nerve end of her being tinglingly aware of what had passed between them, she felt it impossible to sit at table tonight. It was not right that they should share a guilty secret in the innocent presence of Mary Ben.

There was within Leslie, also, a complicating reaction: anger at herself for being vulnerable; anger toward Whitney for taking advantage of the vulnerability. She had, at least, rejected him with all the vigor at her command; she was grateful for that modicum of virtue. Yet something within her, willfully passionate, awaited the promise of the night, and she was uncertain whether she could again muster the courage, the forbearance, to deny him. And herself.

Braced to endure his presence, to face the invalid wife in their guilty sharing, she could not encompass, on first seeing, the sight of Mary Ben alone at the table. Murmuring an apology for her tardiness, she slipped into her place as Mary Ben tapped the bell to summon Martin with the soup.

Leslie dared not inquire after Whitney. Instead, she concentrated on Mary Ben. She had not seen her since their conversation this morning, having avoided their usual afternoon companionship by pleading pressure of the neglected office work.

Mary Ben was pale but calm. She did not allude to their last conversation, only chatted quietly about the macramé she was now working with, detailing the difficulties she was encountering, seeking answers from Leslie's more expert knowledge. Leslie, her mind dwelling on Whitney's unusual absence, could respond only abstractedly.

Finally Mary Ben, in innocent enthusiasm, solved the conundrum.

"Whitney has been invited to a Thoroughbred Breeders' Association dinner," she said proudly. "For the very first time."

"That's nice," Leslie said, lightened by the words. At least he was not avoiding her.

"He was quite set up by it. He's been rather *persona non grata* with the Kentucky horse people." With a smug smile, she added ingenuously, "Because of me, you know; our marriage, I mean. You'd be surprised how many old family friends refused the wedding invitation."

"Didn't it upset you?"

"At the time, I couldn't have cared less. All I wanted was Whitney for my husband. As far as I was concerned, if they didn't like it they could lump it."

She had spoken with spirit. Now a small cloud drifted across her face. "I . . . it *would* be nice to have callers. I get so lonely sometimes."

"Perhaps all that will change, now that Whitney has been accepted."

Mary Ben made a wry face. "Not likely. Whitney was asked to the dinner because of King's Man. They're all interested in breeding to him, he's such a complete outcross, you see, for so many Kentucky mares. And Whitney has been doing some very clever advertising."

She paused, gazing thoughtfully at her plate. They were on the main course now, and with her fork she pushed the bits of meat about like a child stubborn about eating.

"It was all my fault, you see," Mary Ben said gravely. "They could understand perfectly why Whitney would take advantage of the opportunity to marry me. But I shouldn't have been such a silly goose as to fall for him. By doing so, I betrayed Kentucky society, and they'll never forgive me." She smiled faintly. "As my mother used to say, I forgot who I was."

"Whitney should have taken you to the dinner. Or was it stag?"

Mary Ben's face was wistful. "I was hoping he would ask me. But . . . he didn't."

"Must have been stag, then," Leslie said decisively. "I'm sure he'd have wanted you to go, otherwise."

Mary Ben shook her head. "I don't know. I never know about Whitney."

The thought seemed to make her despondent, so Leslie began to talk of more cheerful matters. But Mary Ben ate little, and responded less to various conversational gambits.

When they rose from the table, Mary Ben, with a visible effort, brightened. "What shall it be, Kipling, macramé, or Russian bank? Tonight it's *your* choice."

"Let's read, then," Leslie said gratefully. The interminable card game was beginning to bore her. Mary Ben, perhaps because she won consistently, never seemed to tire of it. Indeed, she had pettishly resisted every new suggestion Leslie had made to expand their limited range of entertainment.

They had just settled themselves to begin the third chapter of *The Light That Failed* when the telephone rang. Leslie, expecting it to be a message for Whitney, had started the reading when Martin appeared in the archway.

"Miss Tallant. For you."

Surprised, she closed the book and arose hastily. Bob Berry's voice came like a gust of fresh air from the outside world.

"Hello there, love. Just checking to see if we're on for Thursday."

Leslie had already made up her mind not to see Bob again; the decision had been an inescapable facet of the self-revelation concerning her love for Whitney.

But now . . . She needed every bulwark that could be erected against Whitney's declared intent. Her wayward flesh, totally against her will, awaited his return. She knew the man; he would, in spite of all denial, open her door. And . . . she could not count on Leslie Tallant.

"Of course," she said into the telephone. "Did you doubt it?"

He chuckled. "Not really. Just wanted to hear your voice."

"That's a nice thing to say," she said, more warmly than she felt.

It made his tone deepen. "I shall be looking forward to it. I'll beat you at tennis, if I have to cancel a lesson to do it, and then I'll dance you off your feet. How's that for your day off?"

He really was very nice—even though he had been less than honest with her.

Leslie wondered why she thought of him as a boy . . . it could not be entirely Mary Ben's influence. At least thirty-five, he carried in his voice and bearing the confidence of successful experience. Mary Ben had named him the most eligible bachelor in the Bluegrass; apparently he had taken full advantage of that enviable status.

"Sounds delightful." She allowed herself a low laugh. "I just hope I can give you a decent game."

He caught the implication. "I'm sure you can," he said. "I'm sure you will." He chuckled again, rather smugly, Leslie thought. "It's suddenly getting to seem like forever until Thursday rolls around again."

Leslie had a bold thought. "Why don't you come out tonight? If you're not busy."

His voice turned cautious. "Well . . . I don't know."

"Mary Ben would *love* to see you."

"I'd like to see Mary Ben. Not to mention you. But . . ."

Her voice urged at his reluctance. "It's a long time till Thursday, remember." She lightened the implication with laughter. "It would be great fun. Mary Ben loves cards; with the three of us, she could have some different games. She really is very lonely, you know. It would be good for her to see old friends."

He remained hesitant. "I'd just . . . rather not run into that husband of hers."

"Mr. Ashe is away for the evening," Leslie said. "We're just two lonely women, palpitating for male companionship."

"I had a little run-in with him at the time of the wedding," Bob said. "I was just a kid, you know, and the idea of Mary Ben marrying somebody like that sent me right over the cliff." He made a sound of laughter. "All night long I went charging up and down the Paris Pike, the cut-out open on my car to make all the noise I could."

Mary Ben had mentioned that episode. Apparently, however, she had not known the full story.

"But how did Whitney . . . ?"

"I don't know how many times I had roared past the mansion. I was just out of my skull, you know." His tone was thoroughly forgiving of such boyish pranks. "The last time I came charging 'round the bend, Whitney Ashe was standing in the middle of the road. I nearly ran him down before I could stop. I think he'd have gone under the wheels before he would have moved."

He was not laughing now.

"He came to my side of the car. He said, 'I don't want to damage you, boy. So I think you'd do best to go home now and sleep it off.'"

Bob's voice had tautened to fit the tension of that past moment. "He spoke very quietly. But I knew he meant it." He laughed shortly. "I had the feeling he could kill me with his bare hands, and would do it if I defied him. I was only a boy, you know, and he . . . Well, I just looked up at him and I said, 'Yes sir.' And when he walked away he left me sitting there in a cold sweat. I . . . went home and went to bed."

"I'm sure it's all forgotten now," Leslie protested.

"I doubt Whitney Ashe has ever forgotten anybody who ever

crossed him," Bob said. "I remember distinctly the tone of his voice when he turned, as he was leaving, and said, 'Don't let me see you anywhere near Manford Manor again.'"

Leslie could visualize the scene. Whitney was fully capable of such controlled and carefully meted aggression. She could imagine its effect on the distraught boy. She had tasted of the violence in Whitney Ashe; she shivered suddenly as she thought of how, tonight, she must attempt to deny him.

"So I'm afraid, dear girl, you'll have to come to me," Bob said lightly. "I'm a tennis player, not a big-game hunter—I have absolutely no intention of braving the bear in his den."

"I'll talk to Mr. Ashe," Leslie said. "I'm sure, if he understood Mary Ben would enjoy receiving you, he wouldn't object."

Even as she spoke, she remembered Whitney's demeanor when she had returned from the first date with Bob. A proud and jealous man, she thought, and I belong to his territory. And again, just today, when she had mentioned the possibility of a revived social life for Mary Ben . . .

She had not been listening. "What did you say?"

"Don't bother," Bob said. "Just be wasting your time."

"All right, then," Leslie capitulated. "But . . . I *will* tell Mary Ben you asked after her. She'll be pleased to hear that, at least."

"Sure, fine, as long as she doesn't expect me to put in an appearance. Until Thursday, then."

"Until Thursday."

Leslie returned to Mary Ben. "Bob Berry." She smiled. "He wanted to know all about how you were doing."

Eagerly, Mary Ben said, "Is he coming to see me?"

"I'm afraid not," Leslie said, reluctant to see the enthusiasm fade. "He's afraid Whitney wouldn't approve."

Mary Ben sighed. "I suppose he's right." Then, rebelliously, "Whitney wants to *own* everybody and everything in the whole world. Especially me." She eyed Leslie. "I'll bet he was just furious about you seeing Bob. Has he said anything?"

Leslie made a show of spirit. "Of course not. I may work for Whitney Ashe, but he doesn't rule my social life."

Mary Ben grinned maliciously. "I'd like to hear you tell him so to his face. I'll just bet you'd do it, too."

"Come on, let's get on with it," Leslie said. She smiled, attempting to restore mutual good humor. "Are you prepared to kipple, Mrs. Ashe?"

It was close to midnight when, faint in the distance, they heard what sounded like the galloping of a stallion. Leslie was first made aware by the attentive tilting of Mary Ben's head.

"What . . . ?" she said. Then she heard it, too.

The ghost stallion, she thought. But that's not right. It's a clear, moonlit night. The ghost stallion is supposed to come only with the storms.

Such thinking was irrational. Because she believed, didn't she, that the ghost stallion was only a distorted figment of Mary Ben's imagination?

Mary Ben held herself rigidly upright. Her face was white, her small hands clenched.

"He knows Whitney is not here to protect me," she whispered. "That's why he's come tonight."

And, Leslie realized with a stab of apprehension, they were alone in the great house; it was Nurse Nunn's regular night off, and Martin had requested a special dispensation, after having served dinner, for a meeting of his lodge.

The noise that sounded like hoofs stopped. There was a piercing neigh; and, incredibly enough, another neigh rang in challenging response, followed by a sudden flurry of hoofs striking board walls. *That's King's Man*, flashed across Leslie's mind like a streak of lightning. *He knows there's another stallion out there.*

She was on her feet, the book slipping out of her lap. The sound of racing hoofs began again, nearer this time, then there was a sudden cessation. Leslie had a vision, as clear as if actually witnessed, of the black stallion soaring over the far paddock fence. The hoofs sounded again. He was on King's Man's turf now, and King's Man knew it; he trumpeted fiercely, showering the confining walls with powerful kicks. There is nothing more proudly territorial than a Thoroughbred stallion; he was frantic with desire to get at his enemy, ghost though he might be.

Leslie knew that her face was as white as Mary Ben's; she might have been looking in a mirror, as each reflected the other's terror. In this moment, Leslie believed, as strongly as Mary Ben, that the stallion was present in the flesh. Not a matter of ancient superstitions; she had faith in King's Man's instinct.

Mary Ben had turned the wheelchair toward the door. "He wants me," she said, the words straining tautly through her rigid throat. "I must go."

"No!" Leslie cried, rushing to forestall her. She grasped the handles of the chair, held it against the furious power of Mary Ben's urge to surrender to her nemesis. "He can't get into the house. You're safe here."

The strained face turned whitely toward her. "You think he can't come through these walls? Let me go!"

Leslie, even as she struggled against the forward impetus of the chair, thought furiously in a calm corner of her mind, *Perhaps Whitney is right, in part at least. Perhaps . . .*

"All right." She was surprised to discover that her voice was steady. "We'll *both* go."

With Leslie's acquiescence, Mary Ben promptly turned coward. "I can't," she whispered in a strangled voice. "I have to. But I can't."

Outside, it sounded as though the stallion was circling the paddock at frantic speed; the galloping hoofs, as loud as small thunder, paused at intervals while the horse stamped and neighed. With King's Man responding to every challenge, the commotion was terrible.

"I don't know about you. But *I* intend to see what must be seen," Leslie told Mary Ben. "You can remain behind if you wish."

"If you leave me, he'll come here," Mary Ben whimpered. "Please don't leave me, Leslie."

"Then come along," Leslie said with a resolution she hoped she could sustain. "I'll help you."

Going behind the wheelchair, she gave it a shove toward the door. Even as she did so, she was thinking furiously, assessing the situation as best she could in the turmoil of fearful wondering.

Surely, out there, they would not be alone. The other hands living on the place were quartered too far away, but Tom Musgrove, who slept in a mobile home behind the stallion barn, should be abroad, if only to protect King's Man from his own rage.

Mary Ben was frantic now that she realized Leslie meant to force her to confront the demons in her mind.

"Don't make me, Leslie, I can't bear it, I can't . . ."

"You must see with your own eyes whatever there is to be seen," Leslie said firmly. "Don't be frightened. I'll be with you."

Speaking so calmly the reassuring words, Leslie wondered if she did possess the courage to confront an authentic ghost stallion. Suppose Black Prince did show himself in the paddock; suppose, upon their appearance, he jumped the nearer fence, descending upon them in all his other-world fury?

Nonsense, she told herself staunchly. There must be a rational explanation.

She pushed the wheelchair into the hallway. She paused to snatch up the flashlight left ready for nighttime emergencies. The same flashlight with which Whitney had made his foray into the storm; Leslie remembered that he had confessed an inability to check King's Man to discover if he had a wet coat. A part of all of us believes in ghostly visitations.

The recollection of Whitney's momentary doubt strengthened Leslie's resolution. She opened the front door and Mary Ben, to her astonishment, of her own volition wheeled the chair out onto the porch.

They gazed at each other in the illumination from the overhead fanlight, left aglow against Whitney's return. Mary Ben's mouth wanted to tremble, forcing her to hold the facial muscles in grim fortitude.

"If you can do it, Leslie, so can I."

Leslie made a smile. "If two women can't face down all the stallions of hell, I don't know what could." Her voice was too shaky for the brave words. "Let's go."

She guided the chair carefully down the ramp. There was no need for the flashlight as they progressed around a corner of the house and down a cinder path that cut across the lawn toward the stallion barn; the moonlight was bright and brave upon the land, dark shadows pooled only under the great oaks.

The noise made by the ghost stallion, the challenging response from King's Man in his stall, continued unabated. Leslie could feel a trembling throughout her body. Mary Ben, she knew, with far greater reason than she, was more afraid. Only that knowledge gave her the courage to keep going.

Near the edge of the mansion grounds, Mary Ben reached back to take Leslie's hand. Her grip was clammy with terror.

"Isn't this . . . far enough?"

"We're going to get to the bottom of it, once and for all," Leslie said stubbornly. "If we turn back now, we'll never know."

They pushed on. Coming out of the tree shadows, they saw the paddock lying before them, green and white in the strong wash of moonlight. There came a piercing, challenging neigh, the jealous anger assaulting them almost physically, followed by a fresh thunder of hoofs as though, sensing their presence, the ghost stallion had launched the final assault.

Mary Ben, putting her hands over her ears as the sound swelled in volume, struggled to rise from the wheelchair. Leslie placed a hand on each shoulder, pressing her down.

"Look," she said. "Look, damn it! There's nothing out there."

Slowly, Mary Ben raised her head. Serenely beautiful in the moonlight, the paddock stretched before them. Even as the neighing raged against their ears, even as, beyond, they could hear the commotion King's Man was making in his stall, Mary Ben realized the truth of Leslie's words.

She rejected the truth. "He doesn't have to be seen," she whispered. "Nobody has ever claimed to have seen him, except that old black man . . ."

"Nonsense!" Leslie snapped. "Be still. Let me listen."

"He's here," Mary Ben persisted. "All around us, you can hear him, he's coming through the curtain from the other side, he'll be upon us in another second."

The fateful pronouncement cast a pall. For a split second, Leslie saw—actually *saw* in her reeling mind—the veil that hung between the real world and the other world. Behind that gossamer barrier, the black ghost stallion named Black Prince ramped and raged in an effort to break through. Leslie swayed backward, as though to avoid the flashing hoofs.

As suddenly as it had vanished, the clarity of her mind restored itself. "If he's there, let him come," she said loudly, as much to herself as to her companion in peril. "We've given him his chance. Let him take it now, if he's ever going to."

She was talking to the ghost stallion, she realized dimly. Challenging him. After she had spoken, she waited, as though convinced there must be a savage response.

Mary Ben waited also, her clammy hand gripping Leslie's. For what seemed forever, anticipating momentarily the materialization, in all enmity, of the great black horse, they gazed upon the moonlit serenity of the empty paddock.

The invalid woman broke first. Turning her face away, she whimpered, "I can feel him coming. He means to kill me."

"Hush!" Leslie said. "Just hush, now."

Somehow, in the midst of the terrible waiting, her mind had continued to assess the situation. Her ears were focused, searching for the source, the direction, of the sound. It had seemed to overwhelm them from all sides at once. But, listening with more discrimination . . .

With an effort, she pulled her hand free. "Wait here," she ordered.

Mary Ben grabbed frantically. "Don't leave me!"

"I won't go far. I just want to . . ."

Leslie, flicking on the flashlight, approached the paddock. Near the fence, she paused to listen, then began quartering back toward the oaks. She stopped once, then again, and each time, with increasing confidence, she quickened her step. Mary Ben, in the wheelchair, watched intently, straining forward.

As suddenly as it had started, the sound ceased. The eerie silence was as loud in their ears as the noise had been. Mary Ben defensively jerked the wheelchair around, as though fearful of an attack from behind. Leslie, chilled to the bone, nevertheless held herself unwavering. She would not be denied in her quest for a rational answer.

King's Man, in his stall, whinnied once, challenging the vanished enemy. Then he, too, fell silent.

Leslie called, "Mary Ben. Come here."

Slowly over the turfed grass, Mary Ben propelled herself to Leslie's side. "What is it?" she said fearfully.

"There's your ghost stallion," Leslie said triumphantly.

She was directing the beam of the flashlight into the tree branches overhead. Obediently Mary Ben's gaze followed. An irrelevant sound intruded upon the ghastly silence of discovery: the quick starting of a car, a grating of tires upon gravel.

Leslie put her arm around Mary Ben's shoulders. "Now do you believe that the curse of Manford Manor is only a myth?"

"Yes," Mary Ben gasped. "Yes, but . . ." Her face was terrible to see. "But someone is trying to kill me."

Leslie waited alone for Whitney to come home. Cold, calm, remote, she had put the newly distraught Mary Ben to bed, undressing her frail body with tender hands, tucking her comfortingly, then sitting with her until the sedative had taken effect. Through it all, Mary Ben's body had trembled; like a lost child she had whimpered in a constant monotone.

Leslie, for herself, was possessed by a cold rage which allowed her to accomplish calmly all that could be done to soothe her charge. As she was strong enough, now, to await the homecoming of the master of Manford Manor.

She heard his step on the porch, the opening of the door. She rose from the bench in the hallway as he entered. Elegantly slim, he was wearing a deep blue dinner jacket, richly brocaded.

He paused, startled by her late-night presence. *He's wondering if I've waited up to welcome him into my bed*, Leslie thought clearly.

Her voice was even in tone. "How was the dinner?"

His reply, surprisingly for Whitney, was jovial with whiskey and residual good-fellowship.

"Couldn't have been better. I booked three seasons to King's Man."

He stopped, suddenly aware of her watchful attitude. "How were things here?"

"We had another visit from the ghost stallion."

His voice quickened. "Mary Ben . . . she's all right?"

"She's sleeping. Come. There's something I must show you."

"What is it?"

"You'll have to see for yourself." The flashlight was ready in her hand. "Come on."

After a hesitation, he followed. Side by side they walked across the expanse of sward. She could sense his wariness; it struck a cold horror into her soul to know she had believed herself, only this morning, passionately in love with this man.

Under the oak tree nearest to the empty paddock, she directed the flashlight beam upward. As she had said to Mary Ben, she told him, "There's your ghost stallion."

Whitney gazed at the sturdy, coned horn of the outdoor loud-speaker tucked secretly into the branches of the oak.

Softly he said, "Well, I'll be damned."

"Mary Ben knows, now, there's no such thing as a ghost stallion." Leslie was surprised her voice could hold so steady. "But she knows, also, that someone means to use that old legend to kill her . . . or to drive her insane."

Whitney faced her. "You believe it's me."

Her voice came as quietly as his. But cold, so cold, out of the remote reaches of her desert heart. "Who else would benefit from Mary Ben being declared insane and put away forever? Or . . . from her death?"

CHAPTER TEN

They stared at each other across the darkness. The beam of the torch, lying between them like a sword of light, revealed a pinched quality in Whitney's face. The lips were thin, bloodless; in the back-glow, his eyes held an obsidian opacity.

Only a moment, but it seemed an eternity. A primordial instinct stirred the hair on the nape of Leslie's neck; she experienced a distinct fear that she stood in the presence of her own death. The deadly quality in Whitney Ashe's regard had caused the adrenaline to start flowing, in the flight response of all creatures in the shadow of a predator.

One step toward her, a touch of his hand, and she would have fled. Immediately, instinctively, not in blind panic but in a rational appraisal of danger made by her body's mechanism for self-preservation.

Forgotten, for the moment, was the passion, each for the other, which only this morning had been given credence.

As though sensing that any movement on his part would precipitate them over the edge into a violence that could never be redeemed, he spoke quietly.

"Give me the flashlight."

She tried to obey. But, as she willed her arm into movement, her hand lost its power of gripping and the torch fell to the ground.

Stooping carefully, he retrieved it. He took a step away; she was grateful for the small sanctuary of an added distance.

"Let's see where the wires from that thing lead us."

The beam of light questing, Whitney walked around the tree trunk. "Here it is," he said. "Look."

Leslie came beside him, touched with one finger the gray-colored wire that, snaking down the bole, disappeared into the ground. Whitney walked away slowly, swaying the light back and forth. A faint trace in the sod betrayed the direction. With absorbed attention, Whitney followed it for a few yards.

He straightened. "Aren't you interested in finding where it leads, Leslie?" he asked. "Or have you already decided what you want to believe?"

Leslie had no answer. Her mind was a turmoil of questions *without* answers. She could not fathom his response to her deadly accusation. That first instinct to silence her; that, indeed, she could understand, in the very fibers of her being. But this calm search . . .

Is it all a charade for my benefit? she thought intensively. Surely he knows where the wire goes; he must have laid it down with his own hands.

"All right," he said. "Don't come. But I intend to find out the truth."

He began again his stalking prowl. Numbly, feeling like a zombie walking through the night, Leslie followed. Whitney moved in a direct line to the nearest corner of the stallion paddock. There, the buried wire made an angled turn, running close along the fence toward the stone barn.

Hidden so well, it became more difficult to trace. Whitney continued beyond the paddock gate, realized he had overrun a turn, came back. He had to scrabble in the soil to discover where it made a right angle to follow the cindered path toward the stone barn.

Assuming that it entered the building, Whitney began to hurry. But, search though he might, he could not discover where the wire crossed the threshold. At last he located an unexpected turn, the buried wire running alongside the wall. Whitney disappeared around the corner, Leslie hastening to catch up.

He was on his knees, digging into loose dirt. The wire could not be found. Squatting, crabbing backward, he raked with probing fingers until he found where the wire veered away from the barn wall to run directly toward Tom Musgrove's mobile home.

Whitney stood up, looked at Leslie. His face showed more grim, the lips a harsh line. Still he did not make the final assumption, but traced the wire with care to Musgrove's doorstep. After he had verified its entrance, he straightened again.

This time he did not look at Leslie. His knuckles rapped firmly against the side of the mobile home.

The door opened so quickly, Leslie had an impression Tom Musgrove, aware of their approach, had been waiting for the summons. His misshapen body, silhouetted by a dim light from behind, looked like that of a troll, the shoulders humped, neck twisted, head tilted to one side. His short legs were bowed, knotted.

He gazed upon them without surprise; Leslie could not read the expression in his shadowed face.

Whitney's voice was blank of feeling. "I'm coming in, Tom."

Without a word, Musgrove stood aside. Whitney, flicking a glance toward Leslie, led the way. Inside, he went first to a lamp, turning the switch to bring more light.

It was a space of shabby plastic, worn and dirtied by the passage of transient lives. On an eye of the tiny stove stood a battered, blackened coffeepot; scattered on the vinyl-covered bench at one end was an array of girlie magazines, rampant with enticing flesh. Leslie felt guilt at their intrusion into the old man's private life.

Musgrove ignored her presence. His eyes were fixed on Whitney as he moved about the frugal space, flicking the beam of light into each shadowed corner.

The equipment was not difficult to find. When not in use, it was obviously stowed away in a cubbyhole. Now, it was pulled out onto the floor. Whitney, expressionless, stooped over the record player, took the single record from the turntable, held it slanted to catch the light.

He lifted his eyes to Tom Musgrove's face. Musgrove stood watching, his battered countenance not showing guilt, but bland, smooth. Like an Indian facing the prospect of torture, Leslie thought.

In a surge of anger, Whitney raised his arm, smashed the record against the corner of a plastic-topped table. The disc shattered into stiff shards, the pieces flying explosively. Leslie tensed, expecting Whitney, in the next moment, to mount a physical assault upon the little old man.

He seemed, however, to have expended the violence that was in him in the symbolic gesture of smashing the sound-effects record. Without taking his eyes away from Musgrove, he said, "Leslie. The telephone. Call the sheriff."

"Wait a minute," Tom Musgrove said hoarsely.

Leslie had not had time to move. In the face of this plea—if it *was* a plea—she remained still. Whitney gazed at Tom with what was almost a speculative look.

"All right," he said at last, "we're waiting."

Tom's eyes skittered from Whitney to Leslie, back again. He moistened his lips with his tongue. For the first time, Leslie realized the fear that dwelled within him.

"I didn't mean any harm," he said.

"Harm?" Whitney spoke violently. "Trying to scare a sick woman out of her wits. You don't call that harm?"

Tom Musgrove's voice had always been harsh, as twisted as his thick neck. Now it carried the sound of gravel, as though he had to push the words of explanation past an impermeable barrier.

"I was trying . . . I wanted to save her from the ghost stallion. Before he finally killed her."

Whitney made a gesture of disbelief. "The ghost stallion? What are you talking about?"

Musgrove's voice was stubborn. "You know what I'm talking about. The black horse. Black Prince, which killed her grandmother and her great-grandmother."

Whitney regarded him. "You're not trying to tell me you *believe* those old stories."

Tom Musgrove was firm in self-defense. "I thought if Miss Mary Ben got scared a little, she'd leave Manford Manor. Then . . . she'd be safe."

Whitney, in the stillness of the confined space, began to breathe hard. "*Got scared a little.* You've always known how she's been about those old tales. You meant to drive her insane, maybe even cause her to die of sheer fright."

Tom Musgrove became agitated. "No!" he cried. "Just frighten her enough to make her leave, that's all." His voice faltered. "I

. . . I always loved Miss Mary Ben. Why, when she was just a baby, her daddy would bring her out sometimes, and I'd tote her around on my arm to see the horses. I was the one to put her up on a saddle, first time in her life; I took care of her little white pony with my own two hands." His face was earnest. "I wouldn't do a thing to harm a hair of Miss Mary Ben's head, Mr. Whitney, and that's the truth."

A faraway look came into his eyes. "She was just the prettiest little thing you ever did see, with them long blond curls and them soft blue eyes. And just as mischievous and full of spirit as a pet raccoon. I watched her grow up into a young lady. After her and her daddy came to live at Manford Manor, I got to see her every single day."

His face darkened. "And then she got crippled by that ghost horse, and had to go away, and I knew I'd never see her again." He lifted his gaze. "It was all right, because it meant she was safe. But then . . . you brought her home."

Whitney's voice was steady, inexorable. "So you rigged your loudspeaker. The night of the storm, you played your sound-effects record for the first time. It didn't do the trick. So you waited until I was gone for an evening, and tried it again."

Musgrove's voice, ironically enough, carried an indignant note. "No, sir, Mr. Whitney. That's not right. Tonight was the first time. I swear to God."

Whitney, Leslie, stared in disbelief.

"But . . ." Leslie said.

Solemnly, Tom Musgrove nodded. "That first time, it was *him*. Black Prince. It was only after I knew he had come home to Manford Manor, too, still jealous of the Manford women, that I thought of faking it."

"Do you expect us to believe that?" Whitney demanded. "It won't make it any lighter on you, take my word."

"Believe it or not, it's the truth," Tom said stubbornly. His tone became a plea. "You don't know how many nights I laid awake, listening to hear if he was in the paddock, trumpeting for Miss Mary Ben. If I could have just persuaded her to leave before he came back again, she'd have a chance. That's when I put up the loudspeaker, and bought that record."

With an immediate, unassailable conviction, Leslie began to

believe the little man. From his viewpoint, awry though it might be, he was telling the truth. He *believed* the ghost stallion had, the night of the storm, appeared at Manford Manor. He had pursued his chicanery in the fanatic conviction it was for Mary Ben's ultimate benefit.

So, for lack of evidence to the contrary, the ghost stallion, in all his evil manifestation, did exist. The discovery of the loudspeaker, the tracing of the incriminating wire to Tom Musgrove's quarters, had solved nothing. It had only added to the mystery.

Leslie felt despair. So triumphantly sure of herself, with Mary Ben she had braved the unknown, had, seemingly, solved the puzzle with a rational discovery. Now . . .

She looked at Whitney. He stood silent, his face sternly righteous. Yet Leslie sensed in him the same uncertainty she knew within herself.

Like me, she told herself, he has not dispelled the phantom of the ghost stallion. The curse of Manford Manor is still as possible of reality as before this hectic night began.

He seemed to have come to a decision. About Musgrove, at least.

"All right, Tom," he said quietly. "I want you off the place by sunrise."

Tom's face twisted. Leslie didn't know how she would react if he wept; he looked as though, in the next moment, tears would show in his eyes.

"Mr. Whitney," he said in his harsh, constricted voice. "You can do anything to me . . . anything but that. I can't. Since I left the racetrack life, I ain't never been nowheres but Manford Manor."

"If you're still here in the morning, I will telephone the sheriff," Whitney said. "Take your choice."

Gathering up Leslie with a glance, he disappeared out the door. Leslie hesitated, wishing for a compassionate word to tender the grief-stricken little man. His deed, though mistaken, had been performed in the integrity of love.

He had never been kind—nor even polite—to her, perceiving Leslie Tallant, she knew now, as a threat to the tranquillity of his beloved mistress. When Mary Ben, in her self-centeredness, is scarcely aware of his existence, Leslie thought sadly.

With a jolt of recognition, Leslie felt that perhaps she *was* a threat, as Tom Musgrove believed. Perhaps, half deliberately, I have been deluding myself in allowing a passion for Whitney Ashe that would not, I believed because of the special circumstances, alter fundamentally the pattern of the marriage.

"Tom," she said sympathetically, "I'm sorry you must go away. You were wrong in what you did, but . . . we all make mistakes. You, at least, made your mistake because of love."

Gratitude flashed in his eyes. But, absorbed in his personal disaster, he did not speak. Leslie, without further words, left him alone.

Whitney, not waiting to see if she followed, was walking on. She hurried to catch up. They did not speak, but moved side by side until they came to the stallion paddock.

Whitney paused. Silently he contemplated the moonlit expanse of grass, the white fences shining with a ghostly luminescence. Leslie shivered, wondering what he was thinking.

She had to break the silence. "King's Man . . ." She cleared her throat. "King's Man thought a rival stallion was rampaging in his paddock. He sounded like he would tear down the stall to get to him."

Whitney was startled. "I'd better take a look," he said. "Make sure he didn't injure himself."

King's Man whickered at the sound of their footsteps, greeted them eagerly when Whitney opened the stall door and flicked on the overhead light.

"How are you, old boy?"

King's Man bobbed his head, saying he was just fine, now that he had routed his rival. Whitney, entering the stall, snapped on a chain shank for Leslie to hold while he carried out the inspection. The stallion, pleased with her presence, whuffed at Leslie, pushed his nose against her arm. Leslie chuckled, patting his muzzle.

Whitney went over the stallion with care, feeling the legs and ankles for bruises, checking the hoofs for shattered edges. He found only one abrasion, on a protruding hipbone. King's Man flinched slightly as Whitney tested it with a probing finger.

"Is he all right?" Leslie asked anxiously.

"Doesn't amount to much," Whitney said. "I'll check it in the morning, put some ointment on, make sure it doesn't become infected."

He turned, looked at King's Man, his head pressed affectionately against Leslie's shoulder. "Quite fond of you, isn't he?"

"Yes, we're great friends," Leslie replied with quiet pride. "He's terribly disappointed if I don't call on him at least once a day."

"Don't forget to be careful," Whitney cautioned. "A stallion can be unpredictable, you know."

"King's Man would never do anything to hurt me," Leslie said confidently.

Whitney regarded her for a still moment. He had never looked at her, for all his intense manner, quite as attentively. A thrill moved along Leslie's spine.

Whitney placed one hand on the stallion's haunch. "A great stallion has in his heart both love and hate," he said quietly. "He can be exceptionally gentle, and extraordinarily violent."

Leslie smiled. "That is a large part of his enormous beauty," she said. "Don't you think?"

"Of course. But don't let his love for you blind you to the danger that's in him."

Leslie's voice was steady. "I won't," she said. "You may be sure of that."

It was a confrontation. They both realized it. The tension between them was a bright ribbon, spanning the empty space separating them like the fragile intensity of a frail bridge arching over an abyss.

Whitney moved, breaking the stasis. "It's late," he said quietly. "We'd better get on."

Again in silence, they walked to the mansion. As they entered the door, the telephone shrilled. Leslie snatched it up before it aroused the household.

"Leslie, is everything all right out there?" Bob Berry asked anxiously.

Startled by the late-night call, Leslie couldn't find her voice. In apprehension, she glanced toward the listening Whitney, wondering how he would react when he discovered that the caller was Bob.

His voice continued in her ear. "I was coming out, you know, decided to risk seeing you and Mary Ben after all. When I got to the gates, I heard the most god-awful commotion." He hesitated. "I decided it was the better part of valor to decamp, so I scratched off before anyone should discover me. I couldn't help but worry . . . is everything all right?"

"Yes," Leslie said. "Everything's fine."

"Listen," Bob said. "I heard a stallion, just as clear as anything. Is that old ghost haunting the premises again?"

"How did you know about that?" Leslie asked sharply.

"Everybody in the Kentucky Bluegrass has heard that old story. A lot of people—including me—believe it. After all, it's an irrefutable fact that . . ."

"Bob, I can't talk now," Leslie said. "Call me in the morning?"

"Is that man with you?" A note of apprehension had crept into his voice.

Leslie evaded the question. "I'm sorry, Bob, but I'm exhausted, and I have to get up early. So good night, please. All right?"

"All right," he said reluctantly. "I'll be talking to you." His voice warmed. "Sleep good. And think about me."

She was not in the mood for sexual games. "Good night," she said, and hung up.

"Why is he calling at this time of night?" Whitney asked sternly.

Leslie refused to go into it. "Oh, just some of his usual gallant silliness."

Whitney seemed relieved by the small lie. He hesitated over the next words. "None of my business, of course, who you choose to see. But I'd . . . rather not receive Bob Berry at Manford Manor."

"I'll keep it in mind," Leslie said, her tone an utter rejection of the intrusion.

He was still looking at her. "Leslie. Do you believe, now, that I had nothing to do with Tom Musgrove faking the ghost stallion?"

Leslie experienced a bewildering confusion. She was, as she had pleaded to Bob Berry, exhausted. She simply didn't want to deal with it. Not now, at any rate, in the middle of the night.

"I don't know what to believe any more," she cried, turning her face away. "I thought I had solved it. But, by discovering the loudspeaker, I've only made matters worse."

His voice was persistent. "You *can't* believe I had anything to do with it."

She looked him in the face. "It doesn't matter what *I* believe," she said wearily. "It's Mary Ben you must convince."

They regarded each other stilly. In the silence, a change of mood came over them. Leslie remembered the warning that, standing in King's Man's stall only a few minutes ago, he had delivered. Had it been deliberate, or only impulsive? She did not know. At this moment, she did not care.

He took a step toward her. "Leslie."

His voice lingered over the texture of her name. She could not endure it. Turning away, she said swiftly, "Good night, Whitney."

She left him. But, halfway up the stairs, with all her will she could not resist turning to look downward.

Whitney had not moved. He had been watching her walk up the stairs; she knew that his eyes, his every sense, had been absorbed in the lithe movement of her body. The fires of desire, which had scorched her only this morning, in what seemed a long century ago, had, in spite of the fast-moving events of the night, come to life again. He had not abandoned his promise—his threat?—to come to her.

A wave of indefinable emotion swept through Leslie's being. She dared not define it in precise terms of feeling and response. She wondered, in the back of her mind, what message her eyes—the shape of her mouth, her very flesh—were sending in response to *his* message.

As though moving against, through, an irresistible force, she made herself go on up the stairs. With each step, she listened for the sound of Whitney, coming closer, closer, closer . . .

She achieved the door to her suite of rooms, opened it, passed through, closed it. There was a large, old-fashioned key that would serve to lock the portal against him. She did not use it. A mere lock could not restrain Whitney Ashe; it would only arouse the violence that was an ineradicable part of the love within him.

In dreamlike movement, she undressed in the darkness and put on the gown the maid had laid out across the bed. Then she went to stand in the moonlight that spilled through the window like molten silver.

Leslie Tallant gazed out upon the Kentucky earth, patterned

in all its neat richness. The white fences embraced the empty stallion paddock, defining this patch of earth where so much of love, so much of hate, had been acted out during the more than a century of Manford Manor's existence.

I am a part of all this, she thought. It is a part of me. I am close to the beating heart of Manford Manor. If there were truly a ghost of the great stallion, Black Prince, he would now hold for me the same love, the same hate, that he holds for all Manford women. He would seek to destroy me, as he seeks to destroy Mary Ben, even though my name is not—will never be—Manford.

She shivered so deeply inside it did not reach the surface of her nerves. For the first time, she could comprehend the compulsion in Mary Ben, when she heard the trumpeting call, to go out into the night. To surrender to the death that awaited her was to surrender also to the Manford Manor earth, be absorbed by it, gratefully relinquishing self-identity for the sake of a meaningful immersion into something so much more powerful than the individual ego.

With fateful prescience, Leslie knew that if, at this moment, the ghost stallion should suddenly appear down there within the circle of the white fences, if he should rear and trumpet, calling out to her: she would go to him with open arms.

Moving like a dream-walker, she left the window, crossed the room, got into bed. Gazing straight up at the ornate canopy, invisible in the blackness over her head, she lay rigid. Waiting.

As Leslie had known he would, Whitney Ashe held to his threat-promise. So suddenly that Leslie was startled, he was in the room, standing between her and the tall, thin rectangle of moonlit window. Her eyes clung to the silhouette of his lean waist, tapered from broad shoulders, the hatchet-edged strength of his profiled head.

She spoke clearly. "Whitney," she said. "No."

Leslie could voice her denial with such firm resolution because, within her innermost being, she was so thoroughly disordered. So much she did not know. She didn't know *anything*, really. She had been convinced, by the evidence of the loudspeaker, that it was all Whitney's doing. But his reaction had been to trace out diligently the wire, to confront Tom Musgrove.

Then there had been Bob Berry's late-night phone call, proof that he too had been present; obviously it had been his automobile departing from the scene. What could she know of *his* motivations and angers? Perhaps he, knowing Tom Musgrove since boyhood days, had inspired the twisted little man . . . ?

Beyond. She did not know Whitney Ashe. In spite of all great passion, he remained opaque. Perhaps there was not love in him, as there was not love for his wife; perhaps only a lust seeking to be assuaged in the most convenient vessel.

Male lust, she knew truly, could not satisfy the female lust that was within her. She must have love also. First. Only then could the lust that boiled in them both be sated.

So she lay tensely in the bed, covered chastely by the white sheet, and the words were defined with clear resolution in the dark air that breathed between them.

Whitney. No.

She held herself stiffly even after they had been spoken, for she could not know his response.

He remained still for a moment that stretched to eternity. When he moved, it was to approach nearer still. She felt herself melt. No longer rigid, defensive, she was suddenly open to his assault upon her flesh.

She had uttered strongly, decently, all the resistance she could muster. Now, if he should touch her, she would not, could not, deny him; she lay not so much at the mercy of his masculine demand but of her female self. It was, in the most profound sense, a willing surrender.

Even as she waited, she accepted that awful knowledge.

Again, for a very long time, he remained still. She gazed up at the profile brooding over her with such passionate intensity. In the next moment, his hand would touch her. And Leslie Tallant would receive, accept—engulf—Whitney Ashe. Against her will, with her will; and, she perceived with a sudden flash of clarity, both with and against his will, also: the thing would be done.

United in spirit, they poised on the brink of the inevitable slide into fleshly union. At this penultimate point, Whitney Ashe turned away, his presence receding as a ghost recedes into that unknown from which it came.

He had yielded to her denial. And Leslie was alone.

She turned over, curling in upon herself. She could not remember when she had last cried. But she wept now, without reserve; for herself, for him, for the bitter necessity of denial.

She did not sleep before dawn had touched rosy upon the Kentucky earth.

CHAPTER ELEVEN

They lived now within the classic triangle; they ate together, talked, went about the tasks of daily living, three beings trapped within the pattern of tensions.

Mary Ben, when Leslie had carefully explained the circumstances of Tom Musgrove's deed, had displayed a most baffling reaction. She had seemed indifferent, saying only, "When I was a child, I never could stand the little man. He was so *creepy*." Afterward, however, more afraid than ever, she dwelled more deeply watchful within herself.

Whitney, too, had withdrawn, scarcely speaking, from one day to the next, either to Leslie or to Mary Ben. Yet there were times when Leslie, without looking, knew that his eyes, all-devouring in their intensity of desire, sought her secretively; and more often, at night, he did not work, but sat solitary in the library, drinking steadily from his bottle of port.

It became a ritual, as the study of bloodlines and pedigree charts had been a ritual. Always he donned the burgundy smoking jacket, arranged his knobby briers in a row at his elbow, along with a tin of fragrant tobacco. Then, feet in slippers propped on a footstool, he drank and smoked steadily until sleep could reach him.

It hurt Leslie, when she and Mary Ben came to say good night, to see him so. Such a virile, self-contained man; she thought the deterioration could only be attributed to her principled denial of his need. Rising at their appearance, swaying slightly, his face flushed with drink, he made a mocking bow of acknowledgement. And always his eyes were fixed upon Leslie, inscrutable, opaque; *waiting*, Leslie thought, *waiting for a signal*.

A sign she could not give, though, with such heavy drinking, she expected him at any moment to step beyond the bounds of discretion. She waited nightly, resistful and yearning at once, until his footsteps had passed her door.

They could be truly together only in the daily riding. They no longer made the long, body-toughening jaunts along the saddle paths; they were working now in the training ring. Leslie, under Whitney's tutelage, had moved beyond her previous experience into a whole new area of competence. Her mentor, she knew from his open approval, was delighted with her progress.

One morning, Whitney, after she had taken Irish Sailor through the pattern of jumps without a flaw, came to stand beside her as she rested the horse. Stroking one hand on her mount's sweaty neck, he looked up into her face.

"You're ready for the show ring," he said quietly. "You'll win some ribbons, too. Take my word for it."

A quiver of delighted apprehension swept through her. "Are you sure, Whitney?"

"You have an excellent seat, and a nice flair," he said. "Far more importantly, you establish a rapport with your mount." He nodded judiciously. "Yes, Leslie. Only competition can season you now."

Leslie, breath caught into her throat, looked down into his face. Their gazes locked. Leslie looked away, seeking relief from the intensity of his eyes. *We are together, at least, in this*, she thought clearly.

She saw Tara Boy standing quietly, reins held by the man who had replaced Tom Musgrove.

An impulse swept through her. Throwing one leg over the withers, she slid to the ground to stand beside Whitney.

"If I'm as good as you think, it's time I rode Tara Boy."

Whitney was taken aback. "Do you know what you're saying? Even *I* have my problems with Tara Boy. As you well know."

"Am I good enough to ride him?" Leslie demanded.

He wavered. "You're good, all right. I won't deny that. But . . ."

"But you don't trust me with Tara Boy. Only with the gelding."

"It's not that. I just . . . don't want you to get hurt."

"Then you don't think I'm good enough," Leslie said. Turning away, she gathered the reins, preparing to remount. "I just wanted to know."

His voice stopped her. "Do *you* think you're ready for him?"

It was not a question lightly asked. Nor was there a light answer; she had to consider deeply before she could reply.

"Yes," she said simply. "If I'm ready for the horse shows, I have to be ready for Tara Boy."

Soberly, contemplatively, they looked at each other. A glow came into Whitney's eyes.

"All right," he said. "Tara Boy is yours."

A thrill struck through Leslie's soul. She did not smile in gratitude, she did not say, "Thank you." The response within her was far more profound.

She turned to gaze at the young stallion, seeing him with new eyes. Unconsciously her hand tightened on the riding whip, lifting it tensely. Whitney forgotten, Tara Boy was all the world to her now; she would mount him, she would know him, they would be together, horse and rider . . .

A movement distracted her attention. Mary Ben, with Nurse Nunn pushing the chair, was coming down from the house.

Oh no! Leslie breathed silently in her soul. *Not just now. Not when . . .*

Mary Ben had never been present during the training sessions; why, at this moment, had she chosen to appear?

I can't go through with it, Leslie thought swiftly, her courage faltering. This is between me and Whitney, between me and the horse. She has no place in this.

But, she realized as quickly, there could be no retreat. She had issued the challenge; it had been taken up. If she did not ride Tara Boy now, the opportunity might never come again.

Nevertheless, she had to will her body to walk across the ring and take the reins.

"Hello, Whitney," Mary Ben called gaily. "Do you mind if I watch?"

Whitney strolled to the fence. "This is a surprise, my dear. You're just in time to see Leslie ride Tara Boy for the first time."

Leslie reached to adjust the stirrups to her length of leg. The horse, made uneasy by her intent to get on his back when she had never done so before, sidled away.

"Easy, boy, easy," she murmured, patting his neck.

Tara Boy, refusing to be soothed, lunged away. Leslie, digging in her booted heels, held on. Whitney was suddenly at her side, speaking to the colt, a firm hand taking hold of the reins. With his accustomed presence, Tara Boy quieted.

"Are you sure you want to do this?" Whitney said.

A quiet tone of question, private. Leslie did not look at him.

"He spooked only because he's not used to the idea of carrying me," she said, her voice as quiet as his had been. "I can't quit now. If I don't get up on him, he'll never let me do it."

Whitney regarded her seriously. Then, with busy hands, he adjusted the stirrups. Returning to her side, he said quietly, "Let me help you up."

In one lithe movement, he threw her up into the saddle. As she took the reins, Tara Boy squatted slightly, muscles quivering. Leslie spoke simultaneously with voice and body, commanding movement.

Tara Boy, obedient to his training, swung into an easy trot. Leslie, suddenly absorbed into the sensation of riding, let her body go with him. Feeling his power, the ease of movement, her awareness of Mary Ben's watching eyes faded.

She schooled him through figure eights until she was sure he had become accustomed to her weight upon his back, her touch on the reins. Then, flowing smoothly into the next phase, she lifted him over the first low jump.

There was, she realized with a thrill of excitement, all the difference in the world between this great colt and the sedate gelding. Enormous power here, flowing from the mount into every fiber of her being as she leaned into the jump, lifting him, feeling the impact as his front feet landed, as he took a gathering stride to ready himself for the next barrier.

She had intended it only as a beginning, to accustom the horse and herself to working together. But Tara Boy demanded that they take the next, then the next and the next, each obstacle more difficult than the one before.

Flowing smoothly through the series, their bodies were united into one body, their will to excel merged with an equal perfection. This, she realized, was what riding is all about. Her heart was hurting with the ecstasy of achievement; it *had* to be perfect, and it was perfect. He cleared the last fence, the highest, like a wild bird in flight, the landing so cushioned and easy it was impossible to believe.

She wanted to laugh, she wanted to cry, she felt herself doing both as Tara Boy slowed to a trot. Passionately she leaned to fold both arms around his sweating neck, his odor strong and sweet in her nostrils.

The high-strung colt, spooked by her unexpected posture, startled out from under her. She was, she realized with a disconcerting abruptness, sitting on air. Just as suddenly, she jarred against the earth.

Humiliated, Leslie got to her feet. Head down, she dusted the seat of her riding breeches. Whitney had caught the horse, was holding him at the fence near Mary Ben. Taking a deep breath, she walked with quick strides to Tara Boy's side.

"That was really very good, Leslie," Mary Ben said graciously. "A pity he managed to dump you after the course was finished."

Leslie looked across the fence into Mary Ben's face. She forced a smile. "I'll do better this time."

"Are you all right?" Whitney asked in a low voice. "Sometimes a simple fall like that can really shake you up."

"I'm fine," Leslie said impatiently. "And don't blame Tara Boy. It was my fault, for doing such a silly thing."

Again Whitney lifted her into the saddle. She gathered the reins firmly, speaking to Tara Boy, letting him know she was again in command. She trotted him in a figure eight, getting the feel all over again.

"All right, Tara Boy. One more time," she said quietly.

The moment she started, she sensed that it was all wrong. Tara Boy was on the bit, fighting the support of her hands, and as a consequence he was rushing the fences. Dumping her out of the saddle had given him the courage of disobedience.

Leslie submerged herself into the ride, fighting with body and with will to dominate the spirited hunter. There was not, this time, the delight of a perfect melding. It was a struggle between Leslie and the recalcitrant beast.

It could only end badly; and it did. At the next-to-last jump, Tara Boy, sensing himself out of rhythm, propped suddenly, swerved aside. Gently, almost gracefully, Leslie continued alone over the fence, her body turning in midair in a slow parabola. Clearing the fence, she tried, too late, to tuck for the fall.

The gracefulness of her solo flight ended with a jarring thump as she landed on her back. The breath knocked out of her lungs, her senses whirling, she struggled to get to her feet.

Suddenly Whitney was kneeling over her, hands against her shoulders, pressing her down. "Don't move," he said urgently.

Leslie obeyed. Dragon, crowding in before Whitney, came to sniff worriedly at her face, so that, laughing in spite of her predicament, she had to push him away. She lay looking up into Whitney's concerned face as his hands probed her arms and shoulders, tested the collarbones, took hold of each booted foot to flex the knees.

"Any sharp pain?" he inquired anxiously. "You didn't land right, you know. You'll be damned lucky if . . ."

Still looking into his face, she said quietly, "I'm all right, Whitney. I think. Let me . . ." Clasping his arm with both hands, she pulled herself upright. Gingerly she twisted her torso. There was pain all right, but only a dull ache.

"Let me get up," she said.

Whitney assisted her. Leslie stood swaying. Dragon, pleased, wagged his tail and left the training ring.

"He was really on the bit that time," she said shakily. "Fighting me all the way."

"That's Tara Boy," Whitney said with a sigh. "I saw you were in trouble with the first jump."

He was supporting her firmly. Leslie wanted to lean against him, but she did not. Mary Ben was still watching.

Her voice came thinly across the separating distance. "Is Leslie all right, Whitney?"

"Yes, she's fine, just shook up," Whitney replied.

Mary Ben turned the wheelchair, then allowed Nurse Nunn to provide the motive power as she left them.

"I ought to get up on him again," Leslie said.

Whitney shook his head. "Not today. You've had enough."

Leslie stood away, took a tentative step. Steady enough. She turned, to encounter again the look of concern.

She smiled at Whitney. "I'm all right. Really. Oh, I'll be black and blue in the morning. But . . . I did ride Tara Boy, that first time, didn't I? Rode him beautifully."

"Yes," Whitney said. "You did."

Somehow, in an obscure way that defied analysis, it was a victory for Leslie.

A victory that carried an immediate aftermath.

From the moment Mary Ben had departed from the riding arena, a change in her attitude toward Leslie was apparent. She became, if anything, more dependent, more affectionate . . . and more demanding, in her sweetly imperious way, of Leslie's love and loyalty. It was as though she were competing with Whitney, so that now there was a triangle within the triangle, establishing a new pattern of emotional tensions underlying the classic pattern of man-and-wife-and-other-woman.

Often Leslie, feeling Mary Ben's eyes upon her, wondered uneasily what thoughts were brooding within her convoluted brain.

Quickly, given Mary Ben's childlike openness, she found out. They were sitting together, as usual, one afternoon, when Mary Ben remarked casually, apropos of nothing, "Whitney is quite enamored with you, Leslie. But of course you know that, don't you?"

Leslie felt herself flush, though Mary Ben's eyes were on the macramé hanging with which her increasingly clever hands were busy.

"Oh, I don't know," she said, aware of the stammer in her words. "He scarcely speaks to me except when we're riding. Or about the office work."

Mary Ben smiled. "But can't you see?" she said slyly. "That's exactly why."

Leslie, alert now, probed the bland countenance. She made a flustered laugh. "Mary Ben, you sound quite paranoiac."

Mary Ben raised her gaze to Leslie's face. Her voice came softly. "I don't mind, Leslie. In fact, I'm rather pleased."

It was Leslie's instinct to flee before the conversation could be further pursued. It was, she realized, an awkward position. She could blame no one else; she had made herself vulnerable to this assault.

She smiled. "Mary Ben, this *is* rather silly, don't you think? I have absolutely no intention of trying to take away your husband."

"That's exactly why I approve," Mary Ben exclaimed. "Whitney is very much a man, you know, and any other woman . . . I know you would do nothing to hurt me. Besides," she continued ingenuously, "Whitney would never leave me for you."

Leslie felt a flash of anger. "I assure you, I have no wish to become the odd woman out in a *ménage à trois*."

Mary Ben's voice was gentle. "I'm sorry, Leslie. I've made you angry, haven't I?" Her face turned sad. "I didn't mean to. I just wanted . . ." Her eyes took refuge in the macramé work, idle in her lap. "I'm not a whole woman any more, Leslie, and I'm so afraid of losing Whitney. It's too much to ask a man like him to . . . And . . ." She smiled appealingly. "I can't really blame him; any man would be attracted to you."

Leslie felt herself assailed from too many vantage points at once. Mary Ben was watching her again. Thoughtfully.

"Of course, I'm not suggesting, if you don't really care for him . . . I know you're seeing Bob, and I think that's very nice."

Leslie fled gratefully into the proffered refuge. "Bob is a very nice person," she said primly. "We have great fun together."

And he was, she reflected, a perceptive person; sensing the essential reserve Leslie brought to their Thursday dates, he had remained amiable and charming—and undemanding.

Mary Ben made a gesture of dismissal. "Well, of course, Bob . . . he's not half the man Whitney is." She grinned. "Believe me, I know."

Leslie had been exposed before to Mary Ben's occasional, but always unanticipated, penchant for ribaldry. Still, bending her head to conceal her agitation, she could not keep from blushing.

Mary Ben regarded her critically. "If you ask me, I think you're terribly attracted to Whitney. More than you want to admit."

Abruptly, Leslie stood up. "Mary Ben, I find this conversation quite . . . unsavory, I guess, is the word. If you don't mind . . ."

Mary Ben stretched forth a hand. She was very grave.

"When I saw you two working together with Tara Boy—as I

can no longer work with Whitney—I realized that you can give him so much that I can no longer give." She paused. "I'm only saying, Leslie, that I love you and I trust you. As I love and trust my husband."

Leslie was moved extraordinarily by the unshielded words. She took Mary Ben's hand, tears springing into her eyes. "Thank you, Mary Ben. No one has ever said anything more lovely."

Her friend's eyes sparkled also with tears. "It's not often that two women can be so, is it?" she said. "But we do understand each other, don't we?"

"Yes," Leslie said. "Yes. We do."

One would have thought the episode would release Leslie from the restraints she had imposed upon her passionate nature. After all, Mary Ben's complaisance had ostensibly removed the last obstacle separating her from Whitney's love. It had, however, the opposite effect. Until now, Leslie had been vulnerable to her own desires, creating the distinct possibility that, against her own best intentions, she might make the subtle signal that would bring Whitney into her arms.

Now, such a consummation was impossible. Mary Ben could not have said anything better calculated to bar Leslie from becoming her husband's lover. Perhaps, Leslie thought in a stroke of paranoia of her own making, as she lay awake that night waiting for the passage of Whitney's footsteps, that had been precisely Mary Ben's intention. She was, at best—or worst—a subtle, devious woman; because she had been reared a southern belle, as well as suffering the emotionally intensifying effect of invalidism.

But no. It was simpler than that complex rationalization. The very fact of Mary Ben's love for her husband, trust for her friend, made it impossible for Leslie to yield waywardly to the desire that raged in her to experience the fateful man named Whitney Ashe.

She was saved, the triangle altered—alleviated—by an unexpected event: the intrusion of a new personality upon the scene.

CHAPTER TWELVE

Leslie fortuitously witnessed the style of his arrival. Leaving Mary Ben in the side yard—one of her favorite situations when the sun, drawing toward the western horizon, cast cool, elongated shadows across the lawn—she had walked upstairs to fetch a new volume of Somerset Maugham's short stories . . . after Kipling, he had seemed the inevitable choice.

The two-volume set was kept in a bookcase in Mary Ben's bedroom. As Leslie took the book from the shelf, she heard a car in the driveway and leaned to look out the window.

The taxi disgorged a slender young man and a suitcase. Digging into the pocket of his rust-colored slacks, he tendered a bill to the still seated driver, saying with hauteur, "Here you are, my good man."

Leslie, amused, recognized that the newcomer was play-acting a British gentleman arriving at a country estate for a weekend. The taxi driver, however, did not take it in that spirit. Out of the depths of his American, democratic soul, he suggested a fitting use for such high-and-mighty words, if only the passenger were clever enough to accomplish it.

Leslie, slightly shocked but cheering on the independent spirit so frankly displayed, could not refrain from continuing to eavesdrop.

His face flushing, the stranger made a belligerent step forward. When the driver promptly unlatched the car door, however, he drew himself to the full extent of his medium height.

"All right, good buddy, you've just talked yourself out of a tip," he said rapidly, turning away.

The taxi driver recommended the same procedure be followed with the tip, and departed, the tires insolently spurting gravel.

Mary Ben, attracted by the sound of the automobile, wheeled herself around the corner of the house. Her voice rang with shocked surprise.

"Howard!"

The young man, his mouth pouting meanly, had been gazing after the departing taxi. He turned, a grin splitting his face, and for a poised moment the pair regarded each other.

Mary Ben propelled her chair forward as Howard, opening wide his arms, moved quickly to meet her. "Hullo, sis," he said, stooping to hold her slender shoulders in both hands as they kissed.

Obviously, great affection abided between the two; Mary Ben's eyes were sparkling, her small hands clung as they embraced.

"Oh, Howard, it's so good to see you," she cried. Then, her face clouding, "But you can't stay, you know. You shouldn't have let the taxi go."

Howard drew away, gazing somberly into her face. "I *have* to stay, sis," he said. "I'm dead broke, and there's nowhere else to go."

The desperately carefree expression returned as suddenly as it had vanished. Plunging a hand into his pocket, he scattered coins in the gravel at Mary Ben's feet.

"The total net worth, my dear," he said, laughing. "It was my intention to arrive with not one red cent, but the taxi driver was so surly, I refused to tip him."

Mary Ben took his hand in both of hers. "Oh, Howard! What are we to do with you?"

Her tone so affectionately chiding, Leslie, watching from above, had the impression he had evoked since babyhood that fond exasperation.

Mary Ben's eyebrows had drawn into seriousness. "You *know* Whitney won't allow you to stay. The moment he sees you . . ."

"Manford Manor is still yours, isn't it?" Howard said with bravado. "If it's your wish to entertain your darling brother until he can get on his feet again, I don't see that it's any of his concern."

"I've never gone against Whitney," Mary Ben said dubiously.

"Isn't it about time, then? Listen, sis, *you* own *him*; he doesn't own you." He laughed. "After all, isn't he only a slightly glorified farm manager . . . with bedroom privileges?"

"You know Whitney as well as I do," Mary Ben said angrily. "Why do you keep getting into these fixes, anyway? There's no doing anything with you."

"I go my own way," Howard said, a flash of stubbornness in his voice. Immediately he lightened the atmosphere with a grin, an affectionate thump against Mary Ben's shoulder. "Just you wait. I'll strike it rich one of these days. I've got my plans. As you will find out."

"Howard," she said despairingly, "you're always going to be rolling in it tomorrow. You just don't have good sense about money, and that's the plain fact. If you'd only kept your mouth shut, the estate would be half yours right now."

He grinned. "It can still be, given a touch of fair-handed generosity on your part, sis. All you have to do is sign it over."

"And see you drag out those old subdivision plans again?"

He shook his head. "You've got that same absurd attachment to the land that Father had, and everybody else in this benighted family." He spread his arms in an expansive gesture. "None of you have ever seemed to realize that, handled properly, Manford Manor could be one of the choicest parcels of real estate in the Kentucky Bluegrass. You're sitting on a gold mine, and don't know it." His lip curled in scorn. "All you can think about is raising those beastly Thoroughbreds."

"Whitney is making Manford Manor what it used to be," Mary Ben said quietly. She put out a pleading hand. "Come, Howard, let's not quarrel. After all, I haven't seen you in *ages.*"

His manner relented. "You *are* pleased that I came, then?"

"Yes, of course. You're my brother, aren't you?" Her face clouded. "I just don't know how I can persuade Whitney . . ." Her tone became exasperated again. "What happened this time?"

He made a deprecatory gesture. "Had a great job, sis, with a publicity firm in Los Angeles. For the first time in my life I was really enjoying the idea of working for a living. Publicity is exactly my line of country."

He chuckled. "Within two years, I had my nest neatly feathered: ample cash, plenty of perquisites, and a pipeline to the Old

Man himself. I was his fair-haired boy, and on my way to the top even if I was the new fellow in the shop."

He shrugged fatalistically. "Naturally, moving up so fast, one makes enemies. Especially if you happen to be dating the Old Man's ugliest daughter. When it looked like I was just about ready to reach for the brass ring, the bloodletting started. And, like that" —he snapped his fingers—"I was out on the street."

Mary Ben said, "I can imagine who started the bloodletting. But you couldn't carry it through, could you? Isn't that the truth?"

"You've hit the nail squarely where it counts," he said with a toss of his head. "Anyway, I didn't have much money saved; in a situation like that you have to put it all out front, you know, make the big impression. So I figured . . . Well, I had plans for going into business for myself. I could have taken three or four of our best clients with me, I had seen to that, right enough. But I needed operating capital."

He shrugged again. "How better than a whirl at Las Vegas? Double your stake in no time, make a comeback in glory. After all, I'd been a good boy for one hell of a long time." He made a mouth. "Didn't work out. I ran wild—too many girls and too much booze, and not keeping my mind on the gambling. So . . ." He spread his hands. "Here I am, a victim of your sisterly charity."

Mary Ben shook her head helplessly. "Howard. Howard."

"Either you take me in, or I don't eat," he said. "It's as simple as that."

She sighed. "I'll try to talk to Whitney."

Swiftly he kissed her, as swiftly picked up his suitcase, and, pushing the wheelchair with the other hand, proceeded triumphantly into the house.

Leslie, selected volume in hand, met them in the hallway.

"There you are," Mary Ben cried. "Come, you must meet my brother. Howard, this is my dear companion, Leslie Tallant."

They shook hands. A gleam of admiration showed in Howard's eyes; clearly, he appreciated a handsome woman.

"I've heard a lot about you, Howard," Leslie said pleasantly.

A small lie; actually, Howard's name had been mentioned in her presence no more than twice—never, so far as she knew, between husband and wife.

"I'll bet you have," Howard said mockingly.

He was a small, compact man, red hair and freckles deceptively conveying the appearance of a country boy. But there clung to him a patina of confident charm that belied his physical appearance. He dressed well, in rust trousers and an open-throated shirt under a linen sports coat. His small feet were elegantly shod in expensive loafers.

His mouth continued to smile, while his eyes warmed in intensity. "You'll hear much more, I assure you. From *my* side."

"Howard, take your things upstairs, I'll send Martin to show you your room," Mary Ben said. "I must talk to Leslie."

Retrieving his suitcase, he started up the stairs. Over his shoulder he said lightly, "Don't talk about me while I'm gone."

Mary Ben moved her wheelchair into the living room, turned to Leslie. Her face was troubled.

"Leslie. I must warn Whitney that Howard has come for a visit. Whitney refuses to have anything to do with my brother." She clasped her hands together. "I'm . . . I'm afraid to tell him."

"If Whitney is so set against him, is it worthwhile to keep him here?"

Mary Ben's voice despaired. "He has nowhere else to go."

"Couldn't you give him money, let him go away?"

Her small chin firmed. "After all, he *is* my younger brother. I love Howard. We were always very close."

Leslie hesitated. "I gather . . . he has no financial interest in Manford Manor."

Mary Ben shook her head. "He and Father had a terrible fight. Last time he got kicked out of college, he brought home this architect friend, had a plan all drawn up to subdivide Manford Manor and sell building lots, with developer approval of house plans and all that, you know, to make them very exclusive."

She smiled faintly. "He's always had these grand ideas. They just never seem to work out. Father, of course, wouldn't hear of it. It made Howard *furious*; he told Father, in great anger, that he'd wait until Father died and then he'd do as he pleased. So . . . Father wrote him out of the will, leaving Manford Manor entirely to me. I had to swear I'd never give Howard any part of the land."

Her mouth quivered. "Whitney . . ." She lifted her eyes. "He feels the same about Manford Manor as Father did, of course. He has refused to let me see Howard."

"What's his reason, beyond mere dislike?"

Mary Ben's mouth tightened. "Whitney says Howard is a bad influence. On me, I mean. And he's a threat to Manford Manor." She shivered. "He's always said he would leave me if ever I gave Howard a share in the estate. Or even allowed him to live here."

"He has a firm conviction in the matter, then."

"Leslie, what shall I do?" Mary Ben cried. "I *can't* send Howard away destitute." She put her face into her hands. "And I can't . . . I can't face the thought of losing Whitney."

Leslie regarded her steadily. "So you want *me* to tell Whitney."

Mary Ben raised grateful eyes. "Will you, Leslie? I simply can't brave his anger."

"From what you say, I don't think anyone could persuade him to accept Howard," Leslie said dubiously. "But, if you wish it, I'll at least tell him Howard has come home to Manford Manor."

Mary Ben grasped her hand. "Leslie. What would I do without you?"

She found Whitney supervising the bringing in of the foals and their dams. He did not look up at her approach. She stood quietly watching as he inspected each foal. Large in size, this time of the year, they were full of themselves. She smiled, watching them prance as the grooms brought them on shanks from the pasture, then stand quietly as Whitney stooped to run his practiced hands over their legs and ankles.

So beautiful in their long-legged grace and strength, Leslie thought. Soon now they will be weanlings, next year, yearlings; the year after that, they will be the two-year-old racing crop. One, perhaps, winning great races, will become known throughout the land. Others will never pass a starting gate. Such devotion, such expert knowledge, to bring them the long road to their destined success or failure.

Whitney inspected carefully a torn shoulder where a chestnut colt had injured himself on a broken railing. "Seems to be healing nicely," he remarked to the groom.

"Yes sir, Mr. Whitney, this colt is going to be all right," the groom said earnestly. "I'm looking after that bad place myself."

Whitney smiled. "We can be thankful there was no damage to the muscle," he said. "Keep your eye on it, now, make sure it doesn't get infected."

"You bet I will. I clean it twice a day."

The groom led the foal into the barn, Whitney turning his attention to the next. "How's she doing?" he asked.

"Still running off a little."

Whitney frowned. "I'd better have the vet check for worms again tomorrow. Can't be too careful about worms."

Only after he had finished did he turn inquiringly to Leslie. "Yes?"

"I must talk to you."

He regarded her seriousness for a moment. "Can it wait a bit? I've still a few things to do."

"Of course. I'll be in the office." The impersonality of the setting would make her message easier to deliver.

As she walked toward the building, she saw King's Man still in his paddock. Whickering, he stretched his neck over the fence. She looked to see if Whitney were coming along yet. There was time; she went to the great horse, speaking affectionately. He tossed his head, anxious for the touch of her hand.

She stood beside the stallion, arm around his muzzle, and gazed out over the land. The sun was just setting, rays stabbing brilliantly against a high bank of clouds, turning them a crimson rapidly fading toward rose. The light slanted against the green earth, causing the white fences to stand out starkly in their rigid patterning.

How could anyone wish to destroy all this? she thought involuntarily. For the first time, she had a true appreciation of Whitney's dream. Since his arrival in Kentucky, the preservation of Manford Manor had been the major force and direction of his life.

He has done whatever had to be done, she thought. He has been calculating at times, rigid when necessary, flexible when nothing else would work. He is aware that Manford Manor, like all old and graceful things, has many enemies. The greed for money; sheer inertia of things and of people; the inexorable process of decay.

Leslie shivered. Not least of all, the inherent curse that lay upon the land itself. No understanding of such a thing was possible; one could only acknowledge it.

Touched to the quick by the beauty, the danger, of Manford Manor, Leslie could let herself know the foreboding which had grown within her. No good could come of Howard Manford's sojourn. Though he appeared only a careless, charming man of questionable character, he carried the same seeds of dark destiny as Mary Ben.

The combination, of brother and of sister, will be so much more potent than Mary Ben alone, she thought fatefully. What forces will that cabal awaken?

She knew, then, that, far less than she wished to be the bearer of ill tidings for Whitney Ashe, did she wish to plead Howard Manford's cause. But she had promised Mary Ben.

Turning suddenly, she threw her arms around King's Man's neck, pressing her cheek against his great head. If only everything could be as simple and as beautiful as you are, she whispered.

The great horse, pleased to accept her passionate caress at the surface level of affection, blew his nostrils in a gratified sound.

Leslie busied herself with paperwork while she waited for Whitney. An easy absorption in mundane detail; she did not have to think about the meeting.

When he entered, he said, without looking at her, "Come on in, Leslie," and continued into the office.

When she had followed, he was seated behind the paper-cluttered expanse of desk. Before she could speak, the telephone rang. She lifted it, listened, held it toward him. "For you."

She took the visitor's chair, amply made of leather, and watched Whitney's face. After a moment he said, "Well, I'm not exactly sorry to tell you that King's Man's book is already full for next spring. So I'm afraid I can't help you out."

He listened again.

"I can only promise to keep you in mind if a season should open up. I wouldn't count on it, though; go ahead and book to an available stallion. You don't want to run the risk of a barren year." He chuckled. "A broodmare eats too many expensive oats for that."

He listened again. "All right." He passed the phone to Leslie. "Put down his name, add it to the waiting list."

Leslie made a quick note on an available pad and hung up. The small business had made it easier to be together in the solitude of the office.

Whitney leaned back. "Well. What is it?"

"Howard Manford is here," she said.

She watched his countenance darken as he took in the news. Putting both hands to the arms of the chair, he pushed himself upright.

"Not for long he isn't."

"Wait a minute," Leslie said.

He regarded her. She was certain he would depart without further words. He sat down.

"Mary Ben begged you to tell me, didn't she?"

"She was afraid to do it herself," Leslie said honestly.

Whitney grunted. "Well she might be. She knows what I think of her brother."

"She's anxious for him to stay. Howard paid his taxi fare with the last money in his pocket. He has nowhere else to go."

He eyed her. "And you're supposed to talk me into it. So . . . talk."

Leslie had to force the words. "I can't see any harm in a short visit."

"Is that all you have to say on his behalf?" Whitney demanded.

She looked at him straightly. "You know how easily Mary Ben can become upset. Her nerves are so fragile, so on edge. Wouldn't it be the better part of valor to let her have her way, rather than get into a major battle?"

"No," Whitney said promptly. "It would not."

"What have you got against the man?" Leslie said sharply. "He *is* her brother, you know."

"He has never been up to any good for ten minutes straight in his life," Whitney said deliberately. "He's a bad one, Leslie, and don't you forget it. The best thing Mary Ben's father ever did was read him out of the will."

Yes, Leslie thought, leaving Manford Manor to Mary Ben. And Mary Ben to you.

"I don't see why it must become a major issue, that's all," she said carefully. "Let him stay a while, and don't make waves about it. Where's the harm in that?"

"Harm?" Whitney echoed. "He can twist Mary Ben around his little finger, that's the harm. He didn't just idly turn up on our doorstep, you know. He's got some scheme in his crooked mind. I'd bet a season to King's Man on it."

He smiled slightly. "He's a ball of fire with the ladies, you know. One of his major stocks in trade. He's probably already got to you, too."

"You have no right to assume that," Leslie said equably.

"Got you pleading his case, hasn't he?"

"My sole concern is with Mary Ben."

He placed both hands palm down on the desk, stared at them. "It's against my better judgement," he said heavily. He lifted his eyes. "If you want the truth, I think it's against yours, too."

Leslie hoped that her face was capable of denying the assertion. She did not have the words with which to do so.

He pushed himself out of the chair. "Come on," he said grimly.

"I'd rather not . . ."

He turned quickly. "Oh, yes. You started this; you're going to see it through. He's your bad penny, and don't forget it."

Leslie followed Whitney, not knowing whether she had won. Or *what* she had won. Whitney stalked ahead through the gathering dusk. His footsteps were loud as he crossed the porch and entered the house. Leslie pressed close behind.

Whitney halted under the archway. The brother and the sister, seated in cozy companionship, looked up with startled faces.

Howard rose, came forward with outstretched hand. "Hello, Whitney," he said ingratiatingly. "Good to see you again."

Whitney ignored Howard, and Howard's hand, to look directly at Mary Ben.

"So your scapegrace brother has come home to roost," he said harshly.

Mary Ben's face crumpled. "Oh, Whitney, don't speak to me in that tone of voice. Please!"

Whitney regarded her. "All right. He can stay. But I warn you. Not for long."

Mary Ben lifted incredulous eyes. With a deft movement of her hands, she brought the wheelchair close to his side, leaned her blond head against his thigh.

"Oh, Whitney, you're so good to me. You don't know how I've longed to see Howard." She paused, a calculating note edging into her voice. "Why, Howard can be your assistant manager, Whitney! You *know* you need someone to take some of the load off your shoulders, now that Tom Musgrove is gone."

Whitney, startlingly to Leslie at least, threw back his head and laughed. "Assistant manager? When he's been terrified of horses since he was a boy?"

"One doesn't have to ride the beasts in order to manage a horse farm," Howard said stiffly. "After all, I was brought up here."

Leslie had a sudden perception this small plot between brother and sister had been laid during her absence.

Whitney, turning on Howard, regarded him with contempt. "The only job I'll give you, Howard, is mucking out stalls for the minimum wage." He continued to regard him for a prolonged instant, then nodded. "Had an idea it wouldn't suit."

"Whitney . . ." Mary Ben said pleadingly.

He ignored her. "So have a nice visit, Howard. Sleep as late as you please, and pass your time entertaining Mary Ben. We will expect you to be on your merry way in short order."

Turning on his heel, he left them.

Late that night, as Howard played cards with his sister—the game was gin rummy, at his insistence, at high stakes—and Leslie gratefully devoted herself to her own reading for a change, it happened again.

Or, Leslie wondered afterward in the security of her bed, did it?

Howard, in the midst of play, suddenly lifted his head. "Did you hear that?"

"Hear what?" Leslie said sharply.

"A horse," Howard said, looking at her intently. "Didn't you hear a stallion neigh? Far in the distance."

Mary Ben, turning white, dropped her handful of cards in fluttering disarray.

"If it was anything at all, it's only King's Man, restless in his stall," Leslie said strongly.

They were all caught into the stasis of listening.

"There it is again," Howard said. "Mary Ben, *you* hear him, don't you?" He lifted his eyes to the portrait over the mantel, forcing the two women to look in the same direction. "It's not a living stallion, either. It's . . . Black Prince."

CHAPTER THIRTEEN

Leslie Tallant disapproved of Howard Manford; yet he could make her laugh, make her feel very much a woman. Indeed, on balance, she was grateful for his daily, indolent presence; Mary Ben's enjoyment of life quickened when he entered the room, her heart was somehow more carefree.

Every morning he rose late, to share breakfast with Mary Ben in her rooms. Because he also devoted the afternoons to his sister's entertainment, Leslie was able to spend the entire day in the office. The barns nearly full now, the work had become more detailed, so it was not at all amiss. At evening they were a jolly threesome, Howard tirelessly organizing absurd word-games, reading aloud with exaggerated drama from swashbuckling novels such as *Beau Geste* and *Scaramouche*, even taking up, with a comic lack of competence, the craft of macramé. With money "borrowed" from his sister, he played high-stakes gin rummy with Mary Ben . . . at which she almost invariably won.

However, to Leslie's dismay, night after night Howard made the ghost stallion omnipresent. At some time during the evening —usually quite late—he would assume a listening posture, a curious, almost anticipatory, smile on his face. His eyes drifting toward his sister, he would say in a low voice, "There he is. Hear that, Mary Ben? He's here again."

Leslie, in exasperation, invariably voiced a loud denial of the ghostly phenomenon. To no avail; Howard would only reply smugly, "I'm quite sure you didn't hear anything, Leslie, though one might suspect you're only trying to comfort Mary Ben. After all, you're not a Manford, are you? Mary Ben is tuned in, all right. Aren't you, sis?"

Mary Ben, white-lipped, would nod jerkily. Yet somehow, in Howard's presence, she seemed to feel so magically protected that she could contain her agitation.

Leslie, attempting to probe into Mary Ben's tense acceptance, elicited from her the answer, "Black Prince doesn't sound as though he's on a jealous rampage at all." She hesitated, her voice lowering. "He only seems to be calling for human companionship."

Leslie, though ever conscious of her responsibility, could think of no way to cope. Did the two Manfords, brother and sister, truly sense what could not be experienced by an outsider? Or was Howard, with deliberate malice, or out of a cruelly perverted sense of humor, playing upon Mary Ben's suggestibilities, hypnotizing her into the belief that her ghostly nemesis was now permanently present at Manford Manor?

First, in all rational common-sense, Leslie made a careful search of the oak trees for another incriminating loudspeaker. Failing to find it, she taxed Howard, in Mary Ben's presence, with indulging in an irresponsible game.

Howard refused to discuss the matter seriously. "After all, it's quite *de rigueur* for a mansion as old as Manford Manor to enjoy a resident ghost," he said lightly. "A mark of distinction, don't you think, for ours to be a Thoroughbred stallion? So boring, the usual sheet-draped, chain-rattling ghoul moaning in the corridors." He regarded Leslie mockingly. "Perhaps, if you stay with us long enough, and play your cards right, you'll become Manford enough to hear him neighing lonely in the distance, too."

Beyond that insouciant comment, he refused, with an air of portentous mystery, to discuss the matter further.

And, with equal smugness, he seemed to take it for granted that his tenure was open-ended. Any awareness that he existed on daily probation showed only in that, so far as possible, he avoided Whitney.

Because of the divergent pattern of their days, the two men saw each other only at dinner, Whitney sitting sternly remote while Mary Ben and Howard, chattering with amiable aimlessness, dominated the table. Leslie, somewhat against her will, fulfilled the role of a buffer between two camps. If Whitney wished to make a communication, he addressed himself to her; Mary Ben, perhaps feeling guilty for neglecting her husband so greatly in favor of her brother, at least once during each meal used Leslie as a intermediary in an effort to draw Whitney into general conversation.

She never despaired of effecting a rapprochement between her husband and her brother. At times subtly, sometimes openly, she pressed Howard's case. Whitney, patently ignoring such gambits, maintained his noncommittal reserve. At least, to Leslie's relief, he made no further mention of the desirability of Howard's early departure. She dreaded the day it would become again an open issue.

Mary Ben, except for her invalidism, had become practically a normal person. Her natural high coloring returned, she ate more heartily, she laughed often. In such burgeoning health, mental as well as physical, she seemed immune to all evil influence. Whitney, Leslie reflected, should be gratified that Howard's unwelcome presence had brought a new health of mind and body into her tenuous, fragile existence.

Leslie, as any woman, was aware that Howard had determined upon a conquest. When his eyes lighted on her, they were eloquent of desire; he had a way of touching her lightly with his fingertips, on arm or back, with casual deliberation.

He was quite open in the flirtation. In the presence of Mary Ben—even of Whitney—the words he directed toward Leslie were ambiguous, lightly provocative, hinting at a hoped-for intimacy which, as far as Leslie was concerned, would never become established. At such times, Whitney would gaze at her with a cool, direct stare, unrevealing of the turmoil of thought which must lie behind it.

Howard employed also more subtle means. Leslie entered the living room, late one afternoon, to find him alone before the fireplace, legs braced, hands linked behind his back, contemplating the twinned portrait of great-grandmother and black stallion.

He turned at the sound of her step. "Ah, the lovely Leslie!" He made an exaggerated, self-mocking gesture. "At last we are alone."

Leslie, ignoring the extravagance, said, "Where's Mary Ben?"

"Taking a nap. We sat up so late last night, she became tired this afternoon."

Leslie studied the portrait over the mantel. "You seem quite taken with your ancestress," she remarked.

He glanced sharply at her, then allowed his eyes to follow hers. "I think I'm in love with her. I always have been."

The simplicity of the statement, at such variance with his usual elaborate, deceptive style of conversation, touched Leslie.

"We didn't live at Manford Manor, you know, as long as Mother was alive," he continued. "I can remember, when Father brought me out, first thing, I'd pay a visit to look at her. My middle name is Brooke, you know. I could stand for an hour, just gazing. Thinking that her blood was in my veins."

"It's a marvelous portrait," Leslie said. "And she was a beautiful woman."

He made a gesture of dismissal. "Not the beauty, so much . . . the world is full of beautiful women. She was, most of all, a remarkable personality. Do you know her story?"

Leslie nodded. "Mary Ben told me."

His words carried a curiously fervent force. "It would call for a truly remarkable woman to do what she did during the time in which she lived. Can you imagine it? Packing that trunk and taking off for Saratoga in the hunt for a suitably wealthy husband." He sighed. "For her, the possibility of failure simply didn't exist. Look at that lovely chin, that heartbreaking mouth . . . great beauty, but also courage and determination. Think how clearly those eyes must have seen; herself, as well as other people."

Leslie laughed. "You really are in love with her, aren't you?"

He took a deep breath. "God, what wouldn't I do for a woman like that." He turned his head to look at Leslie. A deprecating smile showed on his face. "The truth is, we've let her down. Not one of her descendants has lived up to her."

"Perhaps she was like a great oak, never giving the younger trees in its shade the chance to become great oaks in their turn. Certainly, even after dying, she has dominated the history of your family. It was inevitable that a mystical legend would spring up in the wake of her passage through life and death."

"Not as simple as that, Leslie, I'm afraid. If any Manford had

had it in him, her presence in our past would only have goaded us on to outdo her accomplishments."

"Maybe so," Leslie admitted. "I hadn't really thought about it, of course."

"Why not?"

Leslie, bothered by the intensity of the question, made a nervous laugh. "For one thing, I'm not a Manford."

He kept on looking at her. "No. But . . ." He paused. He turned again to the portrait, brooding upon it. "I think I have more of her in me than any Manford has ever had; I'm moved by the same urge to make something great, I inherited her ruthlessness."

Intercepting her reaction of surprise, he curled his lip wryly. "You don't believe it, Leslie Tallant? How do you think she did what she did? By melting kindness, a gentle and tractable nature? Hell, no! She was tough when it counted, she could count the cost and pay it, too, when it had to be paid."

Agitated, he walked to a window, stood looking out. Only after a long minute did he turn.

Across the space between, he said, "Yes. I've let Brooke Manford down. Just like the others. But I'm not done yet. I've not even got started." He jerked his head. "She'll be proud yet, just wait and see. She'll know; all these years she's been waiting impatiently for the Manford she can recognize as her own true blood. When *that* Manford comes along, she'll know it. She'll be on his side, cheering him on!"

Leslie felt a crawl of uneasiness. She had not seen this aspect of Howard Manford, concealed so deeply beneath his surface of calculating charm.

Howard was prowling the room, still talking, his words driven. He had his plans, all right; just give him the chance. Brooke Manford was sending the ghost stallion nightly to remind him the time had come for him to take up her banner, carry it forward into the new times.

He came to a stance before the portrait. Reflectively, he said, "Of course, she'd prefer it to be a Manford woman. Because *she* was a woman. She knew that the female, in every way that counts, is stronger than the male. But she'll have to settle for what she can get. Me."

He looked into her eyes. "Leslie, you have in you more of Great-Grandmother Brooke than any of her female descendants. You could possess Manford Manor as Mary Ben, any of the others, never could." His smile was charmingly self-mocking. "Even if you can't hear Black Prince when he calls."

Leslie looked into the portrait. In this fraught moment, Brooke Manford's eyes spoke to her as never before.

"But I'm *not* a Manford."

"There's an inheritance of the spirit, as of the blood," Howard said. "The spirit is more important."

Swiftly he came to her, took her hands. A timbre vibrated in his voice. "Yes, Leslie. I am the blood-reincarnation of Brooke Manford, you are the spirit-reincarnation. That's why we belong together."

Putting his arms about her, he kissed her. Leslie, enthralled by the magical evocation of the sublime woman named Brooke Manford, yielded to the embrace.

He drew away, laughing. "You know it, you see, as well as I do." He touched her arm lightly. "Thursday, then?" He smiled engagingly. "Don't worry, I have the money for a glorious night out. Mary Ben has made me a secret allowance."

Leslie was jarred by a complex reaction. First, of course, was the gratification of a sincere compliment, the sure sense of being deeply valued, as a woman and as a person, in the flattering comparison to Brooke Manford. Immediately following, she knew anger that he could use these profound meanings in the pursuit of sexual conquest.

Drawing away, she said coolly, "Thursday I have a date with Bob Berry."

He made a gesture of disdain. "That cream puff? Break it."

"I have no intention of breaking it."

Realizing he had lost her, Howard made a bold move. Even as she made a further distance between them, he swooped upon her, clasping her in strong arms to attempt another kiss.

Leslie, as she struggled, heard a step in the hallway. Howard, hearing it also, released her. As their heads turned, Whitney, unexpected at this time of the afternoon, looked in on them.

Leslie, disheveled and panting, sought to muster up a means of conveying to Whitney the truth of what he had seen. It was, of course, impossible; before she could catch the next breath, he had passed on.

Howard, she saw, was pleased that Whitney had surprised them. Though he could not know the emotional involvement between herself and Whitney, he was the kind of man, Leslie thought, prideful of being considered a lady-killer.

And, above all, an optimist. "Thursday?" he queried in a persistent tone.

Leslie was furious, most of all with herself for being vulnerable to this assault. "Not Thursday," she said. "Nor any other time."

His stare was compelling. "Don't kid yourself, love. You'll see me. Sooner than you think."

He started to leave. Cruelly, Leslie said, "Don't you think Whitney Ashe, far more than you, is the reincarnation of your great-grandmother?"

He whipped around in furious denial. "That usurper?" he yelled. "My God, how can you say that, how can . . . ?" The words were strangled in his rage.

"He's the one who wants to preserve and continue Brooke Manford's heritage," she said. "You only wish to destroy it."

She could not have believed such choler in a man who made a fetish of casual comport. "If she were alive today, she'd do what I'm going to do. She'd ride with the times, she wouldn't cling to a useless past."

He recovered himself. Suddenly calm, he regarded her with cold eyes. "All right, Leslie. Believe what you want to believe." He paused shrewdly. "You're in love with Whitney, aren't you? That's *your* problem."

He smiled maliciously, nodding. "I'm glad to know it."

And he was gone.

Leslie realized full well she had made a deadly enemy. She would have expected him, first of all, to use his considerable influence with Mary Ben to undermine the deep attachment existing between the two women. An obvious line of campaign, and Leslie, though she racked her brain, could think of no means to combat it. She must rely on Mary Ben's loyalty to a good friend. But how long could such loyalty endure in opposition to her lifelong love for an errant brother?

Leslie need not have worried. Howard, on the contrary, took every opportunity to praise her, speaking approvingly of her good sense, her reliability, her obvious devotion equally to Mary Ben's welfare and to the success of the breeding establishment.

"Why," he remarked brightly, more than once, "one would think she was a Manford herself."

No. His attack was mounted from an entirely different quarter. And there was nothing Leslie could do about it.

First of all, he ceased the provocative remarks and gestures of an admiring courtship. No longer did his hand caress casually as he gallantly helped her into and out of chairs and coats, no longer did his eyes light with an obvious appreciation when she entered the room.

Not at all. Instead, by subtle means, he conveyed the impression of a comfortable, established intimacy.

He did nothing, said nothing, so openly that it would give Leslie the opportunity for a public denial. Nothing of the sort. The assumption of a sexual relationship was established implicitly by a careful public restraint in gesture and touch; accompanied by the tone of voice, the intimacy of glance, the secret smile of understanding, that inevitably signaled the existence of a passionate bond.

Mary Ben, obviously delighted by the situation, had forgotten her suggestion that Leslie might well pay decent heed to Whitney Ashe. She felt, apparently, that a liaison between Leslie and Howard would enhance his right to reside permanently at Manford Manor.

And what could Leslie do? Nothing. How could she possibly blurt out to Mary Ben, "Listen. I'm not sleeping with your brother."

In the first place, the opportunity for such an open assertion never came about; Howard saw to that. Secondly, it would be accepted merely as the coy denial of an indubitable fact. Leslie could visualize exactly how Mary Ben, bridling archly, would exclaim that, of course, she had never thought of such a thing!

The fury at her helplessness to alter the situation only increased when she discovered, from a casual remark of Mary Ben's, that on Thursday Howard had disappeared for the entire day, returning only after Leslie herself had returned from a tennis-and-dinner date with Bob Berry. Desperately, she sought an opportunity to comment on how fine Bob's tennis game was, how much she was learning from such a superior player. Mary Ben, smiling wisely, refrained from comment.

For the first time in a long while, Leslie entertained the thought of leaving Manford Manor. The situation, she realized, was untenable for a woman of integrity. She could only go away, begin life all over again somewhere else.

However, quite simply, she could not envision another life. So submerged in the twining currents, flowing richly between the living and the dead of Manford Manor, she knew that mere departure, retreat, would not free her. At the beginning, it might have done; but she had long since passed that point of safe return.

If this were true with Mary Ben, how much more so with Whitney? She had now lost the ultimate bonding of intimacy with the man she loved so deeply. The very next day after he had surprised her in Howard's arms, he severed their relationship with an irrevocable gesture.

When Leslie, attired in riding habit, had appeared at the usual time at the exercise ring, it was only to find it empty. Going into the stone barn, she sought out the new stud groom.

"Mr. Whitney, he told me we wouldn't be working the hunters today," he replied to her query. He avoided her eyes. "Told me to tell you that, if you happened to come asking."

An hour later, hearing unmistakable sounds, Leslie went to the office window, to see Whitney up on Irish Sailor, patiently putting him through his paces.

Working the gelding had long since become Leslie's regular duty; the message was cruelly clear. She returned to her desk and put her face into her hands. Her heart was empty. How could he love me? she thought despairingly. Even less than with Mary Ben could she protest her innocence.

Soon now, she thought with desperate acquiescence, he will find an excuse to send me away. It was the only possible solution; and, of course, she must accept without protest such dismissal. She found herself, even, yearning for the release. Then, only then, could she be free of him her lover, of Mary Ben her charge, of Howard her deadly enemy.

In an entirely different matter, Leslie also could only stand aside. With contempt for her inconsequential presence, Howard began to press his campaign to persuade Mary Ben to yield into his hands a share of Manford Manor.

Daily Leslie was forced to listen as Howard, in a thousand different subtle indirections, flattered and cajoled and manipulated his sister's sentiments concerning the ancestral lands.

Mary Ben, Leslie realized with a sinking heart, was greatly susceptible to her brother's blandishments. Skillfully he implanted doubts, reinforced fears, flattered her ability to make the decisions rather than relying upon Whitney. Invoking every familial loyalty, he played artfully on the theme that, from the beginning, ownership of Manford Manor had never been vested in alien hands . . . with the unvoiced assumption that of course Mary Ben, an invalid, would not outlive her strong and healthy husband. He even suggested, without quite saying it, that Whitney awaited impatiently the day he could bring a new wife into *his* house.

At last, one afternoon, apparently confident the ground was prepared, he came out with it.

"Of course, sis, I know that, in your heart of hearts, you have thought of doing justice by me," he said with quiet sincerity. He smiled fondly. "We're so close, you and I, you understand what a bitter pill it was to realize that Father meant to treat my family rights as though they didn't exist."

"Yes, I *have* thought of it," Mary Ben said, her voice trembling. "Often. But I swore to Father . . ."

Leaning forward, he put a hand over hers. "Listen," he said earnestly, "if you, right this minute, handed me a deed certifying that Manford Manor was half mine—as, by rights, it should have been all along—I'd tear it up."

Mary Ben's mouth quivered. "If it weren't for Whitney, I'd *make* you accept it, Howard," she cried.

Firmly, he shook his head. "No. One can't own Manford Manor without earning it." He glanced toward Leslie. To her horror, he tendered a cynical wink. Solemnly, he returned to Mary Ben.

"But . . . I know how it can be done. Without violating your sworn oath to Father. Without destroying Manford Manor. In the process, I will not only receive my rightful share—not by gift, by earning it—but we will both realize enormous capital gains."

He sat back as triumphant as if, by the mere enunciation, it had been accomplished.

"How marvelous, Howard!" Mary Ben said eagerly. She clapped her hands in childlike glee. "I *love* money. Tell me all about it!"

Leslie stared, unbelieving. Did Mary Ben truly not fathom her brother's nature? Or was she, more deceptively than he, made of the same cloth?

Assaulted, suddenly, by the bewildering sense of a new reality, she wondered: Had she been living in a dream world since the day of her arrival at Manford Manor? It did, indeed, seem so. When Howard had come, she had felt within herself the dire prophecy of a cabal between brother and sister. Now, before her eyes, the conspiracy existed; gleefully they were plotting together, Mary Ben as involved, as fully committed, as her brother.

I must warn Whitney, Leslie thought wildly. Go to him, *now*, tell him what is happening. No hope for him here, as there is no hope for me. For we, Whitney Ashe and Leslie Tallant, are the only innocents. Whitney, because of his greatly simple dream for the future of Manford Manor; I, for the great love I bear in my heart.

She half rose. Despairing, she sank down again. No use, she thought dully. Howard has already destroyed me with Whitney, as he has neutralized me with Mary Ben. No channels are open; I cannot speak.

In her turmoil, Leslie realized that Howard was continuing.

"So simple, really," he said easily. "What godly use is all this enormous amount of land, anyway? This day and time, it's financially impossible to populate so much acreage with Thoroughbreds. Far more efficient, actually, to concentrate the breeding operation on, say, half the estate."

He spread his arms. "So? We take the back side, the part farthest from the mansion, you understand—the least productive, too, agriculturally speaking, but marvelously scenic for our purposes—and open it up for development along the lines I visualized all those years ago."

Mary Ben was listening with bated breath.

Howard leaned forward, suddenly intense. "Don't you see, sis, how it solves all the problems? How it changes everything, yet doesn't change anything at all?"

"Tell me!" Mary Ben said breathlessly.

He ticked it off. "You will still own Manford Manor, so you won't have violated your word to Father. You will own a half-share in the real estate development, with me owning the other half. You won't have given me a thing, of course, because I'll *earn* my share by doing all the work of promotion and selling."

"Yes," Mary Ben said, earnestly nodding. "Yes. I see."

"First, we'll set up a corporation to take ownership of half the estate," Howard said rapidly. "That way, you and I can personally realize capital gains on the transaction. Of course," he interpolated casually, "it'll be necessary for you to vest title jointly in our names for me to get capital gains, too. I will take half the shares of the corporation, you'll take the rest. Oh, we might have to cut in a couple of other people for a share or two, just to keep it legal, but that won't amount to anything."

He sat back, suddenly quiet, watchful. "There you have it. As easy as pie. And twice as tasty."

"Howard, it's a *wonderful* idea," Mary Ben said warmly. "You really are clever, I must say."

And you, Mary Ben Manford Ashe, have a memory about as long as a minute, Leslie thought acidly. You have forgotten completely saying to Howard's face: *You just don't have good sense about money, and that's a plain fact.* She regarded the invalid critically. Who could tell whether she was a mere fool, or exactly like her brother?

"All right," Howard said. "The point is, though—*will you do it?*"

Her face clouded. "I'd do it in a minute, Howard. If it weren't for Whitney." Her voice pleaded for understanding.

With sudden vehemence, he struck his hand against the arm of his chair. "What the hell does Whitney have to do with it? It's *Manford* land."

Mary Ben drew back into her chair. "But he's told me, more than once, that if I give up to you one inch of the estate, he will leave me. Instantly. And never come back."

For a moment, Howard sat still. Then, brutally: "Whitney Ashe is a practical man. He married you in the first place for the sake of the land. He's doing his level best to see you dead, right now, while he's still the principal beneficiary of your will."

Mary Ben had collapsed. "No! Don't say such things, Howard. Please don't say it."

Unfeelingly he rushed on. "He's a practical man, I tell you. Like everybody else, he's got his eye on the main chance." He rose, to stand over his cowering sister. "Take my word for it, Mary Ben. He'll settle for half a loaf better than none."

She raised a tear-stained face. "Do you really think so, Howard?" she whispered hopefully.

He changed with mercurial quickness. Tenderly, he smiled at his sister. Tenderly, he cupped an affectionate hand against her cheek.

"Of course. All you have to do is assert your right as a Manford to make the family decisions. To live your own life, instead of letting Whitney Ashe live it for you." He laughed confidently. "Don't worry. He'll come to heel. He'll never leave you as long as you hold in your own name the land he covets."

Leslie's own recent thoughts came anew into her mind. *He has been calculating at times, rigid when necessary, flexible when nothing else would work.* Had Howard Manford, as it seemed to be his evil genius to do, accurately put his finger on Whitney's weakness?

Leslie got up and left.

She had a feeling neither brother nor sister was aware of her departure.

CHAPTER FOURTEEN

Leslie was ashamed; she had given herself to Bob Berry.

But a woman, she knew now, cannot only give; she must also be taken.

Oh, he had taken her, right enough, with complacent expertise. But he had not touched her in the quick, where Leslie Tallant lived. So she had brought away only incompleteness, a sense of unworthiness, when she had sought . . . What?

Embracing him, she had embraced only emptiness. Today, too late—after she had soiled herself ineradicably in a compulsion to learn that which, in her heart of hearts, she already knew—she realized vividly this truth: There can be salvation only from within.

It had been, most of all, a desperate attempt to erase Whitney Ashe from her heart. Which, she should have known, was as futile as trying to stem the tides of the seas. No matter that Whitney had cast her beyond the pale of his regard; no matter that he was now far more a stranger than on the day he had loosed upon her the white dog.

Leslie possessed the unfortunate clarity of self-knowledge capable of recognizing the seeds of her unsatisfactory conduct. Far better to act blindly in unconscious patterns. Such behavior would be, she thought, a certain innocence.

She had never in her life been able to do this; how much less so, here at Manford Manor! As never before, she was responsible for her darker acts and thoughts and feelings. A responsibility that could not be escaped.

The unsavory episode with Bob, she realized also, stemmed in subliminal ways from her new vision of Manford Manor. It was as though a kaleidoscope had turned, the vivid mosaic of life shifting instantaneously into a new pattern. She had viewed—perhaps *wanted* to view—Mary Ben as the innocent victim of her brother's influence. Could that, however, be entirely true?

The salient fact of Mary Ben's daily existence, above all, was that, an invalid, she had withered in the full flower of young womanhood. Certainly there was—must be—something within her which welcomed with evil glee the opportunity Howard had so subtly planted, had assiduously nourished into full bloom. Who can know, Leslie thought, what bitter jealousies, what rages, reign within her crippled soul?

Casting her mind back over her Bluegrass sojourn, Leslie, with a sense of horror, saw that each act, every word, of Mary Ben Manford Ashe could be interpreted in a sinister light. Her eager acceptance of Leslie as an ally; her complaisance over the prospect of Leslie and Whitney becoming lovers; even, awesomely enough, her acted-out drama of terror when she believed the black ghost stallion was again threatening.

Which, indeed, was the crux. Leslie, in her rational mind, had sought a rational answer to the basic mystery of Manford Manor. Gratefully she had uncovered Tom Musgrove's worship-motivated plan to frighten Mary Ben into leaving; she remembered, with an aftertaste of bitter recognition, how relieved she had been. Musgrove's misdirected zeal had been the perfect solution, for his unpunished departure would leave essentially unaltered the pattern of life at Manford Manor.

Next—with good reason—she had suspected Whitney Ashe. Who would benefit more from the destruction, whether through death or incurable insanity, of Mary Ben? That, however, was a solution fraught with the self-destruction of Leslie; it would mean that, under the spell of an abiding passion, she had willfully embraced evil.

She had speculated, even, on the possibility that Bob Berry, out of the personal tragedy of his boyhood love, was the responsible agent. By his own admission he had been present the night the loudspeaker had been discovered. Tom Musgrove had confessed to the deed; yet there remained the possibility Musgrove had been only an agent. Surely he had known Bob, as he had known Mary Ben; perhaps had cherished the fond hope their childhood romance would mature into a suitable marriage. Old family retainers, so often, are the sternest proponents of proper alliances.

Granting Bob Berry's presence at the scene that night, was it not likely that on other occasions he had secretly visited the environs of Manford Manor? Definitely he could not be absolved of suspicion. He, like Mary Ben, was possessed by old hurts and angers. His motivation, if he *were* guilty, would be, however, not the destruction of Manford Manor, of Mary Ben, but of his rival, Whitney Ashe.

There remained Howard. Leslie yearned to place the cloak of villainy about his shoulders. Yet, recognizing her own darkly motivated desire to make him the scapegoat, she suspected the evidence adduced to support it.

Try though she might, she could not fathom the benefit accruing to Howard if Mary Ben should be driven insane. Such a culmination would redound only to Whitney's advantage; as Mary Ben's husband, control of the estate would fall into his hands. Howard could never hope, in that eventuality, to achieve his goal. If Mary Ben should die, her invalid's heart giving out from sheer terror, Whitney was the beneficiary of her will. Howard would be left out in the cold.

There existed, of course, the possibility that he had plotted a devious scheme to destroy Whitney. Driving his sister over the brink of insanity, then successfully fixing the blame on Whitney, as her closest living relative he might well succeed to the management of Mary Ben's affairs. Or, if her death resulted, to ownership of the estate in his own right.

Beyond these multiple considerations, Leslie, in the new vision the kaleidoscope had yielded, had encountered a concept of responsibility breathtaking in its simplicity. The possibility had occurred to her during the first days of her sojourn; now, with ten times the force of plausibility, it had returned.

Mary Ben Manford Ashe was—had ever been—the villain of the piece.

Leslie knew something of the hidden resources of the human mind. Powers existed that were immeasurable by any rational means. She had always been enthralled by reported feats of astounding physical strength, like the account of the ten-year-old boy lifting single-handed the weight of an automobile to free his trapped father.

Such phenomena could not, by any manner of means, be attributed to the ordinary physical resources of muscle and sinew. These deeds can be accomplished only through the involuntary enlistment of powers dwelling in the deeper reaches of the human mind; perhaps, even, far beyond mind; in the pure essence of self. Only from these deepest levels can such power be mobilized.

And if for good, as in the case of the boy saving his father's life, why not also in the service of evil? Power is neither of darkness nor of light; it simply exists, pure and untainted. Its coloring is derived from the purpose, whether of good or of evil, which calls it forth.

In the beginning, Leslie had sensed Mary Ben as the focal point of Manford Manor. Sitting in her wheelchair, she held the center. Like a spider, Leslie visualized graphically, poised alertly in her web, sensitive to the most subtle vibrations.

As a young and willful wanton, Mary Ben had enslaved Whitney Ashe into the service of her maidenly passion. Even now, a hopeless cripple, she held him still in thrall. She had summoned Leslie as a witness—yes, Leslie reflected, I recognize the primordial need I was brought here to fulfill; not companion, friend, so much as Witness; for what can great power avail if there is no one to make a history of its wielding?

Which meant: her decision to come to the Kentucky Bluegrass had been fated. Leslie could accept this truth; all along she had felt sure that she was fulfilling her destiny.

It followed, then, that there was nothing fortuitous about Howard's arrival. He, too, had been summoned. Like Leslie, he had responded because of his own dark needs and appetites.

Suppose, through unknown powers, Mary Ben could evoke also the ghost of the black stallion? A poltergeist phenomenon, perhaps, which Leslie knew from her reading nearly always manifested itself in the presence of a disturbed adolescent girl. Mary Ben, though a woman grown, fitted the definition.

If this be the ultimate truth of the curse of Manford Manor, Leslie told herself, Mary Ben is both villain and victim. To perform such magic, one must tread the razor's edge. Even as that deep center of herself weaved daily the web of fate, the part of Mary Ben that was human knew an awful terror.

Villain. And victim. Which meant that she, Leslie Tallant, must protect the hapless human being that was Mary Ben, even as that human being waged combat against the evil which projected itself through her. I am Mary Ben's only chance, Leslie thought, to escape from herself. As I am Whitney's only chance. And mine. And even Howard's.

She knew, most desperately, that she must talk to Whitney of these matters. But it was impossible. The links of communication had been shattered; not only by the sly machinations of Howard Manford, but, far more irrevocably, by Leslie's own despairing action in giving her body to Bob Berry.

I am not the Leslie Tallant I have always been, she thought. I am not yet the Leslie Tallant I am in the process of becoming. I am in limbo between two selves.

Yet it's up to me, she told herself in a despairing resolution. I am the catalyst; I must precipitate the ending. Whatever that ending may be. I must guard against Mary Ben, and protect Mary Ben. I must guard against and protect my enemy, Howard. I must guard my great love, Whitney Ashe. Then . . . I must relinquish him. And, because I am no longer guiltless, I must guard also against myself.

She had arrived at the break point. She knew what she must do. But she did not, even after such anguished excoriation, know how to begin.

It was still the afternoon of the Friday following her fateful Thursday night with Bob Berry. All day Leslie had moved through the maze of her innermost being, even as she moved through the usual pattern of her day.

Now, returning from her sunset walk, she saw, passing near the exercise ring, that Whitney was working Tara Boy.

It was unusual for him to ride so late in the day. Leslie, thinking longingly of the time when she had been permitted to share these exercises with Whitney and the horses, paused, in spite of herself, to watch.

Dragon, as always, came to lean against her leg, soliciting the touch of her hand. When she caressed his ears, he granted her the one slow wag of tail that was his only betrayal of enthusiasm and love, then sat at her side, his head thrust forward to watch through the lower bars.

Leslie, despite her day-long preoccupation, was captured by the beauty of the scene. The sun, behind a bank of heavy clouds that lay like a rampart across the horizon, was setting redly tonight. Slanted light lay lovely upon the earth. Often the beauty of this land touched her to the quick; never so deeply as now.

The man and the horse were an integral element in today's bittersweet quality. Tara Boy's rich bay hide glistened with sweat. Whitney was one with his steed, savagery melded to savagery, dominance matched to obedience. Dust swirled up from the trodden earth, making Tara Boy's coat and Whitney's face equally grimed, runneled with sweat.

Leslie quickly divined the motive behind this late-afternoon schooling. Undoubtedly Whitney had had this morning an unsuccessful session with the temperamental colt; with grim determination, he had fetched him out again, at this close of the working day, in an attempt to impart the lesson Tara Boy had refused to learn.

Every line of Tara Boy's magnificent body revealed his determination to resist the commands of his master. Whitney's body, lean and tense and strong, was imbued with an equal determination to dominate the contrariness of the talented jumper.

Leslie, concentrated upon the scene, was unaware of Howard Manford's approach until he spoke. She jerked about, startled, to see him standing behind Mary Ben's wheelchair.

He grinned insouciantly. "Thought we'd come down to enjoy the show. Or is it a private exhibition?"

"I doubt Whitney even knows I've been standing here for the last ten minutes," Leslie said coolly.

"Whitney is such a marvelous rider," Mary Ben said. "Why must he *drive* his mount so?"

"Tara Boy is difficult to control," Leslie said. She made a small laugh. "You saw that the time *I* was up on him."

Mary Ben raised her eyes. "You've been strange today, Leslie," she said, mildly complaining. "I've never known you like this."

Leslie gazed into her innocent, pretty face. Through her moved the panorama of recent thinking. One would think the wheelchair is only a convenience, her sensitized mind remarked involuntarily. To all outward appearance, she is a whole and healthy woman. She reminded herself that Mary Ben was paralyzed from the waist down. Even so, on the few occasions she had had the opportunity for observation, the legs, not at all withered from disuse, had the appearance of health and strength.

"I don't know why you'd say such a thing, Mary Ben." She laughed again. "I was Leslie Tallant yesterday. I'm Leslie Tallant today."

"Maybe she's weary from her day off," Howard suggested slyly. "Did you enjoy a real night on the town, Leslie?"

As usual, his light tone carried a cover, as though they shared a secret. Aware of the clandestine gleam of amusement in Mary Ben's eyes, Leslie felt the familiar surge of helpless fury.

Knowing it would be of no avail, she said, "Bob and I had a very quiet evening." Before the subject could be pursued further, she turned to watch as Whitney began a new course.

Howard, leaving Mary Ben, came to stand close beside Leslie, bracing his elbows over the top railing. Dragon rose sedately, moved a few steps away, sat again.

"Look at him!" Howard complained. "That dog just doesn't like me."

Before Leslie or Mary Ben could reply, Tara Boy, balking at a jump, curved away so abruptly he dumped Whitney out of the saddle. Whitney landed with a thump, rose to brush the dust from his breeches while Tara Boy, reins flapping, circled the enclosure.

Howard laughed. Whitney, sharply raising his head, stared in their direction. Leslie was suddenly, acutely, aware that Howard's shoulder was touching hers. She could not, as Dragon had done, move away; not with Whitney looking. It would only appear as if she did not wish him to witness their intimacy.

Helpless again. She felt her jaws tighten. Whitney, turning away, caught Tara Boy and remounted. He put the colt at the barrier with a savage determination beyond anything Leslie had yet seen. He was driving the horse by strength of hand and will.

Tara Boy took the jump in magnificent style, made two long strides, gathering his feet, and took the next jump in a soaring rise. Leslie, remembering how wonderful it had been to feel such power and grace, was thrilled; never had Tara Boy displayed such perfection of form.

As they circled toward a new beginning, Leslie saw the gleam of teeth in Whitney's grimed face, the rictus both savage and mirthful. He has lifted the colt over the ultimate barrier of resistance, and he knows it, Leslie thought swiftly. In this moment, he's astride a champion.

Only for the instant. Circling to begin anew, Tara Boy balked again. Instead of curvetting away, as before, he reared, his front legs striking at the air. Leslie's breath caught; surely, rearing so recklessly, the colt would go over backward, crushing his rider.

Whitney, clinging like a limpet, slashed at the sweating flank. Tara Boy came down, but not to take the jump as commanded. He reared again, walking on his hind legs, eyeballs white-rimmed.

Howard laughed again. The mocking sound, close beside Leslie, was jarring. There was now in Whitney's face a grim fury of rage. Leaning forward almost horizontally, he lashed once, twice, with the crop, at the same time savagely backing the horse in an effort to bring him under control.

Tara Boy, unable to sustain the rebellion, came down to all fours. Black with sweat, he stood trembling. Leslie could hear the sound of his rasping lungs. Whitney, making no attempt to soothe the colt with hand or voice, sat the saddle as erect and still as a statue.

Howard, cupping his hands around his mouth, called out, "Whitney, old boy, if you can't do better than that, you ought to stick to the merry-go-round."

Whitney's response was immediate, irrevocable. His hand snapping a twist into the reins, from a standing start he launched Tara Boy at the fence. Directly toward Howard and Leslie, who were standing side by side.

Mary Ben screamed. Leslie, frozen, could not move as the mass of man and animal rushed at her, larger, more threatening, with each split second. Howard, going to hands and knees, scuttled out of the way.

Leslie, like a camera, registered the scene in frozen snaps of perception. She heard Mary Ben scream again, Dragon's sharp-toned warning bark. Then man and horse were upon her.

Tara Boy took the fence magnificently, clearing it by inches.

Leslie was overwhelmed by the pungent odor of sweat, assaulted by the bulk and speed and violence of the animal. As he soared over her head, there was a flashing perception of hind legs lashing dangerously close. Still erect, she had accepted within herself the peril. If this was the way death meant to come to her, so be it.

The moment passed; she was no longer in danger. She whirled about, as the unbraided tail whipped stinging against her face, to see horse and rider coming to earth.

Suddenly, horrifyingly, Tara Boy stumbled, his front legs buckling, his neck doubling underneath as he cartwheeled. Whitney, thrown from the saddle as from a catapult, tucked instinctively in anticipation of a bad fall. Hitting the ground on his right shoulder, he rolled head over heels.

Tara Boy sprawled grotesquely, struggled to rise. Straining frantically, he got both front feet under him. Then, horribly, he screamed.

Leslie had never heard a horse scream in agony. It shuddered through her, a raw blade of sound.

Whitney was on his feet, running to grasp the bridle in an attempt to restrain the berserk thrashing. Leslie, in that camera-snap of perception, registered that both front legs were broken, the bones protruding whitely through the bloody hair and flesh.

Howard came quickly to Whitney's side.

"We'll have to shoot him, won't we?"

His voice sounded strange to Leslie's ears, as though, out of an immense gratification, he was still laughing.

"Where do you keep your pistol?" he continued to Whitney.

Whitney looked at him, naked hate glowing in his eyes. "We don't shoot horses any more." He turned his head. "Leslie. Bring that kit from the back of my station wagon. Hurry."

Leslie, released by the command, ran toward the vehicle parked beside the stone barn. When she returned, stumbling in her haste, Tara Boy, exhausted by the painful struggle, had become quiet, though his eyes were rolling in terror. Whitney held his head, firm hands soothing the animal in his agony.

"Do you know how to load a hypodermic needle?" he snapped. "The Beauthanasia Special. It's in a dosage bottle."

With fumbling hands, Leslie opened the kit, found the hypodermic and the bottle. Hands trembling, she could not succeed in stabbing the needle through the tough rubber cap. With an effort of will, she made herself calm. Then, with careful precision, she inserted it, with equal care drew the deadly potion into the barrel. Holding it upright, she squirted out air, thinking distractedly, It doesn't matter if he gets an embolism, does it, it's meant to kill him anyway.

Suddenly, the hypodermic needle was snatched from her hand.

"I'll do it," Howard said, the strange quality crawling in his voice. "Always have wanted to kill one of these beasts."

"Get away from my horse!" Whitney shouted, moving with urgency.

Too late. With a quick thrust, Howard stabbed the needle into Tara Boy's neck. As his thumb depressed the plunger, Tara Boy thrashed with an eerie new vigor, the reaction ebbing immediately into tremors as the poison took command of his system. Howard, Leslie saw sickeningly, watched the death throes with gloating eyes.

In the instant, it was done. Painlessly, at least, Leslie thought dully, watching the neck go suddenly limp, the head falling to the ground with a hollow thump. Tara Boy's eyes, moments ago so alive with intelligence and spirit, began to glaze. I will never again ride him, Leslie reflected with an immensely penetrating sadness, experience him in all his glory.

Whitney spoke. He looked somewhere between Leslie and Howard; it was impossible to fathom whom he was addressing.

"I hope you're satisfied. You've just killed the greatest jumper it has ever been my privilege to own and ride."

Leslie took it as meant for her. She accepted the guilt, understanding, as clearly as she had ever understood anything, why Whitney had ridden Tara Boy at them.

Not Howard. He said boldly, "Don't blame me. You were the fool who tried to take him over the fence."

Whitney's fist, in one clean blow, knocked Howard to the ground. Mary Ben cried, "Whitney! How dare you strike my brother?"

Leslie's stomach turned over. She could endure no more. Humiliated, suffering, she fled the scene.

Dinner was in progress when she came downstairs. Their faces lifted in surprise; obviously her appearance was unexpected. On her part, also; upon reaching her room, she had been violently ill to her stomach. Then, trembling, head hidden in her arms, she had stretched herself wretched upon the bed.

Now the reaction had reached a resolution. She arose, washed her face, combed her hair, applied the make-up. Then, steadily, carefully, she had descended to face the people of Manford Manor.

Howard, mockingly, rose to pull out her chair. Though a bruise showed on the point of his jaw, he remained unsubdued. "Delighted to have your company for dinner," he said. "You can't *imagine* what a mausoleum this house has become, now that we have gone into mourning for a dead horse."

Leslie looked at him. She looked at Mary Ben. Then she looked at Whitney.

"Thank you," she said. "I'm not hungry. I only came down to let you know I am leaving Manford Manor tomorrow morning."

She marked the surprise in their faces. It was nothing to the astonishment which dwelled within her. She had not known she meant to speak this message until she had felt the texture and meaning of the words in her mouth.

They were, she knew, the right words. She had been appointed to utter them at this juncture of events. For she was the witness, the catalyst, and within her limited scope it was the only action she could take to precipitate the final events. Whatever those final events might be.

Having satisfied something profound within herself, she turned to go. She would, if those inimical forces controlled and manipulated by Mary Ben did not decree otherwise, follow her words with the announced action. She would not, if she could avoid it, look again upon these doomed faces.

Howard's voice stopped her at the doorway.

"Shall I come to your room again tonight, then, dear? Just for one last time?"

CHAPTER FIFTEEN

Leslie was snatched out of sleep by a tremendous clap of thunder. It brought her upright in bed, nerves tingling, heart thudding. But it didn't look as though it would storm tonight, she thought confusedly.

It was the first storm of autumn. For weeks now the weather had been beautiful, hot days followed by still nights, with perhaps the warning flicker of heat lightning along the horizon. The profound serenity of summer had lain over the Kentucky Bluegrass, marred only here and there by local pools of thermal activity generated by the day's heat, the swift rains sweeping over only limited areas before exhausting themselves.

This, now, was different, as Leslie realized immediately; a major line storm created by the first southward-pushing mass of cool air from the Arctic, in collision with the warm southern flow from the tropics. A major confrontation was taking place.

At sunset, a thick band of clouds lay low along the western horizon. It had not been, however, enough to signal this dramatic change; tomorrow morning, Leslie knew, the first coolness of autumn would reign over the land, and the weanling foals would be friskier with high spirits.

And, Leslie thought, the year will lean imperceptibly toward death and winter. It is a time of ripening and decay, with the resurrection of spring so far away, in perception if not in actual time, that one cannot believe it will ever come again.

She clasped her arms around her knees, hugging herself. I shall not see winter come to the Bluegrass, she thought sadly.

First snow, the large flakes would drift down idly, melting as they touched the still warm earth. However, each infinitesimal crystal of ice would soak up one iota more of the earth's heat, leaving the ground just that tiny bit colder, until at last the snow would no longer be melting as fast as it fell, but beginning to weave itself into a blanket to cover all the land.

In the morning, the sun out again, the paddocks and pastures would gleam in a sparkling whiteness to dazzle the eyes, the landscape rendered suddenly strange, the fences, though they were also white, standing out starkly.

The barns themselves would be warm, the air rich with horse odors; there would be eager stampings and rattlings of halters, because the Thoroughbreds would have sensed the change of season.

Turned out into the pastures, the ungainly weanling foals in their shaggy winter coats would snuff and paw with suspicious inquisitiveness at this strange white substance. And in the stallion paddock, as King's Man galloped through his morning exercise, the warm breath from his lungs would pulse mistily swirling in the still air.

But I won't see it, Leslie thought. Long gone Leslie, scarcely the trace of a memory left to mark her passage. The stark knowledge was a grief to her heart.

Sitting in bed with rounded shoulders, arms clasped about her knees, she realized with an acute ache that Manford Manor had become home. Nowhere else, not even the house in Baltimore in which she had been reared, had possessed for her that peculiarly comforting quality of being the place where she belonged.

The human heart, she reflected somberly, beats from birth to death in an alien world, ever the stranger in its pilgrimage; yet each heart cherishes one tiny corner of the universe, knowing it as home.

Most often, she thought, it is the birthplace. It can, however, be a region never seen before; the heart will throb with painful recognition upon first discovery, and forevermore it will possess its true home place out of all the earth.

As my soul recognized Manford Manor, Leslie told herself. Yet now I must go forth and be forever a stranger in strange lands. For I shall never return.

A distant roll of thunder rumbled long over the land. It jarred the old house, faintly, but Leslie, sensitized in every cell of her being, was aware of the tiny temblors. It awoke in her an uneasiness. Yet there remained also a certain sense of well-being, a recognition of how appropriate it was that tonight of all nights the change of season should be ushered in with atmospheric violence.

The Kentucky Bluegrass is bidding farewell to Leslie Tallant, she thought. It is, at the least, signaling its recognition that I have been here and gone.

Unclasping her knees, she leaned to switch on the bedside lamp. I should go to Mary Ben, she thought. That first great peal of thunder will have made her uneasy. She listened tensely for the sounds of wakefulness. But, with the ancient walls so thick, it was impossible to hear, from one room to the next, anything short of a scream.

Manford Manor was a house designed for a family. Yet these eternal walls isolate us into ourselves, she thought, maintaining our individuality but denying us the protection of a cohesive clan. Murder could be committed, she realized with a shiver, and no one would ever hear the agony of the victim. One would die horribly alone.

So deeply absorbed, Leslie remained yet attuned to the approach of the storm. That first loud clap of thunder had sounded as though the violence would be unleashed on their heads without preliminary warning. It had been, however, only a harbinger; after that first tremendous crack of doom, the storm had seemed to retreat in order to mass its forces for a more devastating advance upon a broad front.

Mary Ben, she knew as surely as if present in the room, was fretfully awake. She wondered about Whitney; for the first time, she did not know whether he had yet passed her door.

Perhaps, she thought, he is still belowstairs, memorializing over a bottle of port his magnificent hunter, now so cold and still, which only minutes before his destruction had exhibited the greatness Whitney had worked so assiduously to evoke. Watching him share Tara Boy's suffering, she had yearned to comfort Whitney, even though her own overriding need had been flight from the harrowing scene.

It was a miracle he had not killed Howard. There had surely been a strong reason behind his restraint in merely knocking the man down. With murder living in his heart, Whitney had dared not unleash the vengeance.

The thought gave her a new insight into Whitney's character. The dominant element was *control*. Control of himself first and foremost; but also he sought instinctively to control events and destinies. He was unafraid of potentiality; at his side daily was the white German shepherd named Dragon, an animal trained to kill. But, Leslie knew, Dragon would perform only upon the command of his master. Perhaps never would he be launched to the deed; meanwhile, obedient, available, ready, he paced at his master's heel.

As Whitney had fought to establish firm control over the wayward Tara Boy, so also he wished to dominate the evil influences dwelling within these ancient walls. It is not mere courage that holds *him* pacing and ready, Leslie thought. It is, far more deeply, the essence of his character.

But does he know, as I know, that Mary Ben is the dark mother of it all?

Seeing Whitney whole rather than, as always before, in the shards of understanding, Leslie knew again, as suddenly and inescapably as the first time she had felt it, the need to be possessed by him. Just one forever-to-be-cherished time, she thought, before I must go away. But, even as she recklessly entertained the dream, she realized how impossible it was of fulfillment. Too much—and not enough—had happened between them.

The single bedside lamp flickered, dimmed to a yellow glow, went out. The room was plunged into darkness. Leslie felt her breath catch. The light came on again, dimmed, steadied finally into reliable brilliance.

Leslie tried to force herself to calmness. I have put all that behind me, she reminded herself firmly. There is no returning. The passion, the love, that existed—could have existed—between us has been destroyed by the circumstances surrounding its existence.

No. By *us*, Leslie said abruptly, so clearly she believed for an instant she had spoken aloud. Most of all, by *me*. I, like Tara Boy, did not trust the man's mastership of himself. Or of me. Like the Irish hunter, I refused perversely the highest fence of all.

If he should come to me, she thought intensely, *now*, on this, my last night at Manford Manor, I would dare all. Risk all, and glory in the challenge. Her heart lifted suddenly; at this moment she owned the courage of her passion.

The lights flickered again. An irrational fear gripped her. Darkness would be absolute. And, within these thick walls, she was so alone. When the illumination steadied, she felt a rush of gratitude.

The storm was perceptibly nearer; a subtle rush of wind came against the house, not flowing outward from the storm center but toward it. Somewhere a shutter creaked, banged, creaked again in an excruciating squeal of rusty hinges. Why must there always be a loose shutter? she thought.

When she heard the scratching at the door, it did not frighten her. It was as though I had sent out a summons, Leslie thought comfortably as she thrust her legs from under the covers to stand barefooted on the oriental rug. At Manford Manor, such strange synchronicities are commonplace events. I thought of him, that small while ago, and now he has come.

She padded barefoot to the door, opened it. Dragon, with the one majestic wave of his tail, lifted his head inquiringly.

"Well, hello," she said. "Come on in."

Dragon graciously accepted the invitation. He paused for a brief moment to submit to the touch of her hand; yet there was in him an alertness unallayed by the friendly caress. Immediately he paced across the floor to sniff at her slippers beside the bed. Then he proceeded to circle the room, gravely intent upon his mission. Whatever that mission might be.

"Surely you're not frightened by the storm," Leslie said.

Dragon lifted his massive white head. They regarded each other for a moment; then Dragon went on to search the corners of the room.

As he explored the open closet, nosing among her clothes, a wryness touched Leslie's mind. "Surely you don't think your master is with me," she said. "Is that who you're looking for?"

The dog ignored her. Assiduous in exploration, he sniffed each corner twice over, worked conscientiously around the edges of the bed.

"Where *is* Whitney, anyway?"

Dragon pricked his ears at the sound of his master's name.

There was a tension in him; it was not idle curiosity that had brought him to her room. There was, in his dog's mind, a definite purpose. Leslie felt a curious shiver of unease.

Dragon came to her. As on that first meeting, he stood suddenly on his hind legs to place his forepaws on her shoulders. Leslie, standing braced against his weight, put her arms about his massive neck, hugging him fervently.

"Oh, you beautiful dog," she murmured. "You can come to my room any time you like. For whatever reason." Then she remembered that after tonight she would no longer be here to receive him. *Or anyone else.*

Dragon let himself down to all fours. Going to the door, he tilted his head imperiously; he might as well have spoken. Leslie, amused, reached over him to turn the knob. The white dog departed as mysteriously as he had come. Rather than going in the direction of Whitney's rooms, however, he started downstairs, still alert for whatever it was he sought in this turbulent night.

Leslie laughed, shrugged. "What was *that* all about?" she asked aloud of the empty room.

Suddenly restless, she went to look out the window, thinking, At least there has been no sign of the ghost stallion. Something within her replied: *Not yet.*

She drew the curtains behind her so she could see into the night. A strange scene. The upper branches of the great oaks swayed gently under the influence of the wind rushing steadily toward the bank of clouds lying blackly to the west. So black it was, so ominous; the tumbled edges of the mass of clouds were illuminated by fretful strokes of lightning. The thunder was a continual, ominous rumble, like the advance of a great army.

However, slanting from the east, a full moon shone serenely in a sky almost clear. Driven shreds of storm wrack did, indeed, sail raggedly across its face, but the silvery light reflected from the moon's benign countenance imparted to the scene a profound peacefulness. Yet, beneath the serenity, lay an uneasiness of anticipation. The shutter banged again, the treetops thrashed suddenly, betraying the gusty passage of a violent wind.

Leslie had never observed such a stark division between the utmost calmness of nature on the one hand, and, on the other, the omnipresence of an impending tempest. The contrast made for an eerie sense of unreality, within Leslie as in the landscape. The serenity of the eastern sky was all the more revealed by the blackness of the clouds; the storm front all the more menacing, lit so deceptively by the fugitive brilliance of the moon.

It was as though the world had divided itself into opposing camps, peace against storm, light against darkness. Good against evil, Leslie thought as the eeriness of the warring elements crept through her. Chill brushed against her flesh, as though the air had turned suddenly colder. It was not, she knew, the ambient temperature, but something bodeful within herself.

Whitney, she saw suddenly, was abroad in the night. As he moved from under the moon-shadow of an oak tree into the deceptive clarity of moonlight, Leslie recognized, with a stab of anxiety, the same poised alertness with which Dragon had searched her room.

He came to a halt, lifting his head. He was looking at the moon. Turning, he gazed as intently toward the black horizon. He was bareheaded, and the wind ruffled at his hair; the white shirt gleamed as though illuminated from within.

He is afraid of the ghost stallion, Leslie thought. So cherishing of Mary Ben's welfare, he is attempting to forestall a new hysteria.

In that moment, gazing down upon him unawares from above, it was as though Leslie had entered into Whitney's mind. He does not know the evil in his wife, she realized as acutely as if he had told her. He is not privy to the mystery of the curse of Manford Manor. It would be his last thought to fix the source in Mary Ben.

He was not a man to endure ambivalence. Yet something within him, even as he sought to discover a rational reason for these manifestations, believed in the reality of the ghost stallion.

Whitney, turning his head alertly, moved suddenly into the shadows. In a moment, Leslie saw why; Howard, abroad also, came up the cinder path from the direction of the stone barn.

What earthly business could *he* have in the barns? It was as though the suspicion had communicated itself in a stroke of thought vibrating between Whitney's mind and Leslie's mind. Whitney moved out challengingly from the shadows.

Whitney must have said something, though Leslie could not hear, for Howard jerked about suddenly. Whitney came closer.

The men spoke together, bodies poised warily. Howard gestured disdainfully with one hand. Whitney moved, suddenly, much nearer; Howard retreated precipitately, hurrying toward the house.

Whitney turned to hasten toward the stone barn. Howard, meanwhile, had halted, looking to see if Whitney still threatened. He stood so for a long time, gazing after him. Leslie wished she could have read the expression of his face.

A great slash of lightning ripped across the western sky. It illuminated the mansion grounds with the intensity of a flash bulb. Immediately following came the peal of thunder, a harsh clap that, reverberating down the canyons of the clouds, raised the hair on the nape of Leslie's neck.

Howard, startled, turned to flee into the safety of the house. Another flash, this time forking straight down at the earth, must have struck a tree; it made a terrible sound, and the smell of ozone burned in Leslie's nostrils.

Howard was suddenly running. Then, as suddenly, he stopped. He raised his head. He looked directly at Leslie's windows.

They stared in each other's direction across the storm-fraught air. Leslie flinched, but recovered quickly, knowing that, with the curtain drawn tightly behind her, Howard could not possibly see her. Nevertheless, fear crawled in her like an evil worm.

Why? She did not know.

He went on and Leslie, seeking the comfort of her bed, retreated to slide between the sheets. Better, much better, in this cocoon of security; still, she did not put out the light.

Her mind, teeming with thoughts and ideas and perceptions, had been moving so swiftly she could only grasp after these fugitive essences in a frantic attempt to possess them entirely. It is because tomorrow I shall go away, she thought, and that inward Leslie Tallant who knows Manford Manor as home is desperately trying to take with her the meanings and feelings and atmospheres of this place.

She did not sleep. She merely lay still, within and without, allowing herself to sense the strangeness of the night; know the almost welcome violence of the coming storm; take in the eerie silence of the waiting house.

It's a bigger storm than the first time the ghost stallion came, she thought, snuggling between the crisp sheets. Somehow the thought did not alarm her; she was too peaceful within herself. Even if I should hear him neigh, she thought on the edge of drowsiness, I should not be afraid.

The question of Mary Ben intruded. She sat up, thinking that, with Whitney out of the house, she should check on her. She settled down again; she had resigned from the thankless task of looking after the crippled woman. It was no longer her responsibility. And she was, she admitted to herself in this new-found clarity of mind, afraid to enter into her presence.

Leslie, secure within her bed, sensed the change as the wind shifted to a new quarter. This, now, was the storm wind, stronger, steadily rising, seeking with a new ruthlessness to test for weaknesses in tree and house and barn. The bulb flickered, but did not go out. She burrowed into the bed, turning her head to keep the light from falling directly on her face.

And Leslie Tallant, as serenely calm as the moonscape juxtaposed against the violence of the coming storm, merged again into sleep.

She awoke with an abrupt jar. The storm was at full rage: continuous strokes of lightning, the wind fiercely irresistible, the rain at full spate. The world outside had gone mad with atmospheric violence, there were surely uprooted trees, the shutter banged madly. The timbers of the house groaned, striving to maintain their ancient invulnerability against the assault of the elements.

It was not the storm, however, that had brought Leslie awake; she had accepted, incorporated, the storm before falling again into sleep. Nor was it the blackness which had once more invaded the room, so deep and dark she could not have seen her hand before her face.

None of these things. With every sensitive nerve ending of her body, she was aware that she was not alone in the room.

She lay tensely still until her senses had verified the presence. Then: a thrilling certainty pierced through her.

Whitney!

Every cell of her being cried out: *He has come.*

In the ultimate darkness of this last wild night of her sojourn at Manford Manor, he would possess her, she would possess him. Now and forever.

She was ready. Like Tara Boy in his last hour, she would brave any jump, risk any peril, she would live one minute of her life in high courage. That one tiny span of time would be worth all the other days and weeks and months and years together.

The sheet was snatched from her body. She reached her arms upward into darkness to embrace his descending weight. She felt his naked ribs under her sliding palms, the smoothness of his back, his breath gusting against her face. She was melting, her senses swooning under the rush of sensation, her perceptions such a tangled swirl she could not bear it.

She must experience this one minute out of all time in utter clarity, possess it as completely as she would be possessed by the man. Fighting to clear her mind, her senses, under the assault of his male urgency, her hands clutched frantically into his flesh as she moaned, "Wait, please, wait . . ."

His hand, caught into the throat of her nightgown, yanked violently. *Wrong,* she whispered deep inside, *wrong, so wrong, not like that, Whitney, I am with you . . .*

"Wait, Whitney, wait . . ."

Her mind whirled again, tumbled senselessly as she was caught in a crosshatch of desire and sensation. Surely this was not the man she had loved with a great passion; he had brought to her bed only a ruthless male penetration, not love, not love at all . . .

And it would be a psychic deflowering as well, she knew within herself sadly even as she submitted. The male can so seldom admit love, and tenderness, and need. When she had expected—demanded—so much more! Out of a world full of males, *her* love, *her* passion, *her* need, had chosen this one man, counting him as capable, as ripe, of love as she.

The neck of the gown ripped, the tearing like a fracture opening in her brain.

"Please, Whitney, please. Take me tenderly. All this time I have been waiting . . ."

Within the continent of her body, an ice age was born. For there in the darkness above her the man laughed; laughed and spoke lewd words she could not allow herself to hear.

Howard Manford.

She lay inert, defenseless. Not for an instant of apprehension had she credited Howard's parting remark, as she had left the dining room, as anything more than his usual insinuation of intimacy. But, she realized bitterly, it was just as Howard had anticipated; she was helpless under his brazen assault, as he had made her helpless against brazen slander.

The walls of Manford Manor were thick, creating about them an isolation. Outside, the storm raged mightily. Even if she should, by crying out, succeed in summoning help, who in this household would believe he had come to her against her will?

Not even tomorrow, she thought fatefully, could she register a complaint. Mary Ben would only smile secretly, Whitney look upon her with open contempt.

Howard chuckled smugly as again his hand clutched at her gown. In the next instant his fingers, ripping powerfully, parted the flimsy cloth. A silent scream echoed inside Leslie. With the heel of her hand, she struck at his unprotected face. Again. And then again.

Howard cursed. His open hand jarred against the side of her head, addling her brain. She fought against succumbing to the physical pain, the mental turmoil. One more split second of submission, and her fate would be sealed.

Silently, ferocious in the darkness, she fought him with teeth and nails, with the furious thrashing of her body beneath his smothering weight. The harsh sounds of their breathing mingled; equally silent, he brutalized her flesh in an effort to subdue her to his will.

Waves of hatred flooded bitterly through her mind, strengthening her body far beyond its normal capabilities. Not a simple hatred for the man Howard Manford; for all men, the Male, the masculine principle itself which ruled the world.

I refuse, Leslie screamed silently inside her mind. I refuse!

The lights came on, so suddenly it was a shock to her vision. Blindly she gazed into his angry face, scratched and bleeding. He stared down at her. His mouth was ugly with thwarted passion. Above their heads, the storm raged, concomitant to the violence within this room.

He smiled grotesquely, speaking softly. "You might as well relax and enjoy it."

She was cold as ice, her voice like iron. "You'll have to kill me first."

Blackness returned as abruptly as it had fled. He touched her. It precipitated her into a new frenzy. With a great surge of her body she threw him off. He was stumbling in the darkness, grasping after her as she fled across the expanse of bed. His hand caught her ankle, twisted it cruelly. She panted against the pain, teeth clenched, but she would not submit, she struggled free once more, kicking him in the face with the free foot until he let go. She rolled to the floor and scrambled toward safety.

She almost made it. At the door, he caught her from behind. His arms circling her struggling body, he lifted her, flung her toward the bed. She bounced, twisting like a cat as he threw himself upon her, her fists beating a tattoo against his face.

The light flashed on again. In the same instant, the door slammed open, banging against the wall. *Whitney!* Leslie gasped in the sudden hope of rescue.

Not Whitney. Again not Whitney. Mary Ben.

She sat beyond the threshold in the wheelchair, her white face contorted as her eyes took in the scene. A strangled sound, compounded of sheer rage, jealousy, hatred, surged from her throat.

As they stared, caught in the stasis of conflict, Mary Ben rose to her full height. She stepped from the chair. She walked toward them, gibbering with rage, her fists uplifted as she screamed at them.

She's dangerous, something cold and brave in Leslie told her. Berserk, gone over the edge.

As though the world was suddenly waiting, there came a lull in the storm. Enwombed within that globe of silence, Mary Ben suddenly lifted her head, listening with a terrible intensity. As clear as a trumpet call, Leslie knew, she was hearing the imperious summons of the ghost stallion. She was strangely, terribly, beautiful as she hearkened.

She gazed upon them once more in their tattered nakedness. Her voice was high and clear.

"You took my husband from me. Now you are taking my brother. But there is one thing you cannot possess. *The black stallion is mine!*"

Her face was pure, white, cold. Her voice was clear in tone, precise with the words. Beyond, however, Leslie knew with cold certainty, crouched a demented mind. Perhaps she had always been mad, her sanity long since destroyed by hatreds and jealousies, by the crippling of her beautiful body.

In this moment of fury, the body was no longer crippled. Borne erect by the powers dwelling within, Mary Ben stood before them whole and strong.

"And now I shall go to him."

With a lithe, quick grace, she fled away down the stairs. To go out into the storm-filled night, there to seek her nemesis, her glory.

Leslie made herself move. Even as she took the first step, strained for the will to force the second, Howard interposed himself between Leslie and the open door.

"You're not going anywhere." His voice was harsh, demanding, sure.

"She's your sister," Leslie said, pleading, not for herself, but for Mary Ben. "Someone must save her."

"You're not going anywhere," he repeated.

And he advanced upon her.

CHAPTER SIXTEEN

I can't make the fight against Howard all over again, Leslie thought despairingly. I summoned it once, I used it; now there is in me no more resistance.

Retreating across the room before his renewed threat, she experienced a terrible weakness; willing herself to get it over with, permit this ultimate penetration, violation, debasement of spirit and of flesh. Then, at least, she could hope to emerge from the trauma, however shattered, and begin to put together again the pieces.

Death is the only ending. Anything less, however terrible, is not the ultimate.

Her weary, battered spirit wanted only to endure him. However, her body refused consent. Her head swung from side to side; she feinted continually for an escape route as Howard, backing her into a corner, narrowed inexorably the angle of opportunity. Grim now, determined, he had moved beyond all civilized restraint; if he could not have her, she knew, he would kill her.

Finally, her back was to the wall. Two walls, for she had crouched into a corner, with nowhere else to go. She watched him reach for her; slowly, too slowly. *Oh God, get it over with!* she screamed deep inside. His hand, clawlike, hovered inches away. Only inches. At the first touch, she would go mad, the only escape from this reality; she would not have to know what he did to her body.

In this moment, she was not Leslie Tallant.

There was a sound. At first she did not know what it signified. Then; she saw Dragon. Standing in the open doorway, he made a second inquiring bark.

"Dragon. He wants to hurt me," Leslie said.

Suddenly wary, Howard pivoted. Dragon paced softly toward them, hackles rising. In his throat rumbled the ominous not-quite-growl Leslie had heard on her first day at Manford Manor.

"If you touch me, he will kill you," she said.

Howard snarled, his eyes darting wildly for a weapon. There was none. Threatening a pace forward, he yelled, "Get out of here, dog!"

Dragon crouched, preparing to spring. Howard halted abruptly. Then, without warning, he rushed to grab Leslie, thrusting her as a shield before him.

"Dragon!" she screamed.

Dragon sprang. His massive weight hurtled into them, Leslie falling in a sprawl on top of her attacker. Her head swimming, she made an attempt to roll over, get to her feet. She could not move.

There was, however, no further need. Dragon's jaws were clamped around Howard's wrist. Howard screeched with the pain as, growling ferociously, Dragon worried at the arm.

Dragon, legs braced, made a mighty pull, dragging the man away from Leslie. Letting go the wrist, he put both front feet on Howard's chest and snarled, his bared teeth only inches from the vulnerable throat. White with terror, Howard dared not move.

Leslie got to her feet. Battered, disheveled, panting, nevertheless she was again herself.

Howard turned his head, fixing her with terror-filled eyes. "Call him off," he begged. "Call him off. Please."

Iron striking into her soul, Leslie lusted suddenly to see the white animal kill her enemy. One command, and Dragon would rip out his throat. Leslie visualized it in graphic detail: the man screaming against the pain, then his voice strangling into the silence of death as the red blood pulsed, staining the dog's white-furred jaws.

Only an instant; then, wearily, she said, "Dragon. It's all right now."

Dragon, feet still planted firmly on Howard's chest, lifted his head. Howard moved, making a premature effort toward escape.

Dragon growled warningly. Howard froze. Helpless, he looked at Leslie, beseeching her intervention.

"Heel, Dragon," Leslie said, not knowing if the dog would obey a specific command from anyone but Whitney.

Dragon did not heel. Leaving Howard sprawled on the floor, he came to Leslie's side, nosing at her hand as if to assure himself she was all right. Leslie knelt, putting her arms around his neck.

"Thank you, lovely dog," she murmured. "Oh God, how I thank you!"

Howard, warily, got to his feet, Dragon stiffened, his yellow eyes fixed on the movement.

"It's all right, Dragon. He wouldn't dare," Leslie said soothingly.

Howard's wordless snarl made Dragon bristle.

"You'd better be careful," Leslie said coldly. Howard prudently held silence. Then, involuntarily, Leslie said, "Why?"

Incredibly, the man threw back his head and laughed. When he had stopped laughing, with his engaging smile, he said, "I just wanted to taste something that belongs to Whitney Ashe, I suppose." His face turned ugly again. "Whitney possesses everything within the reach of his hand. I just wanted to steal an apple out of his tree, that's all."

His eyes narrowed. "I'd have done it, too, if it hadn't been for that damned dog."

There was in him no saving grace. As, almost surely, there remained none in his sister.

With the thought, Leslie was jarred, suddenly, by the realization that Mary Ben was out in the storm—and no one else knew.

She spoke rapidly. "Get out of here. I don't mean just this room. I mean Manford Manor. I'm going to look for Mary Ben. If you're still here when I get back . . ."

Howard remained still. "What gives you the right to drive me away?" he said harshly.

Leslie did not hesitate. "Dragon!"

The sharp command brought Dragon to his feet. He crouched slightly, eyes fixed on his target. Howard, retreating immediately, moved toward the open door. Dragon prowled forward, maintaining the distance between them. After Howard had disappeared, he thumped down, yawned mightily, dropped his chin to his paws.

Leslie laughed at his ostentatious boredom, even as she gratefully noted that he guarded still the entrance to her room.

There was no time in which to assess, encompass, contain, the experience of assault. She hurried to dress, a fresh turmoil of doubt and decision churning in her mind. Now that there was time to accommodate concern, she was oppressed by that last vision of Mary Ben.

There was no one else to do what had to be done. She must, at the least, inform Whitney. Perhaps, she thought hopefully, Whitney, abroad in the night, has already forestalled Mary Ben's frantic flight.

Her body was aching in every muscle. She ignored its protest against further effort, resolutely telling herself, I can do whatever remains to be done. That, at least, has not been destroyed in me.

Passing through the doorway, she said, "Come, Dragon. Help me find Mary Ben."

The dog rose obediently. Leslie ran down the stairs, through the hallway, out the main door. Reaching the lion-guarded steps, she was assailed by the tempest. Gasping, drenched, she paused. The outside storm had receded from her awareness; it was a shock to discover it still at full rage. The rain was cold, numbing, and though she had put on a light raincoat, in an instant she was soaked through. The freshet pounded against her, streamed down her face, blurred her vision. Dragon whined, leaning damply against her wet thigh.

"Come on," she yelled against the downpour. "Let's find her!"

Struggling with every step, she achieved the cinder path. Rounding the corner of the house, she met the full force of the wind. She tucked her chin, held her face averted, in order to see. The dog, pressing close against her side, whimpered against the necessity of being out in such a storm.

The thunder and lightning had marched on toward the northeast, maintaining a vanguard position on the leading edge of the storm front, so she did not have even the dubious advantage of a fitful lighting of the scene. Drenched to the skin, disoriented by the assault upon her senses, she could only grope half blinded.

She blundered suddenly into a maze of fallen branches. She stumbled, almost fell. A great limb, torn from its parent tree, lay across the path, the larger end so splintered it might have been struck by lightning.

She lifted her head. "Mary Ben!" she called. "Mary Ben!"

If there was a reply, she failed to hear it in the din. Extricating herself, she skirted the massive branch and pushed on.

Perhaps Mary Ben had taken shelter under the trees. I will search there first, Leslie decided. I will not have to go to the stallion paddock. Surely it will not be necessary to venture there.

She had hoped it would be better under the trees. But the noise of the thrashing branches demonstrated so graphically the irresistible force of the wind that fear for her own safety trembled in her soul. Somewhere nearby, a branch crashed to earth. The sound brought a whine from Dragon's throat.

Leslie leaned to caress him. "Mary Ben," she said. "Find Mary Ben for me, Dragon. Mary Ben!"

Dragon lifted his muzzle. However, though she repeated the command, he did not seem to understand.

"Whitney!" she said desperately. "Find Whitney, Dragon. Whitney!"

Dragon, barking in a sudden exhilaration of understanding, sprang away from Leslie, braced on the edge of obedience.

"Yes!" Leslie cried. "Whitney. Seek Whitney, Dragon!"

He bounded away, disappearing immediately into the storm. She called for him to wait, wishing fervently not to be alone.

Too late. Stubbornly, she resumed her effort. Each step a struggle, she searched the grounds, time after time stopping in the lee of an oak to call, and call again, until her throat was sore.

So wet, so cold; the soaked shoes had turned her feet to ice. Unless she held her jaws clenched, her teeth chattered uncontrollably, and she trembled in every limb. But she persevered. And she did not even know why.

Why, indeed, should she be wandering in the raging storm, seeking to save the crippled woman from whatever it was that threatened?

Crippled? she thought suddenly. *The last time I saw her, Mary Ben was as sound of limb as I.* Standing on her feet, she had been magnificent, terrifying. When, for all Leslie knew to the contrary —or anyone else, for that matter, she thought—Mary Ben had lived paralyzed from the waist down since the morning she had been found lying senseless in the stallion paddock.

Leslie came to a halt in the lee of a great oak. She put her hand on the wet bark, gripping hard. The thought was like graven words in her mind: Had Mary Ben faked her immobility? If so, for what purpose? Or had she been lifted up by one of those incomprehensible powers buried in the human psyche, and now, with the unholy strength ebbed away, did she lie crumpled under the brutal impact of the storm, her fragile body shivering from cold, perhaps dying . . . ?

Leslie knew that she must search until Mary Ben was found. It did not matter that tonight Leslie Tallant had endured an assault far more devastating to spirit than to flesh; that previously she had forfeited all effort to the simple desire to escape from these multiple, mysterious entrapments of Manford Manor.

Quite simply, she knew, now, the Why of her being.

As she understood clearly, also, the pattern of fate which held dominion over Manford Manor. Somehow, through magic and legend, through the strength of human character, through the very existence during a century and more of this piece of the earth as an island entire unto itself, there was here focused a puissant concentration of good and of evil.

Like the prophetic landscape tonight, divided between the serenity of the moon—and Luna, Leslie remembered, had ever been a symbol of the female aspect of nature—and the black violence of the storm. White and black, good and evil, man and woman. The male and the female, the yang and the yin of Chinese thought which creates the tension of opposites essential to the eternal existence of the universe.

Leslie had dared the storm because she cared deeply for her fellow-woman. However greatly the evil in her warring nature had prevailed over the goodness of her soul, as a member of the human race Mary Ben Manford Ashe was worthy of rescue. Leslie Tallant, in this clarity of understanding, accepted the responsibility.

As she could now accept herself. Summoned to Manford Manor, this estate which had been created by a woman great of soul, Leslie had, as does all humankind, brought along as essential baggage her own lusts and needs and appetites. These, she knew now, must be relinquished. She must go forth as pure of taint as Joan of Arc, like Isolde of the German legends as capable of great deeds and high adventure as any man.

Overhead, the wind moaned in the branches, heightening into a keening note that shivered through her like the passage of a surgeon's knife through quivering flesh. She was cold and afraid; even as she was unafraid.

For she knew what she must do.

With all the instinct for self-preservation inherent in human nature, she had sought to avoid the stallion paddock. When that place, of course, had been Mary Ben's fanatic goal. Leslie, in her coward human heart, had hoped Mary Ben had been unable to sustain the frenzied hysteria of purpose long enough to achieve that doomed circle.

She gritted her teeth against a shivering of the flesh far beyond mere exposure to the elements. No recourse; now she must go the last mile of the long journey she had undertaken when she had determined to come to Manford Manor in the Bluegrass of Kentucky.

Leslie realized that she was gripping the great oak tree with both hands, as though to draw a needed strength from its earth-rootedness. She took away her hands. The white dog, Dragon, was no longer at her side; Whitney was lost to her. She stood alone. But she would go on. Putting her head down against the rain, she began the struggle of making a final passage through the wild night.

The storm, as though aware of her goal, increased its fury. Twice she became entangled with fallen branches, had to back away and circle around. Once a branch came down so near it brushed her shoulder; fortunately, it was not massive enough to cause injury.

She was grateful when she emerged from the oak grove. She paused, leaning on the wind, peering through the murk toward the stallion paddock. Nothing could be seen. There was only the blur of the driving rain; beyond this limited vision dwelled a blackness of night which could not be penetrated. She drove on, cold and afraid and alone. She discovered the white fence by stumbling into it, the impact of her momentum jarring against numbed flesh.

Gripping the top plank with both hands, she peered into the blackness beyond, shouting, "Mary Ben. Are you there? Mary Ben!"

She listened tensely. God, if only there could be an answer. Everything in her being strove against the necessity of passing through this white fence which marked a boundary between the twin powers—the reality of today, the legend of all the yesterdays —reigning over the earth of Manford Manor. If only Mary Ben would stumble out of the blackness of night, the violence of the storm, they could retreat together into the safety of the mansion.

Leslie called, called again. There was no answer.

Though her face was streaming with water, she knew there were also tears—not of pain or anger or fear, but simply an acceptance of fate—as she stooped to crawl between the white planks.

When the hands grasped her from behind, she screamed. For a dizzy moment, the all of Leslie Tallant, body and brain and soul, *knew* that Howard Manford had come again against her, defenseless in the storm. In the next instant, she realized that it was Whitney. She curled herself against him, seeking strength as one seeks a warm fire on freezing nights. Putting her face against the wet shirt, she let herself go into an uncontrollable shaking.

"All right now, it's all right," Whitney said, his mouth against her ear so that, through the turmoil of the night, she could hear the tender words.

"Oh God, Whitney," she said. "Oh *God*, you don't know . . ."

"Hush," he said. He kissed her, not with passion but with concern. His arms were strong and sure, their embrace quelling the chill trembling, he was a safe house, a warm furnace.

"Dragon led me to you," Whitney said. "I had no idea what he wanted, I was holed up down there in the stone barn, waiting for the storm to let up . . ."

"Thank God for Dragon," she said shakily. "He saved my life tonight. Beautiful Dragon."

His arms tightened. "What are you doing out? Don't you have any better sense . . . ?"

Leslie, the urgency suddenly upon her again, stiffened. "Mary Ben," she cried. "She ran out of the house." Turning in his arms in a vain attempt to survey the stallion paddock, she added, her voice trembling, "She's out there somewhere. We've got to find her."

He took his arms away, leaving her bereft. They stood face to face, shouting at each other, the words whipped ragged by the wind.

"Nurse Nunn?"

"She must have already gone to bed. Anyway . . ."

"Did you say Mary Ben *ran out?*" he said incredulously.

She put her hand on his arm. "Whitney, she was in a towering rage. She actually rose up out of the wheelchair, she . . ." Her voice faltered. Now, she decided swiftly, was not the time or the place to tell him all that had transpired. "Then . . . then she ran down the stairs, out into the storm."

"Oh my God!"

Whitney moved against the fence to stare into the paddock. Switching on a flashlight, he rayed it into the darkness. The spate of rain splintered the beam of light before it had penetrated more than a few feet.

Leslie stooped to pass through the fence. "Hurry, Whitney. There might still be time."

His hands, suddenly strong, forestalled her. "No! There's no helping her now. She must fight this battle alone."

Leslie grabbed frantically at his arm. "We have to go. We have to!"

His voice came hard, yet tender. "All these years, I have fought to save her. But I realize, now, it is what she has desired more than anything."

"I don't care!" Leslie cried. "I know you believe in the legend. You're *afraid* to go in there. I'm afraid, too. But I'm going."

His hands caught at her. "I won't let you."

She stood away. "You can't stop me. You can only let me go alone. Or you can come with me."

She stooped through the fence, rose upright on the other side. Treading now upon the magic earth, sacred to the great black stallion Black Prince, she walked toward the center as though in the bright seeing of daylight. She did not look to see if Whitney, if Dragon, followed.

Whitney caught up before she had taken twenty steps. Dragon

remained whining at the fence; then, tucking his tail, he fled away.

Side by side, the beam of the flashlight swaying weakly before them, they pressed on through the storm. They could not speak without pausing to shout into each other's face; they did not touch. But they went on together.

Leslie stumbled over something on the ground. She realized what it was even as she went to hands and knees on the sodden turf.

"Here she is," she called. "Here, Whitney!"

Whitney had passed two steps beyond before he realized she had fallen. He came back, focused the beam of the flashlight. Speechless with the shock of finding what they had sought, they gazed upon Mary Ben's crumpled figure.

Whitney knelt beside her. Yielding the flashlight to Leslie, he straightened the twisted body. Mary Ben's face was white in the focus of tiny light, the rain beating upon it. All about, the earth was trampled into mud.

Whitney stood up. Leslie stood, also. They leaned together over Mary Ben his wife as the storm, seeming now a storm for all eternity, vented its fury upon their heads.

Sad; fated; forever; Whitney's voice spoke into her ear.

"She's dead."

CHAPTER SEVENTEEN

The rain had settled into a steady downpour, the wind diminishing so that it dropped straight down, not driven with slanted force. Whitney stooped, gathered the lifeless body into his arms, lifted it from the rain-soaked earth. She seemed as fragile as a dead bird. Leslie lighting the way with the torch, he plodded stolidly through the storm. Leslie unchained the paddock gate, swung it open, fastened it behind them.

Leaving the magic circle unbroken, she thought in a wild corner of her mind.

Whitney had not paused in his funeral march. Leslie hastened to catch up; he should not be left to walk alone. He kept his gaze straight ahead; at every step, his riding boots squished wetly. Leslie longed to wipe away the rain streaming down his face. It was as though all of nature lent him the tears he himself could not shed.

Leslie followed with head down, forcing her trembling hands to keep focused the feeble flashlight ahead of his heedless feet. Somehow it would be very terrible if he should stumble, and drop the lifeless body.

Leslie could not concentrate on what must have taken place in the stallion paddock. Every time she ventured to edge toward comprehension, her mind, gibbering in terror, skittered like a mount spooking at a fluttering leaf. Had Mary Ben, indeed, encountered the ghost stallion? Had Black Prince, triumphant at his breakthrough, magnificent in murderous rage, reared to attack the female thing he hated with a passion transcending death itself? Around the crumpled body, the thick turf had been broken, the earth trampled into mud.

Mary Ben had summoned the ghost stallion; Black Prince had commanded her forth from the house: they had each called to the other. But: had it been in a ghostly phantasmagoria real enough to result in Mary Ben's death, or had it all been within the crazed circle of a twisted mind?

Leslie's imagination, human and limited, refused the task. There is no knowing, she thought dully. Beneath the not-thinking, a slow fire had lighted in her mind. The boundary line between what was real and what was not-real no longer existed. Perhaps that was how it had been with Mary Ben in those last moments of her life when she had summoned the unfathomable strength to overcome the crippling of her body and run free toward the terrible fate waiting within the magic circle.

What an aweful thing, Leslie thought. Mary Ben had embraced her own death, as she could no longer embrace a lover. But, Leslie thought agonizingly, she should not have had to die alone. No one should ever have to die alone. She shivered, wondering morbidly in what manner death would come to her.

Whitney mounted between the guarding lions into the shelter of the porch. Leslie hastened to open the door. As she did so, Dragon, drenched and shivering, came to them out of the storm. He had been with Whitney, Leslie remembered dimly, when Whitney had found her at the paddock fence. But the dog had refused to follow them into the paddock, instead had tucked his tail and fled. Did he know, Leslie wondered, that death waited out there? So often, animals sense a wider range of reality.

Whitney, Dragon and Leslie following, passed through the portal. In the living room, he laid Mary Ben on the nearest sofa. Standing erect, he looked upon his wife. His face was like marble, the lips a sculptured line. He was motionless, rigid, for a minute that stretched long and long; then, leaning, with the palm of one hand he gently brushed away the wetness from Mary Ben's face.

She was beautiful in death. Her face, too, like marble, but peaceful now. So peaceful. There had been a smile on her lips when she had died, though so violently; a trace of the smile, a sweetly graceful line, remained. The blond hair, soaked wetly, sprayed tangled on the couch, highlights glinting where the light struck it.

Whitney lifted his head. "Nurse Nunn," he said. "She should call Mary Ben's doctor. He must determine the cause of death."

"Whitney," Leslie said.

He had not looked at her when he had spoken. Now he did. "It's all right," he said tautly. "It's what she wanted. It was all that was left for her." He gazed again upon his wife. "I guess I did love her," he said. "More than I knew."

Leslie longed to comfort him; but now was not the time. He had kissed her, she remembered, when he had found her in the storm. They had embraced passionately, tenderly, even as Mary Ben, there beyond, lay wet and cold and dead. With that memory between them, she wondered if he would ever kiss her again; if she could ever allow him to do so.

She realized that, with a steady, minute trembling throughout her body, she was shivering. It's only the wet clothes, she told herself. All I need is a hot bath and a change. Knowing, all the time, it was more. So much more.

Though they were sheltered inside the strong old house, the storm remained with them. From beyond the walls came the sound of rain, flowing out of a black sky with the inexorable energy of all water seeking its own gradient. The creeks will be full to the banks by now, Leslie thought, and overflowing into the low places; the water gathering, massing, flowing on and on.

And it is not over, she thought. There remains also the storm within. And I can endure no more.

"Nurse Nunn," Whitney reminded her patiently.

Numbly, Leslie moved toward the telephone. Before she could reach it, Howard stood in the archway. His eyes found Mary Ben's body. His face twisted under the impact of realization. He plunged across the room, going to his knees beside the couch.

Gathering up the lifeless body, hugging it to him, he shook her limply, as though agitation would restore the life force which had fled. A wordless cry tore from his throat, echoing raggedly in the still room. Burying his head on her breast, he began to sob.

Leslie and Whitney, from their separate places watching the brother in his violent grief, could only hold still. They grew up together, Leslie thought. If Howard could love anyone, he loved his sister.

Suddenly Howard, the body still clutched in his arms, a sodden weight, came to his feet. He turned toward Whitney as though defying him for possession of the corpse.

Whitney laid a hand on his shoulder. "There is nothing we can do now," he said. "Put her down."

Howard's face was ugly. "So you finally managed it. You killed her."

An edge of iron entered Whitney's voice. "Put her down, I said. Have respect for your dead."

Incredibly, so great was Whitney's domination, Howard obeyed. But he would not be forestalled; placing the body again on the sofa, he rose fearless in his grief to confront Whitney.

"You've got it all now, haven't you? The money. The land." His voice snarled, suddenly, as he swung around toward Leslie. "You've even got the woman to take her place."

Whitney's reply was infinitely tolerant of Howard's unbalanced state. "Howard, I have no need of Mary Ben's money. In the beginning, yes. But in Europe I accumulated my own fortune through speculation in currencies. I knew all along that sooner or later we would come home to Manford Manor. I did not want to spend one cent of Mary Ben's capital in the restoration. I have not done so."

"You're lying in your teeth."

Howard, without warning, struck at Whitney's face. Whitney caught his wrist, held him at arm's length.

"I can prove it. If proof becomes necessary. Mary Ben's money is in trust. Has been, since she became crippled."

"Oh, yes, I know that little gimmick," Howard cried. "You manage the trust, you have the control. And now . . ." His head turned toward the sofa. "Now you have arranged to inherit it."

"I am not even a trustee," Whitney said. Visibly, he made an effort. "Howard, let's not be enemies while she is lying there dead. Later, you can think what you please. But now . . ."

Howard's face was ugly. "You're a murderer," he said tautly. "I'm going to prove it. I'll put you in jail for tonight's work."

He had gone too far. Leslie could see in Whitney an anger beyond words, beyond the need for reprisal.

Standing tall, he spoke with restraint and deliberation. "I will ask you to withdraw that statement."

In the face of such controlled anger, Howard wavered. Then, slyly, he said, "You haven't called the sheriff, have you? The sheriff should be called when there's been a violent death."

Contempt showed in Whitney's eyes. "Mary Ben's doctor will examine her body. That is sufficient."

Howard rose bravely to the opening. "Oh, no, it isn't!" He took a step toward Whitney. "You don't *want* the sheriff, do you? No sir. Your tame doctor will sign the death certificate just like you tell him to sign it, Mary Ben will be safely in the ground, and you and this . . ."—his eyes flicked toward Leslie—". . . this *woman* will enjoy the fruits of your labors."

Whitney's voice remained quiet. But there was steel in the words. "I won't hear any more. I will advise you to leave this house. At once."

Howard, heedless of warning, came bravely into a rising frenzy. "You won't get rid of *me* so damned easy. You'll find that out. You'll defend yourself in a court of law against tonight's deed. I'll see to that."

"Howard," Whitney said.

Howard plunged on, the words tumbling over each other. His eyes wild, he was gripped by the reality his words were shaping out of the disaster of his grief.

"I'll strip you to the bone, Whitney Ashe. A convicted murderer can't inherit, you know, and I'm Mary Ben's brother. I'll take this accursed land, I'll chop it up into little pieces. I'll use Mary Ben's land, and Mary Ben's money, to make a million dollars."

The sound of his breathing pulsed in the room. His eyes glared with conviction.

"The first step is calling the sheriff. Which I intend to do this minute."

He stalked toward the telephone. Whitney's hand, snatching at his shoulder, whirled him around. The two men confronted each other. Death, grief, loss, were set aside. Leslie began to be afraid of the anger in Whitney Ashe. Howard's next word, next gesture, might trigger the ultimate reaction.

"We will keep this death private," Whitney said. "It shall not be made into a scandal throughout the Bluegrass."

An old doubt assailed the watching Leslie. Why oppose an official investigation? Calling the sheriff voluntarily was the surest way to disarm Howard's accusations. *What did Whitney have to hide?*

Leslie tumbled the thought out of her feverish brain. She would not let Howard again instill doubt.

Whitney, Leslie thought, is the great man for Manford Manor. I shall not doubt him. Not again. I cannot doubt.

Howard was sure of himself. "What can you do to stop me?"

Whitney put a hand to Howard's chest. Gathering the coat lapels in an inexorable grip, he shook him like a doll. The fury, edging out of control, made his voice tremble.

"You will get out of my house. This minute. If you won't leave, you can't hold me responsible. I warn you."

The possessive phrase triggered a hysteria of rage. "*Your* house?" he screeched. "I'll see you rot in jail for the rest of your life before it'll ever be your house!"

He jerked away from Whitney's grip. In one step he had reached the telephone, a hand snatching the instrument out of its cradle.

It had to be stopped.

"Howard," Leslie said.

His startled face turned. Her presence, in the conflict, had been forgotten by both men; Whitney, too, looked at her.

Leslie's brain was on fire, her senses flickering into and out of comprehension; she had perceived the scene, registered the words, in distorted fragments, like a program coming through on a defective television set.

But her mind grasped her purpose firmly, she forced words into speech on a tongue too numb to perform its duty.

"Go ahead, call the sheriff," she said to Howard. "I want you to. Because, when he gets here, I intend to charge you with attempted rape."

His voice snarled through clenched teeth. "You can't prove a thing."

"What's this?" Whitney said, his startled gaze moving from Howard to Leslie and back again. "What are you talking about?"

"It has nothing to do with you." Leslie's voice was strong and clear. "This is between us."

Howard, distracted by this attack from an unexpected quarter, spoke uncertainly. "You'd be fool enough to accuse me, when everyone knows we've been lovers for weeks?"

"You have never set foot in my room until tonight, and you know it," Leslie said. "You tried to make Whitney and Mary Ben believe that lie, and maybe you succeeded. But you know the truth, as I know it."

Howard tried to make a laugh. "That's still a long way from an accusation of rape. What can you hope to prove, when the only witness was Mary Ben . . . and that damned dog?"

"I may not be able to prove it," Leslie said. "But you can be sure you'll find yourself trying to explain to the sheriff how your face happened to get scratched up like that."

In involuntary self-betrayal, Howard's hand went to the grooves etched deeply into his cheeks by Leslie's clawing nails.

"My God!" Whitney said softly.

"And these," Leslie said. Opening without shame the wet blouse, she displayed the purple bruises on her rib cage. "And this." Tenderly she touched the knot on the point of her jaw.

He was beaten. And Howard knew it. His eyes darted toward Whitney, toward the doorway.

"All right," he said. "All right! I should have known you two were in league with each other."

Still he did not move. Leslie reached for the phone. "Shall I call the sheriff?"

He backed away. "All right!" he repeated. "I'm going! But you haven't heard the last of me. You can depend on that."

An empty threat, and Howard knew it as well as they did. He was hurrying now, saying, "I'll send for my things," saying again, "I'm not through yet," saying, almost pitiably, "It's still storming outside."

Then, under the archway, he turned to look at Whitney. His voice was suddenly shaky. "May I . . . may I come to Mary Ben's funeral service? I want . . ."

"Yes," Whitney said. "Of course."

He was gone, then, and they were alone, their only companion the death that dwelled in Mary Ben. Leslie could not look at

Whitney. Her mouth was dry, hot; tendrils of fire licked inside her head.

Out of some residue of resolution, she lifted the phone, saying, "I never did call Nurse Nunn." She despised the weakness of her voice, the refuge of the banal words.

Whitney came close enough to touch her. "Leslie," he said.

Leslie raised her eyes. They looked deeply into each other. Leslie strove to keep her gaze steady, let him see her, the woman who loved without hope of requital. But, inside this woman she was tonight, Leslie Tallant was shattered, conquered, defeated by the feverish rush of events.

His words, so difficult of speech, were strangely stilted. "All this time, I believed . . . that man tricked me into believing . . ."

He stopped. Words were not needed. He reached for her.

Before his sustaining arms could come about her, Leslie crumpled in upon herself. Red fire lanced through her brain, her senses whirled; then merciful blackness, like a great hand, smothered down over her.

Lying on the floor, she appeared as lifeless as Mary Ben. She did not know it when Whitney stooped to lift her, as he had lifted Mary Ben, into his cradling arms.

CHAPTER EIGHTEEN

Whitney came to her room.

She would not receive him. She pleaded that she loved him, but Mary Ben had not been long enough dead. She begged to know if they would be man and wife, or only lovers. Whitney gazed upon her with cold eyes, and went away.

He is gone forever, she thought brokenly. I have lost him. There is only one true marriage, and however we come together it shall be the true marriage, so why did I ask that silly question to drive him away?

Then there was Nurse Nunn, come to work with nursely efficiency at strapping her arms and legs because she wanted to put a great black thing on her head that struck fire into her brain. *Leslie knew the purpose of this thing was to make her forget Whitney Ashe, remove him forever from her soul, and so she submitted with gratitude to the marvels of modern science.*

So wonderful and free to have lifted these burdens of love and life. In New York she had been free, she had lived through light days and easy nights, the suffering of that unrequited love for her employer only a tidy indulgence.

But what had been the name of that man she had thought to love so easily? Her mind tossed frantically, seeking for his name. It was not anywhere in the crevices of her brain. I have forgotten, she fretted, and one must not forget. One must forget only Whitney Ashe, and though, through the intervention of the black machine manipulated so marvelously by Nurse Nunn, he no longer inhabited her soul, she had not forgotten. Had she? Of course not. She would never forget.

A man came to her. *He said he was Whitney Ashe, but she did not know him. She suspected it was Howard Manford in disguise. Howard was so clever, he had thought to take her in Whitney's stead, pluck her like an apple from Whitney's tree.*

But, as clever as he, she saw through the disguise, and laughed at him because it was so transparent. It made him angry and he attacked her again, flinging his enormous weight upon her body. She struggled against him, calling, "Dragon! Dragon!" and Dragon came to drive him away. But when Howard-Whitney commanded the great white dog to lie down, Dragon, fooled by the disguise, obeyed; for of course, like us all, he always obeyed his master.

So Howard had his way with her at last. He ravished her flesh with great glee, and to her anguish she responded, for half the time he was Whitney, because the dog knew he was Whitney, and half the time he was Howard and he was violating her, destroying all her lovely womanhood, and so she learned the lesson, there is no defeating our master the great Male, and afterward she lay exhausted, weeping bitter tears for the lost Leslie-that-had-been.

Life should not be structured so, she told herself, and wept. It would have been so easy to have it equal and equal, man and woman, yang and yin, the wedding of the opposites. If only Whitney would have wedded himself to me, she sobbed heartbroken, everything would be all right, and Howard and Bob wouldn't have happened. But he looked upon me with cold eyes and went away.

Then he was there again, but this time not alone; another male stood with him and they conversed soberly over her supine flesh.

"Yes, she's like that," Whitney told the man wearing the eyeglasses and the brush of mustache on a long upper lip. "She's simply that way. A pity there's nothing to be done about it."

"Really?" the stranger said in an interested voice. "A strange case. Very strange case indeed. What is your opinion, Doctor?"

"In my opinion, she was born so," Whitney said gravely. "She's a woman, you know. Women are nearly always born that way. Don't you agree?"

"And your prognosis?"

Whitney shook his head. "Incurable. Modern medicine can't cope with this sort of thing."

The stranger turned his head. "Shh . . . here comes the nurse. She's a woman, too, remember. They're always in conspiracy against us."

"Yes, it's definitely a communicable disease," Whitney said. "That's been proved beyond a shadow of a doubt."

Leslie sought to cry out into their hearing. *She knew the disease that dwelled within her, and these men were wrong. But a paralysis gripped her jaws, she could not speak, she could not move, only her eyes could follow their expressions as they leaned, so grave, so wise, over her deathbed.*

Now I know how Mary Ben felt, she thought sadly, confined to that wheelchair for life since the night the black stallion crippled her. How glorious it must have been to rise up and run free into the storm! One hour of ultimate freedom, feeling the rain beating tenderly against tender flesh, sensing one's body afire with life and passion, knowing that beyond the white fence, within the sacred circle where dwelled the tension of the opposites which sustains eternally the universe, the great black ghost stallion waited. A place for a marriage between gods, Leslie thought, and Mary Ben had known it. A place upon this earthly earth where Male and Female can be merged one into the other and thus become the One in place of the Two, where in the heart of conflict lies an eternal core of love.

I am sister to Mary Ben, she thought sadly. We should have gone hand in hand, a twin wedding, and it would not have mattered that there was only one Male waiting for us both.

Now I will have to go alone. I will go. I shall be wedded within the magic circle. And death shall not be in me.

So Whitney came again to her. And *she received him.*

This man with the dark heart had become her life, his hungry passion fed her hungry passion, and her heart was lifted as her body was lifted, on wave after wave of great love. Afterward, he held her tenderly in the darkness, having finished with her and begun with her, and sometime soon, she thought tenderly, I will teach him how to laugh.

Her soul froze. Her body stiffened in his arms. For outside, beyond these safe mansion walls which held her as tenderly as his arms held her, came the galloping hoofbeats, the trumpeting call.

She shivered inside, for she had not known that now she would be able to hear the fateful summons. Her voice trembled. "The ghost stallion has come for me. For *me*, Whitney!"

His answer was strong. "No. You're not a Manford woman. It can't be."

She whispered, "But you've made me mistress of Manford Manor, don't you see? Black Prince knows there is a new mistress. And so he is calling."

"That was all inside Mary Ben's head," Whitney said angrily.

She began to get out of the bed. "I must go to him. I want to go."

His arms held her. "No. There is death in him."

She turned to look into his face. "You see? You believe in Black Prince, too. You always did. You were always as afraid as I was. But I'm not afraid any more."

"*Not afraid of death?*" *he said incredulously.*

"*No more than I am afraid of life and love,*" *she said.* "*You're only a man, you can never know the glory that lies beyond. But Mary Ben knew. And I know.*"

Still he held her strongly. His voice was desperate. "I will marry you," he said. "Now. I promise."

"*No,*" *she said.* "*A marriage made on earth is not enough. There must be a wedding of the gods.*"

Bright afternoon sunlight slanted through the western windows, picking out the intricate pattern of the ancient oriental rug. There were flowers in the room, beautiful flowers, the scent of them strong in her nostrils, *and she smelled them carefully, because if they were flowers for the dead then Leslie Tallant was no more.*

But they were flowers for the living after all, she realized in great relief, and at the foot of her bed stood a man who was to her a stranger. At first she thought it was the doctor who had consulted with Whitney-the-doctor, but then she knew it was not. This man's face was in shadow, because his back was turned to the windows. He wore a clerical collar, in his hands he held a black book.

She saw then, to one side, Nurse Nunn in her white uniform and Martin, the houseman, in his white jacket. That's interesting, she thought clearly, they're going to be married, here beside my deathbed.

Then she realized that Whitney stood at her side, holding her hand, and she was wearing her best nightgown, so sleek and pretty, ruffled at the neck, while Whitney was dressed in a neat business suit with a white shirt and a regimental-stripe tie in black and red.

"Oh, no," Leslie said.

She had spoken aloud, but no one paid attention to the words of denial.

"We are gathered here in the sight of man and God to unite this man and this woman in holy matrimony," the man in the clerical collar said.

Leslie wondered if he really were a minister; she had a suspicion it was Howard Manford again, in disguise. But there was something more important to take account of.

"No, I won't consent," she said. "Whitney isn't even dressed right. He ought to be wearing his riding outfit. He looks lovely in riding clothes."

She might as well not have spoken her heartfelt objection. Apparently they can't hear me, she thought lucidly. *So maybe I'm already dead, after all, and so it won't make any difference, will it, whether Whitney marries me or not? Or even what he wears for the ceremony.*

Comforted by the thought, she listened quietly while the man in the clerical collar spoke the appropriate words. But when it came to the part where she was supposed to say, "I do," she felt a conscientious need to make known her position in the matter.

"This isn't going to be any good, you know," she told them earnestly. She leaned forward from her upright position against the head of the bed. "I don't understand why I have to explain this over and over again. There's the ghost stallion, you see, and there are the Manford women. I wasn't born a Manford woman, of course, but Whitney came to me in the night and made me the mistress of Manford Manor. And Black Prince knows it."

They were waiting. Maybe this time, she thought gratefully, they are really listening.

"You can say the words a thousand times over, with me and Whitney holding hands and saying 'I do,' but it won't count until Black Prince gives his consent. It simply won't count. So this is silly, you see. It's stupid."

They were still waiting. She was beginning to tire, exhaustion creeping blackly out of the corners of her mind. *How can one hope to make them understand? she thought despairingly. Men never understand, so they have to batter at us, use us up, because they're afraid of the great wedding, the true wedding, not a man in a thousand is up to it. And, she thought with a new depth of despair, what else is there for a woman? A man is all that is given to us. Except our selves.*

"Do you, Leslie Tallant, take this man, Whitney Ashe, to have and to hold, in sickness and in health, to love and to cherish . . ."

She listened through it impatiently. At the end, she said, "*Oh, all right, you silly men. I do.*"

And following after, the voice of Whitney Ashe, strong and sure. "I do."

So Whitney Ashe came to her again that night, and she received him.

It was strong and true, this time she knew it for real, the other only a fevered dream, so it was the first time, too, and she had the chance all over again.

Her head was clear, as her body was strong; so it was a pure glory. As he took her, so did she take him, because she could be free, aware even in the throes of passion that there remained yet the black stallion; and the ghost stallion would not be denied.

This knowledge, too, however, made for a core of bitter sweetness within the passion, so that she wept gentle tears, which his hand brushed gently away, even as she surrendered herself as utterly as a woman can surrender to a man. He also surrendered himself unto her.

Later, they slept together, his arms about her and her arms about him. But then she came awake, knowing that she had been called for. She looked into his face in the shadowed night light.

His face was peaceful. One hand tucked under his cheek, the other arm was flung across her hip.

I have been right for him, she thought. He has been right for me. And that, she reflected with a tender sigh, is all that can be hoped for in this world.

Still, she knew what must be done. She yearned to touch him in farewell, but dared not. Awakening, he would forbid her the final adventure of her life. But, she reflected, his arm lies across my body. Cautiously she circled his wrist with the fingers of one hand, lifted the arm, placed it at his side. She watched his face. The eyelids did not flicker.

With equal care, she slid out of bed, stood erect. She did not look for shoes to protect her feet, but glided like a phantom to turn the knob and go out to the head of the stairs. Behind her, from beside the bedroom door where he had been sleeping, Dragon rose alertly.

His nose touched her. She pushed it away. "No, Dragon. You can't go," she whispered.

He wagged his tail, not understanding. When she started on, he followed. She turned again.

"Stay!" she whispered fiercely. "Stay!"

Obediently he sank to his belly.

A moon tonight, she saw gratefully when she emerged, but not the storm. At least she would not have to meet the great stallion in the turbulent blackness of Mary Ben's fateful encounter. Nature is kind to me, she thought, whispering soft-footed through the wet grass.

She paralleled the cinder path, because of her tender soles, and came to a halt upon sight of the white fence, glimmering in the moonlight. It was an old moon now; when she had last seen it, it had been at the full. A puzzle to her mind how the moon could have grown old.

She went on. It was not with courage; she went simply because it was what she had to do. But she went also without fear.

She did not pause at the fence, but stooped quickly through. The bluegrass was thicker here, brushing wetly through her toes, and the faint fragrance wafted up to fill her nostrils. The night was soft and warm and she thought confusedly, But autumn came with the great storm, summer was forever gone. Then she remembered, grateful for the lucid functioning of her brain; there were also Indian summers. It is now Indian summer, she thought happily, and that is very nice indeed, thank you.

She walked steadily, without hurry, toward the center of the paddock. Once she had achieved it, she halted, to begin the waiting.

So peaceful inside herself. A peaceful landscape, too, upon which she gazed. Moonlight lay serenely, making silver-white the fences enclosing her within the magic circle where the marriage of the gods would take place.

Beyond, the stone barn rose up in its bulk; within its walls dwelled the great gray stallion, King's Man. She wished there was time to bid him farewell, as she had bade farewell to Whitney. Too late; she should have thought of it before. There could be no retreat, now that she had reached the center.

This is where Mary Ben stood, she thought. She lifted her head, *the time was now,* and her voice called through the night, clear and penetrating as a bell.

"Black Prince! Here is Leslie Tallant!"

She listened. The universe was still about her. She called again, thinking despairingly, Perhaps he can come only on the wings of a storm. Perhaps it is, after all, the wrong time.

Faintly, very faintly, she heard the drum of racing hoofbeats. Her heart lifted with gladness. She turned to face the east, as though a spiritual compass within her knew the direction of his coming. And nearer and nearer, stronger and stronger, more and more fatefully, the hoofbeats came from the far distance.

She saw him as he took the fence. He soared in a mighty leap, a thousand times more beautiful than Tara Boy at his best, and took the landing without a break in stride. Then he was rushing upon her as she stood braced, he would run directly over her, only one glancing blow needed to knock her into eternity.

Coming to a scattering halt, he reared. As she gazed up at his hovering black barrel, silvered hoofs flashing like knives, for the first time fear struck into her heart, and she knew that she did not want to die.

But one must die sooner or later, she thought. How better than in this moment of glory, when one is beyond, so far beyond, this *earthly self?*

She held herself erect, though she was not unafraid; she waited for his blackness to descend upon her, the hoofs cutting into her flesh as his meaning slashed through her mind, destroying the clarity of decision she had possessed, as the mistress of Manford Manor, ever since the wedding.

But she was also human, and the human does not wish death. So, with a great cry of gladness, she saw that he was wheeling

*away, trumpeting mightily, to face a greater challenge as, over the
fence from the west, came the great gray stallion, King's Man.*

But there is not meant to be a rescue! something fateful within
her cried at the heart of gladness.

He, too, was mighty in his magnificence. The moonlight
transfigured his coat into a silvery white as he galloped to challenge the black horse. Yards away, he halted and reared, tossing
his head, teeth gnashing, mane whipping in his fury. He neighed
his challenge, and the black stallion rose to meet him, their great
voices ringing against each other like swords.

Leslie stood transfixed, feeling helpless in the midst of this
mighty conflict. Aware of the weakness within her, she yearned to
sink into the earth.

But she must see. So, even as her heart stood in her throat, and
she could not breathe, she held herself together by a sheer force of
will.

The two stallions, the moon-white and the black, walked toward each other on straining hind legs. They came together with a
crash, the black getting his shoulder in first, so that King's Man
almost lost his footing. Slipping, scrambling, he arched his neck to
sink strong, yellow teeth into his enemy's neck. Blood showed suddenly on the black hide, running in a darkly glistening stream.
The black stallion screamed and broke away, circling instantly to
come in again from another angle.

Time after time the great stallions crashed massively into each
other, trumpeting and squealing, and it was not possible to discover which held the advantage. At first they were so close to
Leslie she was overwhelmed by the smell of sweat and blood, by
the sheer bulk of their enormous bodies. Then she realized that
King's Man was forcing Black Prince inch by inch away from the
center, where she stood.

Instinct tells him that's where Black Prince's strength comes
from, Leslie thought. The farther from the center, the more
ghostly he becomes, with less presence in this real world.

She began to hope of victory. She began to hope of life and of
love. Though, of her own will, she had relinquished all hope, it
was wonderful to know that Leslie Tallant might continue in her
earthly way—if only her champion, the gray stallion, could prevail.

Then, inexorably, inch by inch, Black Prince, with an enormous

*increase in fury, began fighting his way back toward the center.
Toward her. King's Man was weakening, Leslie saw with clear
eyes; though doing his mighty best, he was not strong enough to
conquer these forces from another world. He staggered now, his
sides heaved, even as with consummate courage he met again and
again the renewed attack.*

*Without that moment of hope, she could have endured. Now
her senses swirled, shot through with red and black, and, because
she could no longer sustain herself erect, she sank to her knees.
She put her face into her hands. She had borne all that could be
borne, and when the gray stallion should fall at last, not to rise
again, she would be defenseless.*

*Nearer and nearer the struggle raged. Though her hands
blinded her vision, she could sense their hovering presences, their
flashing hoofs, and know that at any moment the black stallion
would descend upon her like an evil whirlwind, take her with him
to that other world from which he came. Leaving only the shell of
Leslie Tallant behind, as he had left behind the fragile shell of
Mary Ben.*

*Spent of all courage, she toppled over to lie prone upon the
earth covered so beautifully by the bluegrass.*

Leslie came to her senses to feel Whitney's arms strong about
her. He was kneeling, frantically kissing her face.

Leslie, in a sudden conviction of effort, sat up. "What . . . ?"
she said.

"My God, Leslie, I've been hunting all over," Whitney said, his
face so mingled of love and concern it made her want to laugh.
"It never occurred to me . . ."

Leslie, in dazed wonder, looked about. The dawn was just arriving, brilliant morning light rosy along the eastern horizon. Where
Black Prince came from, she thought with a shiver. Under the
coming light, the thick grass of the paddock spread rich and
green, pristine in its beauty.

"Did King's Man kill the ghost stallion?" she asked wonder-
ingly. "He must have. I thought King's Man was losing the battle."

"What *are* you talking about?" Whitney said tenderly.

Leslie looked toward the westward half of the paddock. As

though a world was fading before her eyes, leaving only traces and glimmers, her senses whirled between reality and unreality.

She saw the gray—almost white—stallion. Quietly, peacefully, he was cropping at the rich grass. There was on his sleek hide no scar of battle. As, Leslie saw, the turf of the paddock remained a solid carpet, untorn by ghostly hoofs.

She looked to her man. "Whitney," she said quietly. "It happened."

"What happened?" His arms were strong about her as he knelt beside her. They tightened. "You've been ill, Leslie, very ill. For a long time. Weeks. I . . . I was afraid I would lose you, too."

Her head whirled anew. The dislocation of time . . . an old moon last night, she remembered, when she had last seen the moon at full.

"But . . ." she said. "I saw it all, I . . ."

"Listen," Whitney said. "It's enough that you're alive. That's all I care about."

She looked at him. Yes. Not knowing what had been real, what unreal, perhaps it was best not to ask. Even if she could know, understand, there was no way to tell Whitney of her knowledge. A mystery, she told herself, a woman-mystery. No man *can* understand.

But, she knew with a great lift of her heart, we can still love the men. In spite of all.

"Let me get up," she said, stirring in his arms.

"No, you've been ill, I'll carry you . . ."

"I'm fine now," she said impatiently, getting unaided to her feet. She looked down at herself. She was indeed wearing her best nightgown, crumpled now, smeared.

On steady legs, she walked toward the stallion. King's Man came eagerly to meet her. She put both arms around his hatchet-sharp head, cradling it, crooning.

"Thank you, King's Man, my love," she whispered. "Thank you for my heart."

Blowing contentedly, he rubbed his head against her arm. Whitney, smiling, came beside her, touching King's Man's shoulder with a gentle hand.

"A great stallion," he said quietly. "He'll make Manford Manor into what it should have been all these years since Brooke Manford lived. And he loves you in all devotion, as that legendary stallion, Black Prince, loved that great woman."

"Yes," Leslie said. "He'll do it. For us." She smiled at the man. "You *are* going to marry me, aren't you?"

He threw back his head. He laughed heartily, freely. And, from somewhere, she recalled a tender thought which had dwelled richly in her mind during a time of travail. *I will teach him how to laugh.*

"We're already married, my love. While you were out of your head, you kept talking about it. So . . ." He chuckled. "I had the minister in, and he pronounced the words over us." He took her, almost violently, into his arms. "Because I feared I would lose you," he said roughly. "And maybe . . . just maybe . . . it might make the difference, it seemed so important to you."

She moved against his chest. "Thank you, Whitney. Thank you, my love."

He put his hand against her temple, holding her close. "If you want to be sure, we can go through it again." He laughed down at her. "Or maybe, now that you're of sound mind, you'd rather not."

She laughed with him, turned in his embrace to put both arms about his neck. Solemnly, then, but quickened into happiness, the promise of passion, they kissed.

The sun, clearing the horizon, rayed the light of a new day across the Kentucky Bluegrass. About them, the white fence encircled the stallion paddock. And the great gray stallion, King's Man, nickered, jealous for a share of the attention, and pushed his nose against Leslie's shoulder.